To Neha

Pirates *of* Provence

TG Snowball

Terrence G Snowball

25 December 2015

Happy reading ...

BECKSIDE BOOKS

First Published in Great Britain in 2015
by BECKSIDE BOOKS

A CIP catalogue record for this title is
available from the British Library.

ISBN 978 0 9933886 0 6

Printed & Bound in Great Britain by
Clays Ltd, St Ives plc

BECKSIDE BOOKS
Publishers

www.BecksideBooks.co.uk

Dedication

For my two daughters MC and DC

Acknowledgements

My sincere thanks to Pam and Mick Boyle for reading the
manuscript and suggesting changes

Chapter 1
The arrival

'Grandad!' It was Laetitia escaping from the arrivals hall at Hyères airport, dragging her rucksack.

Grandad caught her and gave her an enormous hug. 'Where are the others?'

'They're waiting for their cases. Mum only let me take hand luggage and one doll. That's not right, is it?'

'Don't worry, I've got a box full of dolls,' replied Grandad amiably.

Laetitia, who was six, had her unusual name given to her by Grandad, something his daughter-in-law, Jo, had always resented.

'Here they are,' Laetitia shouted.

'Hi, Grandad!' Jessica was having difficulty with her huge case, held together with masking tape. She appeared to be undressing. 'My case was overweight, so I had to wear it all on the flight – fucking *AirJet!*'

Jessica was Laetitia's sixteen-year-old big sister.

'Mum said she's going through her awkward period,' explained Laetitia.

'Grandad!' shouted Lucy and Ewan. They were twins and cousins of Jessica and Laetitia.

'And who is this?' asked Grandad.

Behind the others was another girl, unexpected, about Jessica's age. While Jessica was slim, the other girl was fat.

'It's Ellie,' said Jessica.

'Little Ellie, I didn't recognise you.'

Except she wasn't so little now!

'She's coming for the summer. Didn't Mother from fucking Hell tell you?'

'I don't remember her saying so, but you're very welcome, Ellie.'

'Thank you Mr err—' said Ellie hesitantly.

'Call me, Charlie.'

1

'Mum says you're Charles, because Charlie sounds too common,' was Lucy's contribution to the introductions.

'Next time you see your mother, tell her from me, it's Charlie.'

Both Jessica and Ellie had recently finished their GCSEs. Their respective parents were hoping both would continue at school to do their *A*-levels. Ellie was okay with the idea, mainly because it was a better option to working. Jessica, on the other hand, had other ideas, although she wasn't sure what those ideas were, not yet anyway.

'What's with all the hair, Grandad?' asked Jessica.

'Do you like it?' answered Grandad genially.

'What, with a gross ponytail?'

'And a scraggy beard?' added Lucy, who wasn't at all impressed.

*M*other from Hell, Jo, hadn't informed her father-in-law, Grandad, of the extra arrival.

A week before departure, Jessica categorically stated she wasn't going anywhere without her best friend, Ellie. In fact, she said she would just stay at home. The thought of having her daughter, who was going through her awkward period, at home for the summer, was unthinkable. Mother from Hell quickly booked an extra flight at extortionate cost for Ellie, whose mother was quite happy with the arrangement. What mother of a teenage daughter wouldn't be? Mother from Hell was so relieved she neglected to inform Grandad in case the extra arrival was inconvenient.

As many a parent would confess, particularly mothers, when one talked about their daughters going through their awkward period, the euphemism was instantly recognised. Mother from Hell regarded her daughter to be the most devious, deceitful conniving shitbag ever to walk the planet.

'*Y*ou don't expect me to get into the back of a baker's van?' queried Jessica while adjusting her new Ray-Ban sunglasses in the middle of the car park. 'It's hot in there.'

'It's the best I could do,' said Grandad. 'I had to find something big enough to get you all in.'

'If we must...'

'Can I go in the front?' pleaded Ewan.

'No, it's my turn,' retorted Lucy.

'Just get in the back,' said Grandad cheerily. 'It's only a short journey. Come on, little ones first.'

'I'm not little,' stated an indignant Ewan.

'If he's not little, then I'm not little,' added Lucy, who was sensitive about her height, but more of that later.

Grandad managed to squeeze them all in, including their luggage. In the front, on the passenger seat, he had a couple of bags of baguettes he had to drop off at a small supermarket – that was the deal for borrowing the van. Grandad neglected to mention he was going to fill the back of the van with les enfants of the English variety because he wasn't sure of the insurance situation.

After dropping off the baguettes, getting slightly lost in the back streets, Grandad finally arrived at his destination. When he opened the back of the van, he met a hostile, mutinous bunch of children because, as correctly drawn to our attention earlier by Jessica, it was hot in the back of the van.

'You could have put the air-conditioning on,' muttered Jessica while squinting in the bright afternoon sun.

'It doesn't have any,' replied Grandad. 'I think it's bad for the bread.'

'What are we doing here?' queried Lucy.

They were standing in Port du Lavandou, near the Quai d'Honneur, staring at all the boats and yachts that moored there for the summer. Behind them, moored on the Quai des Pêcheurs, were a few small fishing boats having finished their work earlier that morning.

'Are we going for a swim?' Laetitia asked.

'So where is the villa?' queried Jessica.

'Where's my swimming costume?' added Laetitia.

'We have a slight change of plan,' replied Grandad evasively. 'We're going on a klipper.'

'A kipper?' Ewan was never the best at listening.

'Klipper, it's a boat.'

'What, for a trip or something?'

'Yes and no,' answered Grandad. 'What I mean is, we are going to spend the summer on my klipper.'

3

'Ace.' Lucy was impressed with the thought of living on a boat. Her imagination began to run riot on what exploits she might plan.

'Awesome,' added Ewan.

'Aren't we going for a swim then?' Laetitia was only six, remember, and lived in the present time. What the consequences were of living on a boat for the whole summer she would find out soon enough.

'Later, I promise.'

'So where is the villa?' Jessica repeated.

'I sold it.'

'You sold it?'

'Yes, and bought the klipper.'

'I don't recall Mother from fucking Hell mentioning anything about a klipper.'

'I'll explain later.'

They all stood and glanced around the port, all wanting to know the answer to the same question. Which one was it? What did a klipper look like?

There were mainly small boats in the port, some with sails, and some without. You could hear the distinctive clinking of rigging and metal shackles banging against masts that you always heard in a yachting marina, particularly when there was a wind blowing. There were some motor boats, perhaps up to forty feet in length, though nothing outlandish or exotic such as seen in the more chic ports of Saint-Tropez or Cannes. Le Lavandou was a comfortable holiday town for French workers. They were searching for a boat that matched up with what they thought Grandad would buy.

At the end of the quay, past the Capitainerie and near the station carburants, was something completely different, with two masts and a long bowsprit. On the quayside, tourists and locals were admiring it and taking photographs. There was nothing else quite like that in the port – or the south of France for that matter. It appeared old and in need of some maintenance. At the stern, on a flagpole was a large Red Ensign. Below that, painted on the stern, was its port of registry – Hull.

Everyone gazed at the unusual looking klipper, hoping that was the one. Even Jessica had to admit to herself that if she were to stay on a boat for the summer, then that one would do just nicely.

'What do you think?' asked Grandad.

'So that's a klipper,' said Jessica reflectively. It looked a cool party boat. It had potential.

'The one with flippers?' asked Laetitia, getting all excited.

'They're leeboards and yes, that's the one.'

'Can we go aboard?'

'Julien,' shouted Grandad.

Julien was the teenage son of the couple who owned the boulangerie and van. He had admired the klipper earlier and wanted the chance to get on board and explore. He and Grandad knew each other as their paths often crossed when Julien delivered baguettes. Since Grandad didn't want to leave the klipper unattended, a deal was agreed. Grandad borrowed the van, made the baguette delivery, while Julien minded the klipper.

Julien enjoyed the brief spell of notoriety while having his photograph taken by tourists. If it were a film, then he would have been tall, handsome, and bronzed with a physique of a Greek warrior. It wasn't a film. He was bronzed and not bad looking, but that was where the similarity ended. Being the son of a boulanger had taken its toll so average height and plump would be about right. Julien helped the family business when he could, particularly at weekends and school holidays. He had recently successfully completed his baccalauréat, bac to the French, and planned to study music at the Université d'Aix-Marseille, in October, when the summer holidays were over.

Julien waved and gave a lovely smile when he saw Jessica and Ellie. It was his lucky day. He let down the gangway so everyone could board.

'Rule one, all shoes in the basket,' instructed Grandad. 'Only bare feet allowed on board.'

'It's called, *Black Pearl*,' screamed Lucy with joy.

'I'm a sailor, I'm a sailor,' shouted Laetitia while she skipped up and down on the gangway and was in danger of having an early swim. 'Quick, I need a wee.'

'Shoes off first.'

'The skull and crossbones,' shouted Ewan, pointing to the flag at the top of the mizzenmast. 'It's a pirate ship.'

'House flag,' explained Grandad.

5

'We're pirates,' Lucy informed the others.

Julien helped to carry Jessica and Ellie's luggage aboard, while Grandad struggled with the rest. The new arrivals disappeared to explore their summer home and make claim to their cabins. It was better that way, Grandad believed, and no one could blame him if she or he didn't get the cabin of her or his choice. Grandad's own cabin, the stateroom, had a double bed and adjoining bathroom and since it was full of his own belongings, wasn't available. Lucy and Laetitia were quick to claim a cabin opposite the stateroom, with two single beds and a bathroom next to it. Jessica and Ellie claimed the cabin with bunk beds opposite the galley with its own bathroom. This was for'ard of the saloon and other cabins and was more secluded.

'That's not fair,' complained Ewan. 'Where do I sleep?'

'I have a special cabin for you,' explained Grandad. 'It's in the crew accommodation near the front. It is self-contained and all yours.'

'Awesome,' said Ewan, running to find it.

'You didn't tell us about that,' commented Jessica.

While Ewan's cabin was separate from the rest of the accommodation, it didn't really matter. Unless it was raining, Grandad slept in a hammock on deck because it was cooler. Nobody came or went without him knowing.

The much-photographed boat that Grandad had bought was an old Dutch klipper, built in Papendrecht, Holland, in 1895. Ignoring the ten-foot long bowsprit, it was about sixty-six feet long and nearly sixteen feet wide. It had a metal hull, much like a barge, with two masts for sailing around the Dutch coast or along the inland waterways of Holland and Europe. It needed the huge leeboards to reduce the tendency to slip sideways and heel over with a side wind, particularly in canals and rivers. At some stage in its life, an added engine made sailing an easier task.

Someone lovingly converted what was the cargo hold into comfortable living accommodation, with wooden panelled walls, a Dutch tiled fireplace in the saloon, and oriental rugs on the floors. It had teak decking with seams and butts caulked with oakum and black pitch. Years of scrubbing the decks with a holystone, a soft and brittle block of sandstone, had scoured and whitened the decking to a light honey colour. It had a white hull with a black stripe around the upper part, much stained with rust giving the klipper a neglected appearance. Its flat bottom, with a draft of around five feet, was well suited for the canals and rivers. In the open sea, with a heavy sea or slight swell, it rolled like a drunken sailor. While it had seen better days, if you looked closely you saw a striking old klipper, full of mystery and adventure.

Grandad had bought the klipper on a whim. It was like meeting his late wife all those years ago; it was love at first sight.

'It's time to go,' shouted Grandad.

'Aren't we staying here?' queried Jessica. She and Ellie had been exchanging telephone numbers on their mobiles with Julien who knew all the best places to go, and we're not talking about boulangeries.

'We have to leave or I'll have to pay port fees.'

'Fuck,' said she who was going through her awkward period.

After Grandad returned the van keys to him, Julien left the klipper waving at Ellie, Jessica, and the others.

'Furcuff,' shouted Laetitia, waving back.

'What did you shout just then?' queried Grandad.

'Dunno. It's what Jessica says.'

'Let go fore-and-aft,' shouted Grandad, 'and pull up the gangway.'

'Metoo, metoo.'

'Yes, you can help as well, Laetitia.'

Grandad started the engine and was amazed that his new crew appeared to do things; at least, the three younger members did. They undid every rope in sight and let them go. He then spent the next ten minutes retrieving his mooring ropes from the harbour and recovering his Zodiac, which acted as tender and lifeboat.

They needed nautical training, decided Grandad.

They left Port du Lavandou without damaging other boats. *Black Pearl* was all of ninety tons in weight and not the easiest to handle. They headed down the coast in an easterly direction. Grandad used the engine, although his aim was to use the sails as much as possible once he had trained his new crew.

'Laetitia, why are you climbing the mast,' queried Grandad.

'I'm the lookout.'

'Be careful.' Having a lookout seemed like a good idea. The klipper had ratlines, simple rope ladders close to the masts, making it easier for climbing, attending to the sails, and routine maintenance.

'Where are we going?' asked Lucy.

'Pramousquier.'

'Ace.' Lucy was pleased because the villa Grandad had sold to buy the klipper was at Pramousquier and she had friends she met on the beach there every year. In fact, everyone was pleased with his choice of destination, including Jessica.

'You can unpack if you want,' said Grandad.

'We'll unpack later,' Jessica said, while she and Ellie fiddled with their mobiles.

'Don't phone your parents yet,' Grandad said quietly. 'I want to talk to you all first.'

'Phone parents, I don't think so, fancy thinking that, Grandad,' replied Jessica. 'They aren't in my address book.'

'Have you got reception?' Grandad tended to have problems with his mobile when at sea.

'I've got an iPhone, so no problem.'

'It's still a mobile?'

'It's an iPhone 6s, Grandad, every girl's must-have accessory.'

Grandad had never heard of an iPhone 6s.

'Are we in a bay or something, because there is land on both sides?' Ellie was delighted with what was happening and wanted to know more.

'We're sailing between the coast and the Îles d'Hyéres, a group of four islands a few miles off the coast,' explained Grandad.

'I'll show you,' said Jessica, indicating to her iPhone with a GPS map displaying the coastline, sea, the islands, and the position of *Black Pearl.*

'You get that on your mobile?' Grandad was impressed.

'Get a life, Grandad. You've got to get the right apps.'

'Apps?'

'You better get used to it because they'll soon have them attached to Zimmer frames. I'm not saying you need one, not yet anyway.'

The voyage to Pramousquier was about four nautical miles sailing. It wasn't a difficult journey because visibility was excellent in the late afternoon and there was little or no wind. Being at sea, the air temperature was in the mid-twenties although it would have been much warmer further inland.

With the exception of Ellie, everyone knew where she or he was. Having spent every summer at the villa, they knew the coastline, be it from the land. They sailed past all the beaches of the Commune du Lavandou, clearly marked by inner and outer yellow buoys. Ewan took particular interest in the workings of the binoculars when they sailed past Plage du Layet, which was the local plage naturiste.

'Perve,' said Lucy.

'I'm not,' Ewan replied guiltily. 'I'm helping with the navigation.'

'The beach is a long way, Lucy,' said Grandad, trying to be impartial.

'Anyway, I'm older than you,' stated Lucy.

'So what, I'm taller,' countered Ewan.

They were not identical twins.

Ewan was taller with dark, unruly hair. Lucy had light coloured hair easily bleached by the sun and was the older by a couple of minutes or so. The trainee nurse assisting the midwife noted the exact time of Lucy's birth but, when Ewan arrived, she forgot to record the event. Later, the trainee nurse had thoughtfully amended the records and noted Ewan's time of birth as a couple of minutes or so after his sister. It might have been ten minutes, who knows?

Marina was the mother of the twins and daughter of Grandad. Regrettably, her marriage didn't last long. Whatever attributes Marina's ex-husband had, quickly diminished, and after the divorce, he would allege that it was a good thing because he now had more time to spend in the pub with his chums.

Lucy and Ewan were brought up by a single parent who was a busy and successful barrister specialising in women rights. Were they disadvantaged in any way? They were two happy quarrelsome twins who excelled in most things they put their minds to and had, until recently, two doting grandparents to contend with, so the answer to that last question was probably not.

Once Lucy was old enough to understand she was the oldest and that Ewan's birth went unrecorded, initially anyway, she never let Ewan forget this. Comments such as, 'They didn't even bother recording your birth,' and, 'I'm the oldest,' will give you a flavour of their squabbles.

Despite the discrepancy of his birth, Ewan generally got along with his twin sister. Their common passion was singing and acting. Their fondness for the performing arts probably originated from their late grandmother who loved the theatre and musicals. Before the age of five, both Lucy and Ewan knew most of the best-known songs from West Side Story, Joseph, Godspell, Hair, Jesus Christ Superstar, and the like. By age six, they produced and directed their own productions, playing the starring roles, of course.

By the age of seven, the disparity in their voices became evident. Lucy had a pleasing voice, and although not strong, could hold all her notes to perfection. Ewan's voice was something else. To call it a caterwauling would be unfair, but you get the meaning. It was strong and tuneful in a way, a mixture of Tom Jones and Mick Jagger.

Placing Ewan in the crew accommodation at the front of the klipper was probably one of Grandad's better underhand acts, because Ewan liked to sing first thing in the morning.

'Enemy on the cliffs,' shouted lookout Laetitia, pointing to the turreted villa above la Pointe du Cap Nègre.

'That's the Bruni place,' Jessica explained to Ellie.

The previous year Jessica had paddled in the kayak to la Pointe du Cap Nègre from Pramousquier. She had jumped off the Pointe into the sea, risking breaking many bones and possible death. The Pointe was high and it was a dangerous jump. None of her friends dared to jump. Her aunt, Marina, had done it many years before, but not her father, Dominic.

After France elected Nicolas Sarkozy president a few years ago, he parted from his second wife and married Carla Bruni, model, singer, and one-time friend of Mick Jagger. Sarkozy and Carla took their holidays, including odd weekends, at the villa on Cap Nègre, which belonged to Carla's parents.

'You're getting close to the cliffs, Grandad,' warned Jessica.

'The water is deep here,' explained Grandad while scrutinising Jessica's iPhone. 'Useful gadget that.'

'iPhone 6s, Grandad, not any old gadget.'

'Can you see the commemorative plaque, Ellie?' queried Grandad, pointing to the blue and yellow markings on the cliff face.

'What's it for?' Ellie had been ecstatic since arriving in France. She had had a clandestine journey in the back of a baker's van, met Julien who had possibilities, and then sailed on a pirate ship. She was actually quite elated by the turn of events and if that was a taste of things to come, then she was all for it.

'Not the Commandos d'Afrique story,' moaned Jessica while scanning the cliffs of Cap Nègre.

Grandad was sailing close to the cliffs, well inside the outer yellow buoys, which he wasn't meant to do. It was the only way to see the plaque properly.

'About two months after the Normandy Landings in June 1944, the Allies had a major landing along the coast here, 'explained Grandad. 'Some refer to it as the forgotten D-Day.'

'It was World War Two,' added Ewan, who, like Jessica, had heard it all before. 'The American tanks smashed up the old railway line along the coast, and the French never repaired it.'

'Just after midnight on fifteenth August 1944, shortly before the Allied landings, French commandos, on a secret mission, climbed the cliffs, and demolished German artillery emplacements,' continued Grandad. 'It was a strategic lookout position for the Germans with views of the approaches to the port of Toulon. If you look closely, you can still see the old lookout walkway along the cliff.'

Grandad sailed *Black Pearl* safely past Cap Nègre, rounded la Pointe du Souffre, and entered Pramousquier bay. The beach itself was about three hundred yards in length and faced southeast. Cap Nègre sheltered the bay from southerly and westerly winds, including the mistral, which occasionally blew in that area. Just inland, the high and wild Maures Hills blocked any winds from the north. It was a good bay for anchoring. If by chance a strong wind blew from the east or southeast, which it occasionally did, then you quickly rounded Cap Nègre and sheltered in the next bay. As for swimming in the bay, there was no safer place. There were no nasty currents or undertows, and the beach itself was sandy with rocks both ends for snorkelling, diving, and jumping. It was perfect for children.

Because of the imposing height of the Maures Hills inland, the sun sets early over Pramousquier bay. Despite that, there would still be at least two more hours of daylight.

Anchoring *Black Pearl* singlehanded wasn't easy. It involved Grandad running from the helm at the stern, where all the navigation controls were, to the bow, where the anchor was, then back to the helm and so forth. With a bit of training, Grandad thought, anchoring would be a useful task for Ellie, who seemed to have the right build for it. *Black Pearl* anchored in a sheltered spot in deep water less than two hundred yards from the beach and fifty yards off the eastern cliffs of Cap Nègre. Grandad had estimated the distances, because he didn't have radar or any other such navigation equipment.

'Can I see your gadget, Jessica?' Grandad confirmed his position to be where he had judged it to be. Who needed gadgets?

'It's an iPhone, Grandad, iPhone 6s.'

Now came the difficult part.

Chapter 2
A few months earlier

His family said he was bad, particularly his daughter-in-law, Jo, who was also known, by Jessica, as Mother from Hell. That was probably too strong a word, so perhaps misbehaving a little would be more generous.

Maybe misbehaving a lot was nearer the mark. You could never have described him as an angel.

His so-called bad period started after his wife of forty-five years died. He and his late wife had planned growing old disgracefully. They had a game plan, which included making life difficult for their two children, payback, and enjoyable for their grandchildren.

They didn't think they were old despite what everyone said. Seventy was no age at all. They were getting into the rhythm of doing what they wanted, when they wanted, and keeping within their generous pensions and savings. Life was good, very, very good.

Then his wife died. It was breast cancer.

He buried his wife in the village church graveyard, leaving plenty of room for himself. He didn't have a church service, only a simple prayer at the graveside with close family and friends. That was what his wife wanted. She didn't want acquaintances and distant relations gawping at her coffin mouthing the usual platitudes. She wanted people who would miss her.

After the brief ceremony and a few drinks at the family home, everyone left and carried on with their lives. They expected him to do the same .He executed the probate and eventually sorted out his wife's clothes. He took them to the local charity shop where his wife had been working as a volunteer for the past fifteen years. All he said was, 'Here are Jean's remains,' in a light-hearted manner, and the others working in the shop, again as volunteers, were upset.

His daughter and son said he was being insensitive and he should have chosen a charity shop where his wife wasn't known. She loved working in that shop and he believed she would have been quite happy with what he did. Until then, everyone said how well he was coping. Now they said he was misbehaving, was being awkward, and couldn't even iron his own clothes. What did they know?

He missed his wife.

They had had a small villa in the south of France with direct access to Pramousquier beach. They loved that villa and together looked after the grandchildren for the summer holiday each year. Their daughter, Marina, and son, Dominic, had also spent every summer at the villa when they were children, with all the good and bad memories. They now had important jobs and rarely took holidays.

After his wife died, he was supposed to carry on as if nothing had happened. How could he do that? He couldn't face living in the villa without his wife, so he sold it and bought *Black Pearl*.

It was just the incentive he needed, a new challenge, a change in lifestyle.

He knew he couldn't sit around feeling sorry for himself. His wife had died, and he couldn't change that. Sad as it was, he had to pull himself together and get on with life. While buying *Black Pearl* wouldn't have been the sort of thing his late wife would have approved of, not with her susceptibility to seasickness, he believed his action would have made her smile. Despite what others might think, Grandad and *Black Pearl* were well suited, a match made in heaven.

It was regrettable he neglected to tell anyone.

After the charity shop episode, he was cautious with what he told his family. They might have had strange ideas that he needed looking after or locking away in some hellhole care home in the Shetland Islands.

When the summer came, the grandchildren flew out as normal.

'Isn't he good with children,' everyone said.

That was true.

His grandchildren gave him the excuse to be himself. They saw a like-minded spirit and when with him they could do things their parents would never allow. He wanted his grandchildren to enjoy being carefree for as long as possible before the pressures of adulthood took over; and they eventually would, he knew.

Chapter 3
The difficult part

Before Grandad did his explaining, they had had an evening swim in the warm, clear turquoise-blue sea. Even Grandad had a swim because he wanted to check that his cable and anchor were resting on the seabed as he intended; they were. Once Grandad was in the water, Laetitia gingerly climbed down the ladder into the sea, armed with her water wings. She wasn't confident in the water, not deep water anyway.

Lucy and Ewan had swum ashore to see if any of their friends were on the beach, and then swam back with their friends and climbed aboard. It was an easy swim for them all, particularly with the aid of floating crocodiles, body boards, and other such modern aquatic paraphernalia.

The deck of *Black Pearl* was a good height for diving and jumping.

Jessica claimed the padded sunbed immediately behind the bowsprit as her own. While she was an excellent swimmer, getting wet wasn't what Jessica had in mind, not yet anyway. Looking cool, in her new skimpy bikini and Ray-Bans, on the most admired boat in Pramousquier bay had higher priority.

Ellie was hot and bothered and lounging on a hot padded sunbed wasn't her idea of fun. While not a strong swimmer, she gamely launched herself off *Black Pearl* dive-bombing poor Grandad who didn't know what hit him.

'Are there sharks, Mr err Charlie?' she asked.

'We get the odd méduse, although I can't see any around at the moment. And it's Charlie, just Charlie.'

'Odd what?'

'Jellyfish.'

After a while, Grandad got everyone back on board, and then sent back to the beach all the friends that didn't belong.

'Furcuff,' shouted Laetitia, waving happily, as they left.

15

Black Pearl had a large top-loading freezer and a separate fridge that Grandad had stocked in advance. That evening they were to have gourmet pizzas specially prepared by Olivier, who owned the pizza van nearby. They also had plenty of fresh baguettes, which Grandad got from Julien, and a good selection of cheese for those who were still hungry. Earlier, Grandad had baked a large tarte aux pommes, which he planned serving with Italian limoncello-flavoured ice cream for pudding. With Orangina for the three youngsters and local rosé wine with ice cubes for the others, it was time for tea.

'Tea's ready,' shouted Grandad. 'It's on deck.'

He had earlier sent everyone to wash and change before tea, having explained rule thirty-one, only one shower, or bath, per day to conserve water; and rule thirty-two, they must wash before the evening meal.

'Do we have to wash?' complained Ewan, 'that'll save water.'

'It's up to you really,' replied Grandad amiably, thinking it was quite a good idea.

'Put it this way, Ewan,' explained Jessica, 'I don't want any smelly little boys on this klipper.'

'I'm not little,' answered Ewan indignantly.

'He isn't little,' said Lucy supporting her twin brother, because if Ewan was little, then she was definitely little.

'Metoo, metoo.'

'I was only asking.' Ewan knew it was best not to antagonise Jessica.

Last year, when Ewan threatened to throw a bucket of cold seawater over Jessica, she had said, 'You dare.' What made Ewan throw the water was still puzzling. Was it a moment of boyish bravado or a lapse in juvenile judgement? Let's not be too hard on Ewan, because he was only nine at the time. He tried to run but he wasn't quick enough. Jessica easily caught him and gave him a Chinese burn to his arm, which hurt. He knew not to mess with Jessica.

Tea was on deck, where the saloon skylights opened into a large dining table. Grandad had erected a canopy over the mainmast boom to provide shade over the dining table from the sun during the day, and rain, if ever it did. It also added atmosphere during the evening. *Black Pearl* was a convivial, sociable klipper, which, according to Jessica, had potential as a cool party boat. She was already planning how to hold a party and invite all her friends.

'Mum said we don't have tea, it is supper.' Lucy was first to arrive.

'Then tell your Mum from me, it's tea.'

'I'd better write these down in my notebook,' said Lucy. She considered Grandad a better source of information than her Mum and wanted to get her facts right for when she got home.

When they got to the cheese, Lucy panicked, thinking she wasn't having a proper pudding. She had already seen the large tarte aux pommes in the galley. It was delicious.

'Mum said that cheese should be last, not pudding,' explained Lucy to Grandad.

'Tell your Mum from me, in France, cheese is always served before pudding. She should know better.'

'...should know better, got it.' Panic over.

Tea was a success and laid down the foundations for Grandad explaining all.

'...and that's why I bought *Black Pearl*.'

'And Mother from fucking Hell doesn't know?' queried Jessica.

'No.'

'Cool, Grandad, good one.'

'Doesn't anyone know?' asked Lucy for further clarification.

'No.'

'Mr err Charlie, what about my parents?'

'It's Charlie, just Charlie, and the answer is the same. Nobody knows.'

'Metoo, metoo.'

'What do we tell Mum?' asked Ewan.

'We use our mobiles or Skype, so we can be anywhere, and parents will be non-the-wiser,' explained Grandad. 'They know I no longer use the villa landline and now use a mobile.'

'Why don't you get an iPhone, like Jessica?' asked Lucy.

'Because, Lucy, my simple, ordinary old Nokia works fine.'

'Mum said that ordinary mobiles are dead old fashion.'

'Then tell your Mum from me, there's nothing wrong with a simple, ordinary mobile. I can talk to people, that's what I want.'

'Okay,' said Lucy, scribbling in her notebook.

'Whatever we say to your parents, we never lie. For example, when you phone home, say things like; yes, you have arrived safely; yes, the weather is good; yes, you've had a swim; yes, the water is warm; no, there are no méduses. Tell them you've seen some of your friends on the beach, had an enjoyable meal, that sort of thing. They are all things true. Don't mention the villa or *Black Pearl*. I'll let your parents know in the fullness of time, but I need to pick the right moment.'

'Not a problem,' said Jessica, 'I lie to Mother from fucking Hell all the time.'

'Where can we use Skype?' asked Ewan, 'I want to speak to my friends.'

'Go to Chez Claude and ask Max,' replied Grandad, pointing to the beach restaurant at the Cap Nègre end of the beach. 'Tell him you're with me.'

'We all know Max, Grandad,' added Lucy with that tone of exasperation perfected by children. Max was a plagiste and the owner of Chez Claude.

'I thought you had a laptop, Grandad,' enquired Ewan. 'You let us play games on it last year.'

'I dropped it and it doesn't work so well now.' That was true. Grandad was using his laptop while in his hammock and then fell asleep, so no need to explain what happened next.

'So how do we get online and check emails?' asked Lucy.

'Ask Max, that's what I do.'

'If you're really stuck, Lucy, you can use my iPhone,' Jessica offered. 'Ace.'

'Awesome,' said Ewan.

'I said Lucy, not you Ewan. Your track record with electronics isn't too good, is it?'

'That's not fair.'

That was true.

Ewan had received the latest Xbox for Christmas and one of the so-called child friendly educational games, which involved a sea safari. Initially, Ewan thought the game was boring until he added an additional feature. He set up his Xbox so he could use it in the bath, making it all more true-to-life, until he dropped it. How he wasn't electrocuted was a miracle.

'That's not fair.'

'Rules one, thirty-one, and thirty-two are reasonable,' said Jessica cautiously, 'what about all the ones in between. You haven't told us them.'

Jessica had a thing about rules. Mother from Hell had rules, school had rules, and there were even rules on the school bus.

'I haven't made them up yet,' explained Grandad, 'I like to keep my options open.'

'Fuck—'

'Rule two, if you are heard swearing by the others, you have to wash the dishes. That goes for everyone.'

'Ace.'

'Awesome.'

'Metoo, metoo.'

Jessica regretted her query about Grandad's rules and learned a salutary lesson. There were times when you shouldn't ask. From the point-of-view of the others, they didn't swear anyway, so it wasn't a problem. Each day, to avoid the miserable task of doing the dishes, they waited patiently for Jessica to break rule two.

Grandad didn't much like rules himself.

Because others perceived anything that floats, like a boat for example, to be dangerous, he believed he had better have a few practical rules as a matter of expedience. In any case, Grandad had a theory that children often needed some rules. Rules gave them something to moan about and feel aggrieved. To avoid the imposition of further rules, children changed their behaviour, thus reinforcing self-discipline and that alleviated the need for further rules. Admittedly, not many others had signed up to Grandad's theory.

Mother from Hell had an alternative theory. Rather than reinforcing self-discipline, a lack of rules encouraged children to become devious, and she had a deceitful conniving shitbag daughter as proof.

Grandad explained about the batteries on *Black Pearl*, not leaving lights on, not to flush paper down the toilets but to use the baskets provided, and things like that.

'I can't work the toilets because I'm not strong enough,' was Laetitia's response. The toilets needed a strong pumping action to make them work.

'That's okay, when you've been, shout help, and someone will come to your rescue.'

'No way,' complained Ewan, 'I'm not pumping her poo.'

'Rule two, Ewan, that's swearing,' said Lucy.

'That's not swearing, tell her Grandad.'

'Dishes...'

'That's not fair.'

'I'll help Jessica with the dishes,' volunteered Ellie.

'Thanks, Ellie.'

'Mum, it's me.' Lucy was on the mobile.

'xxxx'

'Weather's hot and sunny.'

'xxxx'

'Yep, everything is fine, no problems with the flight.'

'xxxx'

'Grandad's okay.'

'xxxx'

'Ewan's a pain.'

'xxxx'

'Ewan can't speak right now, he's busy.'

'xxxx'

'I'm sharing a room with Laetitia, and yep, she's okay too.'

'xxxx'

'Pizzas, they're ace.'

'xxxx'

'I'm sure we won't have them every night.'

'xxxx'

'I won't forget the sun cream.'

'xxxx'

'There are no méduses.'

'xxxx'

'We've had a swim before tea, that's how I know.'

'xxxx'

'Grandad said it's tea, and that's final. Speak to you soon, bye.'

'xxxx xxxx'

*H*aving done the dishes and the three younger ones had completed their exploration of their floating summer home, everyone ended up on deck lounging around the dining table, with Grandad in his hammock.

'Tell us a story, Grandad?' demanded Laetitia, who loved stories.

'Yeah, one about pirates,' requested Ewan.

'And Paddington Bear,' added Laetitia.

'Paddington Bear wasn't a pirate,' interjected Ewan in a derogatory manner.

'What do you know?' retorted Laetitia indignantly.

Grandad enjoyed telling his grandchildren stories in the evening. He never had television at the villa, and there wasn't one on *Black Pearl*, so stories in the evening were a feature of life in Pramousquier. He rarely read stories from children books. He made them up, some true, others fantasy, mostly a mixture of both.

While preparing tea, Grandad had had a couple of pastis as an apéritif, so was feeling mellow, particularly as everyone had agreed never to mention *Black Pearl* to their parents. Laetitia did what she always did at story time and climbed onto Grandad's lap and snuggled down into a comfortable position, smelling that familiar smell of salt, cooking, and pastis. Both Jessica and Lucy felt pangs of jealousy, because that was what they used to do before getting too old for that sort of thing.

'Most people think of pirates as only men,' Grandad began, 'but that's not true. About three hundred years ago, when the Caribbean Sea was full of brigands, there were two notorious female pirates, Anne Bonny and Mary Read.'

'Ace,' said Lucy, who reckoned being a female pirate would be an excellent career choice for her.

'Anne Bonny was born in Ireland to a lawyer who became socially disgraced and then escaped to the Caribbean, taking Anne with him. Anne was a fiery young girl and was known to beat up men who made inappropriate advances. With one thing or another and being a bit wild, Anne ended up a pirate with Calico Jack Rackham.'

'Why did they call him Calico?' asked Lucy.

'He wore brightly-coloured clothes made from calico, a cheap cotton fabric from India. Anyway, Calico Jack was a minor pirate, raiding small ships and fishing boats near the coast. He stole the odd sloop as his preferred pirate ship. He had some lucky escapes from the authorities.

'Mary Read was born in London and her father never lived with her or her mother. Her mother deceived her father by dressing Mary as a boy so she could receive money for her upbringing. If her father knew she was a girl, she would have received nothing. After a while, Mary became used to being a boy. When she grew up, she was footboy to a wealthy French woman, but she didn't like doing that.

'She then became a cabin boy on a warship and to cut a long story short, she met a good man and they were married and her days pretending to be a male were temporarily over. Unfortunately, Mary's husband unexpectedly died.

'Mary returned to the only other life she'd ever known and once more pretended to be a male. She signed up as a sailor aboard a Dutch ship bound for the Caribbean. That was where she fortuitously met Calico Jack, who captured the Dutch ship and took Mary and some others to increase his crew.

'Eventually Anne and Mary became friends. At first Calico Jack was jealous, thinking Mary was a man but then Mary's true identity was revealed. It wasn't long before one of the pirates fell in love with Mary and that caused a quarrel with another pirate but Mary killed him in a duel, with sword and pistol. They said that Anne and Mary only dressed as men before and during a battle. They were both ferocious pirates and fought alongside the men.

'Like most pirates, Calico Jack and his crew were eventually caught by the authorities and found guilty in court of piracy. They hanged Calico Jack on Deadman's Cay, an island in the Bahamas.'

'What happened to Anne and Mary?' asked a worried Lucy.

'They didn't hang because Anne and Mary said they were pregnant and it wasn't allowed to hang pregnant women. That was when Calico Jack gave Anne a Paddington Bear as a present for the baby. It must have been one of the last things Calico Jack did before he was hanged.'

Laetitia poked her little tongue out at Ewan and loved her Grandad even more, if that were possible. Ewan rolled his eyes high into their sockets so only the whites were visible, which wasn't an easy trick.

'Some say Anne Bonny's father bought her freedom and others say that on her acquittal, she ran off with another pirate, but no one really knows what happened to her. They say poor Mary Read contracted an infectious virus and died while still in prison. They were the most infamous female pirates of their time.'

Lucy's enthusiasm for being a female pirate was now on the wane. She didn't want to hang or die in prison.

'One more story, pleeease,' demanded Laetitia, who loved Grandad's stories.

'That's enough for now.' Grandad was contented at having got Paddington Bear into the plot and congratulated himself on a job well done.

Two hurricane lamps under the canopy gave a warm, comfortable light, not too bright, not too dim. Insects, attracted by the light, buzzed around the lamps until too close, burnt, then died. The lamps didn't hang over the table directly, so they weren't bothered by dead insects. High on the mainmast was a bright light, visible for miles, revealing the presence of *Black Pearl* to any other boat that might approach. The moon provided additional light, making it a fairy-tale evening on the deck of *Black Pearl*, eating on the deck table, sipping Orangina and wine, listening to Grandad's stories.

'Can we go ashore?' asked Jessica half-heartedly.

'Not tonight,' said Grandad, 'you need to know how to work the Zodiac. I'll show you tomorrow, and then you can come and go when you want.'

'Okay, thanks.' Jessica was pleased with the answer, because Grandad hadn't dismissed going ashore in the evenings. It was a matter of being able to work the Zodiac.

'When is it bedtime?' asked Lucy.

'When you're tired,' answered Grandad, 'that's the best time.'

Grandad knew from experience that children, when given a free hand, never purposely lost sleep. If they were up late in the evening, then they invariably slept late in the morning. Tell them to go to bed then they never slept a wink.

Grandad peered down at Laetitia, who was already fast asleep on his lap. He left her there for the time being as he didn't want to disturb her.

'Tomorrow morning it's nautical training,' declared Grandad.

Chapter 4
Nautical training

'**Help**, help…'

It was dark, the exact time unknown.

Grandad fell out of his hammock, bruising his leg and arm before he ran along the deck and nearly tripped over the side railings into the sea. After stumbling into the chartroom, he grabbed his hefty wooden rounders bat and made his way into *Black Pearl*'s accommodation, ready to jump the first intruder he came across.

'It's Laetitia,' explained Lucy all in a dither, 'I think she's seen a ghost. You didn't tell me there were ghosts.'

Laetitia sleepily walked out of the bathroom, climbed back into bed, and promptly fell asleep.

'It's okay,' whispered Grandad. 'Laetitia's been to the toilet. I told her to shout, help. I didn't mean in the middle of the night though.'

'Why are you playing rounders, Grandad?'

'Go back to sleep, Lucy, there are no ghosts.'

Grandad hadn't planned on little girls going to the toilet several times in the night. He then remembered the large amount of Orangina Laetitia had drunk the night before. She had wanted to match Grandad drinking, which was a lot.

Shortly after sunrise, which was early, Grandad queried his flippant comment to Lucy about there being no ghosts when he heard a howling noise from the fo'c'sle. He didn't fall out of his hammock this time. He clutched his ethnic bed cover up to his nose until he could work out where the noise was coming from.

'Is breakfast ready, Grandad?' It was Ewan, singing, as he always did first thing in the morning.

'It's early, Ewan.'

'It's not, I can see the sun.'

Ewan was right, the sun had risen, and he was hungry. It was still early though.

'Go and raid the fridge in the galley, but don't wake the girls.'

'Okay.'

Ewan was a happy soul, and like most ten-year-old boys, had a very short-term memory. In the galley, he grabbed a piece of pizza left from the previous evening, a bottle of Orangina, and believed life on a pirate ship was awesome. Why he decided to sing Gershwin's 'Summertime' outside Jessica's cabin was puzzling!

'You're dead meat, Ewan.'

'Help, help…'

'Grandad, Laetitia's seen that ghost again.'

'Grandad, she's giving me a Chinese burn, arrrr…'

'Mr err Charlie, will it be like this every morning?'

Grandad decided it was time for his morning swim, a little earlier than normal. He dived from the side of *Black Pearl*, going under the warm, calm water to escape the bedlam, enjoying seconds of glorious solitude, though he knew he had to eventually surface.

'Grandad's abandoned ship,' shouted Lucy, 'I think he's seen a ghost.' She was first on deck, still not sure about the ghosts because pirate ships always had ghosts. If Grandad was abandoning ship, then she wasn't going to be left behind, so into the sea she jumped.

Ewan finally managed to escape the clutches of Jessica, made a rapid dash to freedom, and followed Lucy into the sea.

'Don't think you can escape me, little boy.' Jessica did an almost perfect dive into the sea and, after easily catching Ewan, gave him a ducking to remember.

Grandad had noticed that about girls, they followed their actions through to the end, no half measures, like boys, who couldn't be bothered.

'Metoo, metoo.'

'Don't j—'

Too late.

It was Laetitia's first jump and she did it without thinking. Perhaps she really had seen a ghost. She hit the water with her arms and legs already doing a frantic doggy-paddle, and when she surfaced, she shouted, 'I can swim, I can swim.'

Jessica quickly went to her aid. 'Laetitia, what do you think you're doing?'

'I can swim.'

'Mr err Charlie, before I jump, should I let down the ladder, because I can't see how we can get back aboard?'

'That's a good idea, Ellie.'

Grandad was never an early bird and not at his best in the morning, particularly after a disturbed night. Grumpy would be a kind adjective to describe him. Once he saw the others all happily swimming around in the water, and Ewan had recovered from his ducking, he climbed back on board and prepared breakfast. Grandad viewed breakfast as the most important meal of the day, so he always took care in its preparation.

Lunch, however, was the meal he enjoyed most, taken at leisure, with all sorts of bits-and-pieces to snack on, with fresh baguettes and fruit. Tea, or supper if you were Lucy's Mum, was the meal the grandchildren liked most, because it was Grandad's bath meal, and they loved bath meals.

Gran, when she was alive, had never cooked a meal in Pramousquier. When the children were little it was Gran's job to wash and dress them, and immediately after, they wanted feeding – so Grandad made tea. When the children got older, they could wash and dress themselves, so Grandad used to have a leisurely bath himself and change for tea. Grandad still preferred baths to showers. Accordingly, Grandad prepared tea before having a bath, and it had to cook itself and be ready to serve by the time he had finished his bath, hence the term, bath meals. To begin, Grandad's meals were a bit hit-and-miss. However, he was an advocate of that old adage.

If at first you don't succeed, try, try, try again.

He did.

And the meals got better.

Gradually his bath meals became quite good and his cooking at least equalled, if not surpassed, the chefs in the restaurants around Pramousquier. Consequently, his children, Marina and Dominic, were superb and adventurous cooks. Mother from Hell, Jo, who was Dominic's wife, could trace her husband's ability to cook back to

Grandad. You would think that having a husband who was a competent cook was a positive attribute but this just added to her resentment of Grandad.

You don't get cereals with Grandad. It was warmed-up baguette left over from the night before, freshly baked pain au chocolat and croissants from frozen and they tasted just as good, and brioche, which he got from Julien the previous day.

Grandad had that DIY trait common to his generation, and provided honey-flavoured yoghurts he had made himself, along with marmalade, and plum jam, all made when Gran was alive. He also had fig conserve, which someone had given him.

He served a huge pile of sliced melon de Cavaillon, because they were local, in season, and were mouth-wateringly good. Melon de Cavaillon can be a bit of a lottery regarding taste. One can be tangy and full of flavour, and the next tasting like a limp courgette. To alleviate some of the risk, Grandad had honed his technique of sniffing the skin for obvious fragrance, pressing the ends, checking that the stem had cracked, and weighing the melon carefully in his hand for it must feel heavy for its size. While impressing many at the market stall where he normally bought his melons, buying melons was still a lottery.

'Breakfast is ready,' shouted Grandad.

Five wet and hungry bodies clambered aboard and rushed towards the table, as you would expect, wet, hungry children to do.

'Rule three. Dry yourselves before sitting at the table. You don't want to eat soggy croissants. At the end of the table is fruit juice, coffee for those who want it, tea, and milk. Just help yourselves.'

'Grandad, Mum says we should only have skimmed milk,' declared Lucy. Her Mum had so many silly rules about what you can or can't eat, what you can or can't do, that she wanted some trustworthy facts to present to her mother. Lucy knew it didn't come more reliable than from Grandad.

'Full-fat milk actually tastes of milk, particularly when fresh and chilled, whereas skimmed milk tastes of rancid calcium dregs, from a female donkey, left in the midday sun too long. I've nothing against donkeys, either. Next time you see your mother, tell her from me.'

'Okay.' Grandad was not only reliable. He was also informative. Lucy didn't know you could get milk from donkeys. 'Is it the milk or the donkey that's been left in the midday sun too long?'

'The milk,' clarified Grandad.

Lucy was relieved with that answer because it would be cruel to leave donkeys in the midday sun.

'Rule four, whenever you empty a bottle from the fridge, replace it with another. That way we always have cold drinks.'

'Good idea.' Jessica was up in the night and there was no cold water in the fridge.

'Rule five, a special one for Laetitia, you only shout, help, in daylight hours.'

'Can't I have a wee at night?' Laetitia was worried.

'It's okay, you can go,' explained Grandad. 'We'll flush the toilet in the morning.'

'I'll try and remember.'

'One last thing, there are no ghosts on *Black Pearl*.'

'You never told us about ghosts,' said Ewan, 'and I'm all alone in my cabin.'

'I didn't tell you because there aren't any, that's why.'

'See,' said Lucy, 'I told you he would deny it. Grandad doth protest too much, methinks.'

'I'm impressed, that's from Hamlet,' said Grandad. 'Where did you learn that?'

'At school,' explained Lucy. 'We had to learn famous quotes.'

'No we didn't,' stated Ewan. 'I don't remember doing famous quotes. She's just making it up.'

'We did, you just never listen. I know because I'm older, so there.'

Grandad let that go, accepting that females always like to get the last word in.

'Don't forget, after breakfast we have nautical training.'

'I'm the lookout,' shouted Laetitia. She already knew what to do.

'I'm the pirate king,' shouted Ewan, who had seen many pirate films. He knew the pirate king was the leader of all the pirate captains who, according to the pirate code, was the only captain who could declare war against the enemy. What more did you need to know?

Lucy and Ellie said nothing because neither knew what nautical training involved and they didn't want to commit to anything untoward. That's how girls are, unlike boys, who can be a bit impulsive.

Jessica knew exactly what to say. 'Fuck...'

They all dawdled over breakfast because they could see the beach was empty, so it must still be early. They saw an early morning swimmer. She was wearing a blue bathing cap and was making a big splash doing the backstroke, and you could hear her cheerfully chanting, '*Eins, zwei, eins, zwei,*' in rhythm with her strokes.

'What's she saying?' asked Lucy.

'She's batty, if you ask me,' added Ewan.

'Furcuff,' shouted Laetitia, waving at the lone swimmer, who waved back. 'She's a nice lady.'

*F*or children, life on the beach was simple. At least it would be if it weren't for parents.

Firstly, there was dress code. They woke up, put on their swimsuit, and didn't take it off until some unreasonable parent told them to do so, usually at bath-time, before the evening meal, or, if they could get away with it, bed time. Out of choice, they would prefer to keep their swimsuit on all the time, including when asleep, which seemed a sensible thing to do. Would parents listen? Until then, Jessica was quite happy with the dress code. Now she had complications, such as being cool and noticed by boys.

Secondly, there was feeding code. Children wanted feeding when they got hungry, a simple enough request. Even so, parents had that unreasonable habit of wanting to have meals at specific times, which, believe me, could be very inconvenient.

Thirdly, children wanted leaving alone to get on with things, their things, and this was a concept parents had difficulty understanding. Children didn't want any of that shopping nonsense, or making beds, or visiting boring museums, or seeing distant relations, or keeping quiet, or not getting dirty, or being polite, or speaking proper. Parents didn't have a clue.

If asked, nautical training would not have been high on their list of must do activities.

29

In preparation for nautical training, Ewan had dressed as a pirate. He was having difficulty walking because he had one leg tied behind and kept talking to an imaginary parrot on his shoulder. Ewan obviously mixed up nautical training with being a pirate, an easy mistake for a boy!

Ellie enjoyed talking to Ewan's parrot. She wanted adventure, and Charlie seemed like the chap to provide it. Jessica tagged along, seemingly bored.

Laetitia didn't need training, because she was already up the mainmast being lookout.

'Enemy on the beach,' shouted Laetitia. The enemy in question were friends of Lucy and Ewan, the ones who boarded *Black Pearl* the previous evening. Laetitia recognised them and decided she had better remind the others that she was the lookout on that particular pirate ship.

'Come on,' shouted Ewan, 'let's attack the enemy.' He didn't need training. He knew what to do because he was the pirate king.

'We'll attack later,' said Lucy reluctantly, because she didn't want any nautical training either. While she wanted to support Grandad because she loved him, she wanted to attack the enemy with Ewan, with the element of surprise. That's what pirates did. She also wanted to talk to Ewan's parrot, though she would never admit it. Despite that, she was ready with notebook and pencil in hand.

'Come down, Laetitia, we don't need a lookout during nautical training,' pleaded Grandad, who was quietly impressed how one so small could climb so high. 'You can be lookout after, I promise.'

'Okay.'

'Grandad,' queried Jessica, 'what do you know about boats?'

She wanted to know his credentials for conducting nautical training because nautical knowledge wasn't something she had observed he possessed, not until now, anyway.

'I spent several years as a navigation officer on supertankers.'

'Supertankers!' exclaimed Jessica. 'Aren't they the ones that spew oil all over the beaches?'

'Not the ones I sailed on.'

'You never said we'd spew oil!' exclaimed Lucy, who had changed her initial enthusiasm for a more cautious attitude.

'We won't,' Grandad explained. 'This isn't a supertanker, is it?'

That seemed to placate poor Lucy, even though she didn't know what a supertanker was.

'Can we attack the enemy now?' Grandad ignored Ewan's query.

'When was the last time you sailed on a supertanker, Grandad?' asked Jessica, not dropping the issue of competence, because she was trying to wriggle out of this nautical training nonsense because she had other plans in mind.

'Let me see, it must be about forty-five years ago, maybe longer.'

Jessica did some quick calculations in her head and worked out that was before Mother from Hell was born. 'That's a long time ago.'

'You don't forget these things. I learnt to talk when I was little, and I haven't forgotten how to talk, have I?'

While Jessica didn't buy that argument, the others agreed it was a valid point. Ewan could remember learning to spit nearly six feet ages ago, and he hadn't forgotten how to do that.

'I give in,' said Jessica. 'Let's just get on with it.

'It won't take long,' said Grandad, who decided to give the abridged version of nautical training. 'In that box over there are the life jackets, I'm the cook, Jessica and Ellie are the navigators, Laetitia is the lookout, and Ewan is the pirate king.'

'What about me?' Lucy queried.

'You're the pirate princess with the additional responsibility for entertainment.'

'I won't be hanged or get pregnant and die in prison?' Lucy queried. To be honest, Lucy wasn't sure what getting pregnant entailed, because she hadn't done that at school yet.

'That won't happen, I promise.' Grandad questioned his choice of story the previous evening, but after a few glasses of wine, his tongue was much quicker than his brain.

'That's okay then.'

'Test time now,' Grandad informed everyone, 'where do we keep the lifejackets?'

'You just said,' said Lucy incredulously, 'in that box.'

'Correct, you all pass, you can go now.'

'Is that it?' asked Lucy with even more incredulity.

'How do we learn things, then,' asked Ewan, 'like how to tie pirate

31

knots and sharpen daggers?'

'Look it up,' explained Grandad, directing their attention to two books on the table.

Ellie picked up the nearest book and read its title on the spine, *Nicholls's Seamanship and Nautical Knowledge*. She opened it up and noticed it was the 1953 edition.

'It's a bit old,' said Ellie.

'I had a hard time getting it,' explained Grandad. 'You might read the section on anchoring, Ellie, because if you want, you can help me with that.'

'Okay.'

'You'll find every knot a pirate will ever need in that book, Ewan.'

'It better show how to tie a hangman's noose.' Ewan knew his priorities.

Jessica was suspicious. 'You said me and Ellie were navigators.'

'I did,' answered Grandad, ignoring Ewan. 'You should read the other book, the one about chartwork.'

'So how do we work the Zodiac?' Jessica was eager to learn how to get ashore without having to swim, 'that's nautical, isn't it.'

'I haven't forgotten about the Zodiac, I'll show you in a minute,' said Grandad. 'One last thing, rule six, we keep our own cabins clean and tidy.'

'That's not fair,' grumbled Ewan, as any ten-year-old boy would. 'I'm all by myself.'

Nautical training took all of three minutes. Grandad had suddenly decided that learning by discovery was a much more suitable method of training. If they were stuck, they would work it out, if they really were stuck, they would ask. Everyone was on holiday and didn't want to hear him jabbering on about how to do this, do that, and spoiling their day.

'I've launched the kayak,' added Grandad.

Lucy and Ewan's surprise attack on the enemy didn't go as planned.

Their delay was due to the demands of having to make a pirate princess outfit for Lucy. Ewan borrowed Jessica's makeup bag, clearly without Jessica knowing, which was a dangerous thing to do, even if you were the pirate king. They would put the makeup on later. Lucy borrowed one of Jessica's black frilly skirts. It was either a petticoat or a disco-dancing miniskirt, so take your pick. No, Jessica didn't know and yes, it was a dangerous thing to do, even if you were a pirate princess.

By the time that Lucy and Ewan came on deck, it was too late. Their friends, the enemy, had boarded, captured the cook, made a tentative attack on the fo'c'sle, but were stopped in their track, which wasn't surprising, considering the circumstances.

'One more fucking step will be your last.'

While the enemy didn't fully understand what the murderous older girl said, they got the meaning. They remembered her from last year, when she had done over poor Ewan. Unsure of their victory, they happily fraternised with the cook, who was always entertaining.

'Laetitia,' shouted Ewan angrily, 'why didn't you warn us we were being attacked by the enemy?'

'I was playing with my dolls.'

The pirate king and princess accepted defeat. With the enemy, they planned their day while sitting on deck outside the chartroom. Planning involved finding snorkel and masks, blowing up a dolphin and mermaid, topping up on biscuits and Orangina, and—

'Lucy, that's my fucking tutu skirt you're wearing.'

'Abandon ship, *tout de suite*,' ordered the princess pirate, and they did, over the side they went with dolphin, mermaid, snorkel and masks, and biscuits, which got wet.

'I give the orders, Lucy, not you,' shouted Ewan on the run while leading the abandonment of ship. He certainly didn't want to be caught by Jessica.

'Metoo, metoo.'

Laetitia, having seen the striking-looking pirate princess, had earlier climbed down from the mainmast quicker than a monkey. She wanted to dress like a pirate like the others. They always forgot about her just because she was little, which wasn't right, was it? She found Jessica's makeup bag on deck outside the chartroom and quickly blacked her face, with purple stripes, and promoted herself to pirate lookout. When she heard the call to abandon ship, off she went, dropping the makeup bag, joining the others.

'I bet Ewan put you up to this, you're dead meat, little boy.'

Daughter who was going through her awkward period couldn't have been nearer the truth. Ewan had indeed recommended the black frilly tutu skirt to Lucy. It was partly for revenge because of his ducking earlier, and partly because it seemed more appropriate for a pirate princess rather than for Jessica, who merely looked silly. Lucy loved her new pirate outfit. She wasn't going to give it up without a fight.

'Lookout, don't forget your water wings,' advised Grandad.

'It's pirate lookout now.'

'Is that so?'

It was too late. They'd all gone. Grandad viewed this abandonment a useful lifeboat practice, and he would have entered it into *Black Pearl's* logbook, if he had one.

'Keep an eye on Laetitia.'

'Furcuff,' shouted the pirate lookout, waving wildly while hanging on to the tail of the mermaid, which was being hauled towards the beach by Lucy and one of her friends. Lucy was having difficulty swimming while wearing Jessica's black frilly tutu skirt, although she managed.

Grandad watched carefully until they were all safely inside the inner yellow buoys. There was very little wind and a clear blue sky, a perfect day for the beach. He had already phoned Max, the plagiste at Chez Claude, and had ordered moules mariniere, which always came with lots of frites, for their evening meal. Grandad also ordered several baguettes, which would be freshly baked for the Chez Claude and delivered by Julien or his parents. He arranged to pick it all up in the Zodiac later that evening. Max also said he would keep an eye on the children and give them ice cream and plenty of water, if needed. Chez Claude was a good example of a French restaurant situated on the beach, also it was one of four plagistes on the beach offering locations de parasols, matelas et transats, meals, and drinks for those prepared to pay.

What Grandad had in mind was an easy morning in his hammock, possibly a little reading, with little dips in the sea to cool down. What he actually did was stumble across Jessica's makeup bag with whatever was inside melting and making a horrible stain on the teak decking. Grandad didn't know it was Jessica's bag. He thought it was Lucy's makeup for her theatrical productions, or something like that. He put the bag in a corner of the chartroom. He decided to give the teak decking a good going over with a holystone, and then did other nautical tasks you would expect to see on an old Dutch klipper.

He switched on the generator to top up the batteries, which, surprisingly, weren't too bad. He then remembered he had used the main engine the previous day, when he had collected the youngsters from the airport. The main engine drove an alternator, which automatically topped up the batteries.

Grandad then made a tarte au citron for pudding that evening because he had a surplus of lemons he had bought from an old man who had a small lemon grove. He didn't make his own pastry. He bought it ready-made from the supermarket and kept it in the freezer. He defrosted a couple of homemade loaves of wholemeal bread for lunch, which everyone liked. Grandad enjoyed cooking, and he had been busy preparing meals before the youngsters arrived. He checked the fridge and restocked it with essentials, like water, Orangina, and wine. He planned to restock with food once a week, with baguettes daily from Max.

In the meantime, the two cool teenage girls, who were laying on the padded sunbed immediately behind the bowsprit, got restless. Jessica realised that no one was close enough to see them, except Grandad, and he didn't count. Ellie had the Nicholls's Seamanship book and read about anchoring, and found it somewhat absorbing, sort of.

'That can't be interesting, Ellie, surely?'

Ellie tossed over the other book to Jessica. 'That's about chartwork.'

Even a teenage girl who was going through her awkward period can get inquisitive. When thrown a book, one tends to open it, flick through a few pages, close it, and then forget all about it. Jessica reached the second part of that process.

'It was printed in 1956, and it's called *Modern Chartwork*.'

Jessica, despite going through her awkward period, when inclined, was quite intelligent, as was Ellie. They both thumbed through their respective books, drinking chilled sparkling water.

'This is elementary geometry, like what we do at school.' Jessica made a mental note to check out the chartroom later.

According to Jessica, Grandad, who was thumping the decks with a lump of stone, was generally being a nuisance.

'Ellie?'

'What?'

'It's got to go.'

'What?'

'The gross ponytail, that's what. We can't be seen in public with him with it dangling from his head, particularly if he's wearing that black bandana. What does he think he's doing? If Gran were still alive, she wouldn't allow it, that's for sure.'

Ellie decided Jessica wasn't getting the hang of being on ~~a pirate ship~~ an old Dutch klipper. Despite being sixteen, she would much prefer to be playing pirates or dive-bombing the enemy, because her splashes were second-to-none. However, she was sixteen, and knew that she had to be cool and noticed by the boys. Being noticed by the boys wasn't a problem, not when you were her size. Being cool was a different matter.

'Why don't we go ashore and have a walk around,' Ellie suggested.

'What, and get wet.'

'Can't we take the kayak? I've just had a text from Julien and he'll be on the beach soon.'

Chapter 5
Life on the beach; morning

Life might be hard for some, but not for those aboard *Black Pearl.*

Both Lucy and Ewan have had two friends at Pramousquier for as long as they could remember. Out of habit, parents stayed in their respective villas or apartments for the summer at the same time each year. Children therefore knew each other and grew up together. When they met the following year, it was as if they had never parted and things simply continued as before.

While the twins were English and their friends were French, German, and Italian, their command of French was quite good. Over the years, while playing on the beach, speaking French just came naturally, without warning, and they weren't aware of it.

Ewan's two friends, Noé, who was French, and Hans, who was German with fair hair faded by life on the beach, didn't think it proper when Ewan declared he was the pirate king. According to Hans, that wasn't democratic. While not really appreciating what it meant, Ewan argued it was democratic, because his Grandad had promoted him that very morning. That was a compelling argument for the other two because they could see the skull and crossbones flag flying from *Black Pearl's* mizzenmast. Sensibly, Hans elected himself German pirate captain, and similarly, Noé reluctantly became French pirate captain.

Lucy's two friends, Virginia, who was Italian, and Nina, who was French and younger sister of Noé, didn't think it proper when Lucy declared she was the pirate princess. Lucy explained her Grandad had given her that title that very morning. That wasn't a compelling argument for the other two despite being able to see the skull and crossbones flag flying from *Black Pearl's* mizzenmast. It wasn't fair, simple as that.

'So what does a pirate princess do?' Nina wanted to know.

'I do pirate things and I can't sleep on a pea,' explained Lucy without conviction. 'It's all on Max's laptop.' She failed to mention about the possibility of being hanged and dying in prison.

Any reason to visit Max never went neglected. Despite having ages of only nine or ten, and without knowing why, they knew Max was special. Lucy took off her black frilly pirate princess outfit, because it was wet and soggy, and put it on the rocks near Chez Claude to dry.

Max was in his early thirties, a worldly kind of man burdened with being tall, handsome, and bronzed with a physique of a Greek warrior. For most women his own age, his attractive appearance and physique were intimidating and they assumed he had other women lined up and waiting their turn, and they didn't want to join the queue. His history with love and romance, therefore, wasn't good. Regrettably, women of a certain age and disposition often came on strong, particularly customers. This he politely ignored because didn't want a bad reputation.

Teenage girls, who often came and stared wantonly, were an additional problem. He knew most of their parents, who were good customers.

'Tell your parents that the fish is good today,' was Max's usual remark and they would blush guiltily and continue on their way.

Laetitia had friends on the beach last year but couldn't remember what they looked like. She hoped she would recognise them when she saw them. As she walked down the beach, following the others, she examined at all the usual spots where she thought her friends might be. She ambled along following the others, dragging the giant mermaid behind her, because Lucy couldn't be bothered.

'I'm a pirate lookout,' said Laetitia to anyone nearby.

'No you're not,' said Ewan, 'you're a simple, plain, ordinary lookout, and a rubbish one at that.'

'I told you, I was playing with my dolls.'

Nobody, not even Virginia, who considered Laetitia as cute, thought that playing with your dolls was a compelling excuse to neglect your lookout duties, pirate or otherwise, and miss an enemy attack.

'Is she really a lookout?' Hans asked.

'Uh huh,' answered Laetitia, ignoring that the pirate bit was missing.

'Yeah, I suppose,' answered Ewan grudgingly. 'Grandad said so this morning, although I don't know why, because she's rubbish.'

Ewan was aware that Hans' question might be a trick. Since his pirate king position depended on Grandad, then he couldn't deny Laetitia's claim of being lookout, could he. That might jeopardise his position.

'She's not rubbish, not like you, because you're useless,' countered Lucy. 'She can climb the mast higher than you, and she's properly recorded, unlike someone I know. Isn't that right, Laetitia?'

Ignoring the bit about not being properly recorded, Lucy had hit a sore point with Ewan. Laetitia could indeed climb the mast higher than he could. It seemed easy at first. It did when Laetitia did it. When he tried, he found he didn't like heights, not that high anyway. Everyone eyed Ewan, waiting for the robust rebuff, which didn't come.

'I haven't tried properly yet.' Poor Ewan knew he had suffered a loss of face. 'I was busy at the time planning pirate things.'

'We could do with a pirate lookout,' said Hans, 'it might be useful.'

Hans was the best boy ever, thought Laetitia, not like useless Ewan. She didn't have her dolls with her, so wouldn't be distracted. She pledged to herself that she would be the best pirate lookout ever.

The gang returned to the end of the beach near Chez Claude, sat on the rocks, and decided what to do next. They dropped their things on the beach, making their claim so no one else could pinch their spot.

'Enemy on the beach,' whispered Laetitia for all to hear.

Hans surveyed the beach with his piercing blue eyes and reviewed the dangerous situation. 'Good work, pirate lookout. Keep a close eye on them. Keep us informed if they do anything wrong.'

Laetitia almost burst with pride, and if the enemy took another step in their direction, she would run down the beach and kill them all single-handed.

'Let's climb round the rocks,' said Noé.

'I haven't got my flip-flops,' said Lucy, because the rocks were sharp at the beginning of the holidays although not a problem after a few days, when the soles of their feet became hardened. 'We're going to see Max.'

'Metoo, metoo.' She needed a wee.

Laetitia seized her chance because she was secretly jealous of Lucy's new outfit, so she quickly took the black frilly tutu skirt from the rocks and put it on. Putting it on were kind words to describe what Laetitia did, because Jessica was much bigger. It would never fit her. It therefore hung neatly around Laetitia's neck, despite partly obscuring her field of vision, which wasn't the best thing for a pirate lookout. As any pernickety female would confess, swimming in the sea can play havoc with your makeup. This was particularly true for Laetitia and her blackened face with purple stripes, although one could never accuse her of being pernickety.

'Let's swim round with our masks,' said Ewan, who also had no flip-flops with him.

'We'll go hunting for pirate treasure,' said Hans, taking charge.

Ewan was feeling aggrieved because he was the pirate king, not Hans, who was only a pirate captain. It wasn't his fault Hans was older. Hans was becoming too bossy for his liking. He would have thought of going hunting for pirate treasure, given time.

The three boys put on their snorkels and masks and off they went, ignoring the four girls, who were in return, ignoring them.

'Charrrrge…'

Everyone on the beach stopped to watch the little six-year-old girl, blackened face with purple stripes, and black tutu skirt with drooping frills around her neck, run down the beach, armed with a snorkel, shouting…

'Let's get'em, pirates, this is our beach, furcuff.'

Lucy was baffled with Laetitia's behaviour and decided not to hang around.

'Charr—'

Justifiably, you would expect a little six-year-old girl, blackened face with purple stripes running wildly down the beach, to trip over her black tutu skirt with drooping frills.

She did.

That little girl was brave, with a heart of a lioness, and despite hurting herself with her fall, stood up, forced back her tears, and continued her advance on the enemy.

'—rrge.'

It appeared that one member of the offending enemy had taken a step in the wrong direction while playing beach volleyball with his friends. Laetitia soon sorted them out, all six teenage boys. She splashed them good and proper, letting them know who was in charge of that particular part of the beach, then threw their ball as far out to sea as she possibly could, which wasn't far, obviously.

'Furcuff,' shouted the pirate lookout in true pirate fashion, which took the enemy by surprise.

She didn't go as far as hitting any of the boys. She wiggled her snorkel under the nose of the biggest in a threatening manner, if such a thing was possible for a six-year-old girl, blackened face with purple stripes.

The six teenage boys lost heart in their game, because everyone was staring at them, and they were still at the age of being easily embarrassed. They had only recently become teenagers. They went and sat at the back of the beach where it was hottest, and the sand dirtiest. That was where they always sat.

Laetitia only hoped Hans was watching her heroic act and was mildly indignant that he hadn't joined in her annihilation of the enemy. Having made amends for her dereliction of lookout duty earlier, she turned round, and proudly marched back, head held high. Others nearby on the beach applauded Laetitia because the six teenage boys playing volleyball on the beach were too noisy, taking up too much space, and were being inconsiderate.

Laetitia, who had no doubts that her position as pirate lookout was incontestable, was feeling pleased with herself on two accounts.

Firstly, her surprise single-handed attack on the enemy was a complete success. In fact, it was probably the highpoint of her short-lived six years of life. It was definitely better than being potty trained, which Mum always said was a big relief, so must be quite a highpoint. Learning to talk was also a highpoint, but Mum always said she was born talking, so that probably didn't count. Yes, doing over the enemy was probably the highpoint. Then again, she liked playing with her dolls, but she did that all the time, so that probably didn't count either. Such were the trials and tribulations of the decision-making process of a six-year-old pirate lookout, something parents simply didn't understand.

Secondly, she was getting the hang of saying, furcuff, because from her experimentation, she could detect two meanings, although she didn't grasp what those meanings were. There was the nasty way of saying it, like Jessica, and it sounded plain nasty. Then there was the nice way of saying it, like when she said it to Grandad, who smiled and rolled his eyes, though he couldn't do it as good as Ewan.

Despite being bossy, Hans wasn't a hero. When he said to Laetitia, keep a close eye on them, he meant just that and nothing more. He could see the enemy were teenagers, bigger than they were, and best kept at a distance. While Laetitia was busy with her annihilation of the enemy, Hans kept his head low in the water, hoping they didn't spot him or his two companions as they swam steadily away in the opposite direction.

When Laetitia got back, the three older girls had disappeared not wanting anyone to think that the little girl with a blackened face causing mayhem on the beach had anything to do with them. Laetitia looked around, and then saw Max at Chez Claude; he waved and indicated where the other three girls were.

'Furcuff,' shouted Laetitia, the nice way, because she liked Max. He had been on the beach for as long as she could remember, and that must be a long time. Max, who had known Laetitia before she could walk, was taken aback by her mode of welcoming, because she smiled and seemed happy.

Having witnessed Laetitia's annihilation of the enemy, Max was impressed. It had solved a problem he had. Some of his customers had complained that the six teenage boys playing beach volleyball were disturbing their peace and tranquillity, and they had paid good money for their matelas and parasols. Max politely explained that they were on the public part of the beach and entitled to do what they wanted, including playing volleyball.

Chez Claude was positioned a few feet higher than the beach, behind a wall built of local stone, thus providing, from the terrace, stunning views along the beach and out to sea. Laetitia climbed the steps onto the terrace to join the other girls.

'Hi, Max.'

'*Bonjour*, Laetitia,' said Max while giving her a kiss on each cheek.'

Laetitia loved all that kissing routine because, in Pramousquier, it's what everyone did, and it made her feel nice.

Exchanging kisses on both cheeks, faire la bise, is the customary French greeting or farewell to a friend. It can be a complicated business. Unless on very familiar terms, the lips never touch the skin, it's merely a touch of two cheeks accompanied with a kissing sound made by both parties. This amiable social tradition is fraught with endless perils, social pitfalls, and awkwardness. When in doubt, let the other person decide.

'I like your costume,' complimented Max. 'Lucy and the girls are at the back using the laptop. They've got some water if you're thirsty.'

'Thanks, Max,' said Laetitia while handing him the black frilly tutu skirt, which by now had seen better days. 'I think it needs drying.'

Laetitia gazed across the terrace to the covered salon at the back, and saw the others gathered around Max's laptop. She ambled over, forgiving them for not waiting for her on the beach while she did over the enemy. They were only princesses and she was a pirate lookout. Who wanted to be a princess anyway?

'That my water you're drinking,' said Lucy by way of welcome.

'Max said it's okay.'

'What were you doing on the beach, you're embarrassing.'

Laetitia didn't answer. What did you expect from cissy princesses?

'What are you doing?' queried Laetitia.

'It's no concern of yours.'

'Let me see,' demanded Laetitia, who plonked herself immediately in front of the screen and had a good peek.

'It's the *Perils of the Pirate Princess*, if you must know,' said Lucy.

'Wow!'

'It's on *YouTube* and we're the buccaneer beauties now.' While Lucy was proud to be the pirate princess, she hadn't quite worked out what it entailed, and what were her responsibilities. She also wasn't sure about being a pirate, not if they are hanged, like in Grandad's story. One thing for sure, from what she had seen on Max's laptop, buccaneer beauties beat up pirates, who were men, and ugly. What more could a buccaneer beauty want?

'Metoo, metoo.'

'I thought you wanted to be the pirate lookout?' Lucy had a

43

dilemma. She would dearly like Laetitia to be one of her buccaneer beauties, so that they would outnumber the boys. Laetitia was hardly a beauty, though.

'I'm the best pirate lookout. Hans said so.'

'If you're so good,' said Lucy, 'then how come you missed—'

'Leave her alone,' said Virginia, 'she's cute. She can be a buccaneer beauty and pirate lookout at the same time.'

'I can think of lots of ways to describe my little scrote of a cousin,' said Lucy, 'but cute isn't one of them.'

Laetitia wasn't sure she wanted to be cute. Being a scrote sounded okay.

'I think Lucy's right, Virginia, I'm a scrote.'

That appeared to settle matters, and the four girls huddled around the laptop screen and downloaded all the quests of the *Perils of the Pirate Princess*, which, believe me, were riveting. Every now and then, they went into the sea to have a splash, and Laetitia did a bit of looking out, just in case.

'What's a buccaneer?' asked Laetitia.

Lucy thought about this and glanced at Virginia and Nina for support, which wasn't forthcoming. She examined at the pictures on the screen and noticed that the buccaneer beauties were all wholesome, clean looking, with super makeup, dressed like pirates, posh.

'They're middle-class pirates, like us.' Lucy's Mum was always saying they were middle-class. 'And they don't get hanged.'

For Max, it was a quiet time of day.

His customers were on their matelas and provided with drinks. The rush for lunch hadn't begun. He had prepared his tables, checked his wine stock, made sure he had plenty of chilled carafe d'eau, just as his customers liked. He was a little worried about the table bookings logged on his laptop, but whenever he approached, Lucy gave him that can't you see we're busy look. He resorted to using his iPad, and despite what everyone said it wasn't as convenient to use as his laptop.

'Help, help…'

Max woke from his feeling-good reverie with the words he never wanted to hear. He quickly scanned the sea and his domain on the beach, and all appeared to be in order. He saw Chef, his dependable cook, dash down the stairs, armed with a meat hook, and then realised that the voice was the little girl, blackened face with purple stripes, Charlie's granddaughter, Laetitia. In a panic, he followed Chef down the stairs, declaring he would kill anyone who laid a finger on her.

'It's Laetitia,' explained Lucy outside the toilet, 'she's probably seen a ghost.'

'A ghost?'

'Yep, she sees them all the time,' added Lucy by way of further explanation.

'Are you okay, Laetitia?' asked Max, who couldn't see a spot of blood anywhere.

'Hello Captain Hook,' said Laetitia leaving the toilet, seeing Chef who was still clutching his meat hook in a menacing manner. She certainly knew her Peter Pan. 'Can you flush the toilet for me, Max?'

'I'll get you all some ice cream,' said Max, wearily, after doing what was requested of him.

'Thanks, Max,' said Laetitia while holding his hand climbing up the stairs.

*E*wan and the two pirate captains were skilled explorers with several years' experience under their belt. They knew the beach, sea, and rocks better than most. Nonetheless, they found finding treasure wasn't as easy as they hoped, not pirate treasure anyway.

They could find octopus, starfish, hermit crabs, shells, and many other things in the sea. We weren't talking about those bright orange starfish, because anyone could see them, but those brown hairy ones difficult to detect in the rocks. They knew where to find the big fish, where the little baby blue ones hid, and where young fish gathered in huge shoals.

Flatfish camouflaged on the sandy seabed they could easily find. Sometimes they weren't camouflaged, so they would frighten them and watch them change colour. Grandad said they were left eyed flatfish, which didn't sound right. Noé called them barbue. Anyway, they could see some had two eyes. They were odd, because they sometimes swam around the bottom with a long skinny fish, with two fiddly things by its nose grubbing away in the sand for worms and things.

They didn't know the names of all the fish. They could recognise a cuttlefish and garfish because they were easy. There were several types of sea bream, daurade to the French, so if you weren't sure what fish it was, you called it bream.

Spears and harpoon guns they never used, not like other tourists, because Grandad didn't let them. You only kill if you're going to eat it, Grandad said, and they weren't eating any octopuses or fish they've seen alive. Some tourists swam around in wetsuits, with long flippers and harpoon guns. You made sure you kept out of their way.

Tourists rarely found an octopus.

Grandad explained the secrets of where octopuses hid.

They liked shallow water, hid in a small hole barely big enough, and were difficult to see. Octopuses had a tell, like a gambler, which gave their position away. In front of their hole, they collected a pile of stones to hide behind and these you could see, because they liked clean, white stones, and they appeared out of place. If you were lucky, you might see an octopus moving between holes under a ledge. Grandad said that they were having a hard time finding a decent hole to hide because sea urchins were increasing in numbers and taking residence in all the holes. Those were the secrets of an octopus and you were never to tell anyone.

After swimming out to sea for about a hundred yards or so, the gang of three climbed ashore near the jumping cliff to have a secret pirate meeting. Only the foolish ever jumped from the cliff where the water was deep and the top of the cliff overhung the sea. Although it seemed easy, the jump was into a narrow inlet, which didn't give any daredevil jumper much of a target to aim for. While Jessica had done it many times, it wasn't a jump for Ewan or his two friends, despite them being fierce pirates.

'We'll have to swim deep in the sea and check the underwater holes,' suggested Noé.

Ewan and Hans didn't think it a good idea, mainly because they had already been trying their hardest to swim deep. It was all very well for Noé to say that, because he was the best at swimming deep.

Something else bothered Ewan. He remembered Grandad once saying that while swimming underwater around the rocks he poked his head into a hole, and had a fright. A big conger eel put its face right up to Grandad's mask and looked him in the eye.

'Never be bitten by a conger eel because they can be ferocious, so be careful whose hole you poke your head in,' Grandad had warned.

'We need a wreck,' said Hans. 'That's where we'll find treasure.'

Ewan and Noé knew that was a great idea. They also knew there weren't any wrecks in the bay. A couple of years ago, in a bad storm, a yacht had parted from its mooring and been wrecked on the rocks, and they had meant to explore and examine it. When the storm stopped, a rescue launch came and towed the wreck away, spoiling their plans.

'There aren't any wrecks,' said Noé, stating the obvious.

'Pirates always bury their treasure on beaches or desert islands and you need a map,' declared Ewan seriously.

'We haven't got a map,' said Hans.

'Grandad might know where to find one.' No one disagreed, so left it at that for the time being.

'Let's explore the beach for signs of hidden treasure,' Noé proposed. 'That's the easiest place to start.'

'We'll pretend to play football so people won't know what we're doing.' Ewan wanted to exert his authority over the other two. They seemed to forget he was the pirate king. 'We'll need bamboo sticks to poke the sand and spades to dig holes.' In places at the back of the beach, bamboo grew profusely, so that wasn't a problem.

'We haven't got a lookout,' declared Hans, still worried about the six teenage boys who were bigger than them, and best kept at a distance, unless, of course, you were Laetitia. 'Those other boys might still be around.'

'My little cousin sorted them out,' said Ewan, with a touch of pride. 'Before breakfast, I gave her some training on things like that when I was teaching her to climb masts.'

Ewan had recovered some of his pride, even if the other two were a little doubtful of Ewan's early morning training regime.

The three boys returned to the beach and started their exploring.

Hunting for treasure on the beach, particularly hidden pirate treasure, was a tricky business using techniques only known to boys. You've seen them on the beach being a bit of a nuisance, with sticks, poking here and there, digging odd holes, hot and sweaty kicking a ball about, sitting down discussing things secretly, acting suspiciously, up to no good. Now you know why!

If you were a teenage girl like Jessica, then looking cool was a complicated affair, particularly if you were venturing onto the beach. It entailed a change of skimpy bikini, and...

'Where's my fucking makeup bag, I know I packed it.'

'Are you sure?' asked Ellie.

'Yes, I am sure, no question. It's more crucial than my passport.'

'You can use mine if you like, although I didn't bring much.'

'What's all the noise about,' shouted Grandad, hearing the commotion below decks.

'Have you seen my makeup bag, Grandad?'

'Is it silver with coloured twinkles?'

'Yes.'

Grandad paused before answering. 'No, I haven't seen it.' He decided to hide the offending item, which was then in full view in a corner of the chartroom, in a drawer.

'I've got a text from Julien, he's just arriving,' said a delighted Ellie, which was fortunate, because that distracted Jessica enough not to query Grandad's knowledge of the colour of her makeup bag. Jessica had noticed Ellie's interest in Julien.

After some feminine preparations, Ellie gingerly climbed down the ladder into the kayak, which Grandad had made ready. Jessica followed. Grandad passed down their beach bags, which contained all sorts of mysterious items known only to teenage girls, particularly those going through their awkward period.

'If you synchronise your paddling you might get somewhere,' Grandad advised the two occupants of the red kayak, which was zigzagging here and there.

'It's another text from Julien,' Ellie informed Jessica. 'Who's Max?'

'You'll soon find out.'

Jessica remembered in previous years sitting on the hot sand with her friends, staring at Max. All he did was to tell her to inform Grandad that the fish was good that day. Max needed to get a life.

The two inhabitants of the red kayak landed on the beach, near Chez Claude.

'Wow,' said Ellie. 'Julien's waving from that terrace with that gorgeous—'

'That's Max.'

The two girls climbed the few steps onto Chez Claude's terrace.

'Hi, Julien,' said Ellie enjoying the kisses on the cheek. She was hoping for something more intimate when the time was right. Max shook hands with Ellie having only met her for the first time.

'*Bonjour*, Jessica,' said Max, '*mon dieu*, you've—'

'I know, I've grown a bit since last year, and don't worry, I won't forget to tell Grandad about the fucking fish.'

It was true. Jessica had grown a lot since last year. Call it a growing spurt if you want, but she had grown in all the right places. If only Jessica were ten years older, Max pondered.

'I can only stay half-an-hour but I am free tonight if you can make it,' said Julien. 'My friend can come along.'

'I'm not sure…' started Ellie hesitantly, because she didn't know how they'd get ashore or if Charlie would allow them.

'Make it about nine,' interrupted Jessica.

Jessica saw the four younger girls, heads glued to the screen of Max's laptop. She walked over to see what they were up to, leaving Ellie and Julien some serious bonding time.

'Where's my tutu skirt, Lucy?'

'Max has got it,' explained Laetitia. 'He's drying it. I think the seawater did it no good. It's my pirate lookout costume now.'

'Is it your skirt?' asked Max incredulously to Jessica 'The black one Laetitia was wearing.' Max then remembered that Jessica was still an adolescent girl, with a body that defied her age and pubescence.

Jessica blushed. The problem was, she had had that skirt for two years, and it had never let her down. She loved that skirt. Perhaps it was time to move on, thought Jessica.

'I brought it along for the others to use for dressing-up,' said Jessica.

'So the tutu skirt is now mine. Jessica did say that, didn't she Max?' Laetitia wanted to clarify things. She had always wanted that skirt.

Max was noncommittal because he had learnt from experience never to join an argument with females, whatever their age.

'Didn't she Max?'

'I think so, maybe.'

'That's okay then.'

'What are you doing, Lucy?' asked Jessica, seeing that Lucy and her two friends hadn't moved their eyes from the laptop screen, not once.

'Grandad said I was responsible for entertainment, so I'm writing a show about the buccaneer beauties and pirates.'

'Sounds cool, Lucy.'

'We need Ewan alive, not dead meat, cos he's gotta sing pirate songs.'

'I'll only pester him a little, just to keep him on his toes.'

'Thanks, Jessica.'

Having done enough bonding for now, Ellie and Julien came across to see what was going on.

'A musical,' exclaimed Ellie, once they had told her what they planned. 'Julien can play the guitar, so he can help.'

'I can also play the keyboard and violin,' added Julien.

'That's settled then,' declared Ellie. 'Let me know when your rehearsals are and I'll make sure he's there.'

'Thanks Julien, that's ace,' said Lucy, who was delighted.

Ellie was also delighted, because she had now ensured she would have plenty of bonding time with Julien. Julien was delighted for the same reason. Besides, he would have more chances to get aboard the grooviest boat he had ever seen, and escape from his parents' baguettes.

'I have to go,' said Julien. 'I'll see you tonight.'

Those in the know will appreciate that a farewell in France wasn't a quick affair, because it involved handshakes, kisses on the cheek, and so on. From Julien's point-of-view, there were six females of varying ages to attend. Understandably, he wanted to kiss Ellie mostly. When it came to Lucy, she pulled a face as if she were going to be sick. She just didn't get it. While she believed the custom to be disgusting, she went along, begrudgingly.

Jessica and Ellie returned to the beach and did what Jessica always did. Having brought their flip-flops, they climbed round the rocks to a flat, isolated spot. They also brought bottles of water, and were set up for an hour or so, or until they got hungry.

Out of prying eyes of those on the beach, Jessica forgot about being cool. She was just another girl, who loved diving from the rocks, swimming and sunbathing, and there was no one to see her being herself. Except Grandad on *Black Pearl*, who, while grabbing a quiet few moments in his hammock, glanced across and saw the two girls, being that, just two girls on the rocks, gossiping about this, scheming about that, relaxing, and generally taking time out from being awkward.

Ellie wouldn't dive from the rocks but did a few jumps instead.

Jessica did a few backward dives.

'Who taught you to do those?' asked Ellie, who was impressed.

'Grandad.'

'Isn't he getting a bit old for things like that?'

'If he shaved, cut his hair, got rid of that gross ponytail, and put on some proper clothes, then he would scrub up not too bad. All he ever wears are dog-eared old shorts, which were probably okay thirty years ago, and those faded, shabby t-shirts. He refused ever to iron them, which used to irritate Gran no-end.'

'Isn't that our red kayak going back to *Black Pearl* with the others?' asked Ellie.

I think we can guess what Jessica said!

Chapter 6
Life on the beach; afternoon

Everyone was hungry and Grandad had prepared a help yourself lunch. At one end of the deck table, he had all sorts of pâtés, cold meats, cheeses, crisps, tomatoes, and salads. These he covered in plastic shower caps that he had collected from hotels on his travels. His homemade bread was warm and ready to eat. He had a bucket with ice to keep the drinks cool.

*T*hat was something else Mother from Hell couldn't cope with, allowing children to choose what they wanted to eat, that's to say, allowing them to help themselves.

Grandad's theory was that hungry children, with good fresh food placed in front of them, will happily tuck in, copying each other's likes, competing with each other, not wanting to be left out. By contrast, Mother from Hell would take a plate and fill it with what she decided her children would eat, and then hand it over accordingly. What happened? They left half.

Last year, Jessica had upset her mother, the one from Hell, by informing her with a high degree of sarcasm that if it was a help yourself lunch then the clue was in the name. It didn't help matters when Laetitia decided to add her contribution to this family discussion. 'We help ourselves, get it,' and then went ahead and filled her plate with crisps.

*B*efore lunch, Lucy took Jessica aside and explained about Laetitia beating up boys on the beach. 'It was embarrassing.'

'I am sure Laetitia had a very good reason for doing it,' explained Jessica, 'she usually has.'

'That's okay then.'

'Lunch is ready,' Grandad informed everyone from his hammock, while sipping a glass of rosé wine.

'Grandad?'

'Yes, Ewan.'

'You wouldn't have a pirate treasure map, would you?'

'A treasure map?'

'We've been treasure hunting all morning and we didn't find a thing.'

'Pirate treasure maps are difficult to get hold off.'

'This is an old ship, isn't it? Pirates must have been on board at some time?'

'Good point,' pondered Grandad. 'I'll have a good hunt around this afternoon when you're on the beach. How do I recognise one?'

'It'll be real old.'

'It'll be written in blood,' added Jessica, 'your blood if you touch my things again. Where's my makeup bag?'

'Yeah, probably written in blood, and burnt a bit, with slashes made with a cutlass when they were protecting it from other pirates who were after their treasure.' Ewan ignored the comment about the makeup bag because he worked out that if Jessica were going to do him over and inflict a Chinese burn, she would have done it before now.

'Ewan, please don't make conversation,' commented Lucy with disdain, 'it's really not your area.'

'What do you mean?'

'Grandad?'

'Yes, Lucy.'

'The entertainment is sorted. We have to practice at Chez Claude.'

'Don't make a nuisance of yourself.'

'Max don't mind.'

'Grandad?'

'Yes, Ewan.'

'Can me and my friends use those flipper things—'

'They're called leeboards.'

'Can we use them as assault craft for invading the beach?'

'No.'

'Grandad?'

'Yes, Laetitia.'

'Lucy says I'm too old to take my bikini bottom off on the beach.'

'She has a point.'

53

'I don't like the sand getting everywhere, it scratches.'

'See what the others are doing, and then do what you think's best.'

'Okay.'

'Grandad?'

'Yes, Jessica.'

'Can we take the Zodiac ashore tonight? We're meeting Julien.'

'What time do you plan to get back?'

'Is eleven okay?' challenged Jessica.

'That's fine.'

I should have said midnight, Jessica thought.

After lunch, Laetitia, Lucy, and Ewan disappeared in the red kayak, to continue whatever they were doing. Grandad never knew what they did, not exactly, because if ever he asked, he always got the same answer, 'nuffin,' which, when roughly translated into adult language meant, 'mind your own business.'

Jessica and Ellie decided to explore the chartroom, armed with Grandad's two books. It was too hot to do anything else and they felt lethargic.

'That Ewan, I'll kill him.' All sense of lethargy had suddenly left Jessica.

'You've found your makeup bag.' Grandad did a quick disappearing act into the galley, not wanting a Chinese burn – while he supposed it unlikely, he didn't want to chance it.

Jessica and Ellie spent an interesting hour investigating the chartroom, opening this drawer, switching on this and that switch, being inquisitive.

'It's got an echo sounder,' Ellie revealed, amazed at finding such a thing on *Black Pearl*.

'What's a fathom?' queried Jessica, while scrutinising the dials. 'It doesn't make any sense.'

Ellie rummaged through Nicholls's Seamanship and found what she was looking for.

'It's six feet, or so it says,' exclaimed Ellie, amazed.

'Feet,' echoed Jessica, 'and why six?'

'It doesn't explain that in the book.'

'This is, like, life before the Rolling Stones, isn't it?'

'A nautical mile is longer than a mile on land.'

'You're joking.'

'And it changes length as you sail.'

'Now you really are joking.'

In the chartroom, which was situated at the rear of *Black Pearl*, were two day beds, one each side. Jessica took the starboard day bed, armed with the *Modern Chartwork* book, and Ellie took to the port side, with her dependable Nicholls's Seamanship.

You might wonder why two normal healthy sixteen-year-old girls, particularly one going through her awkward period, took an interest in matters nautical? They had recently completed their GCSEs, were waiting for their results, and were bored. Was that the reason? While that may have been partially true, it wasn't that. They were two intelligent girls, and needed intellectual stimulation and that was the best available; it wasn't that. Were they merely inquisitive? No.

Grandad made an error in judgement in stating they were the navigators, however patronising or flippant the comment. Grandad appeared not to want to move *Black Pearl* far, having anchored it in a secure position. The two girls had other things in mind. If you were on a cool party boat, much photographed by tourists, and admired by boys if Julien was anything to go by, then there was only one place to be.

Saint-Tropez.

If Grandad wasn't going to go there, then, as navigators, by any means, they would get *Black Pearl* there themselves.

'Have you found any charts?' Jessica was rummaging around drawers and cupboards and had only found a lot of dust and a copy of Swallows and Amazons.

'There are these,' replied Ellie.

They were staring at a Michelin road map of France, admittedly essential if driving a car. They found tourist maps of the coastline and beaches issued by the local tourist office, undeniably useful if you were a tourist, and on land. Then there were printouts of the coastline from Google Earth, which clearly showed the coastline.

'You're joking?' was the verdict from Jessica. 'How come he's still floating? What does he think he's doing?'

Jessica and Ellie went on deck, where Grandad was busy burning the edges of some greasy paper with weird markings.

'What you doing Grandad?'

'Nothing.'

Jessica let that one go.

'Grandad, you haven't got any charts, not proper ones.'

'I know this coastline like the back of my hand.'

'Your hand isn't necessarily much help, is it?'

'I can't get the charts I want.'

'There are dozens of boats around here, they all seem to manage.'

'They probably use French charts.'

'What's wrong with French charts?'

'I want to use Admiralty charts because they're dependable.'

'Grandad!'

'Did you know that little over one hundred years ago the French insisted on using the Paris Meridian and didn't recognise the Greenwich Meridian? Knowing the French, they probably still use the Paris Meridian. They're not known for following international conventions. Anyway, they use metres and my echo-sounder measures fathoms.'

'Everyone uses metres, Grandad. I bet even the Admiralty does.'

'Mr err Charlie, can you explain to us how to steer and use the compass.'

'I'll do it now if you like, it won't take long. And it's Charlie, just Charlie.'

Grandad took the two girls to the helm positioned behind the chartroom. Immediately in front of the helm was the mahogany binnacle, on which the liquid magnetic compass stood. The compass, mounted in gimbals to keep it level in rough seas, had a traditional mariner's compass face, displaying both cardinal points and degrees.

'The cardinal points are easier to see,' explained Grandad.

Covering the binnacle was a brass dome-shaped cover for protection against the elements, with a viewing window so the helmsman could see the compass card.

'What's with the *P* and *S* you've painted on the binnacle?'

'Port and starboard, I get them muddled sometimes.'

'Grandad, port and left both have four letters. That should do it.'

'Left and right, they're the ones I get mixed up. When your Gran was alive, we had no end of arguments in the car. She insisted on saying, turn left, turn right, while I insisted on, turn your way, and turn my way.

'Grandad!'

'You have to remember that the compass points to magnetic north and not the North Pole. Also, *Black Pearl* is metal and had its own magnetic field and that can influence the compass.'

'Are you saying the compass isn't accurate?'

'I've made a correction card and I'll explain.'

Grandad explained what he could about navigation and how *Black Pearl's* controls worked, which wasn't hard, because there weren't many. Ellie was interested in how to sail *Black Pearl*, and things like anchoring. She had once spent two weeks on holiday with her parents on a Turkish gulet, so understood a little bit about sailing and nautical matters. Coastal navigation intrigued Jessica because it appeared to be no more than basic geometry, which she enjoyed and understood at school, although she would never admit it.

'That's settled then. Ellie is sailing master, and you, Jessica, are pilot,' decided Grandad.

'When can we have a go at sailing *Black Pearl*,' Ellie asked, impressing Grandad with her willingness.

'Tomorrow, after breakfast, weather permitting.

Grandad returned to his greasy paper, with weird markings.

'What's with the ketchup?'

'Nothing.'

'What's with the used teabag?'

'Nothing, honest.'

Jessica had experienced her first lesson of adulthood when speaking to a child! When asked a question on what they are doing, a child will never provide a straight answer. It's against their nature, particularly when they are up to no good. She will also learn at some time in the future that ketchup is an excellent substitute for blood, and a used wet teabag the best aging solution available. Ask any forger!

'Jessica, does that gadget of yours do translations?'

'Of course.'

Why Grandad wanted to write things in Turkish was anyone's guess.

Jessica and Ellie swam back to the rocks to pick up their things. Since the sun had lost its heat, they decided they would grace the beach with their presence.

Jessica knew the best place to sit on the beach was near the water's edge, where the sand was cleanest and temperature coolest. If boys were to walk down the beach, then they would do so on the water's edge, where they were. She could observe the boys, discreetly, from behind her Ray-Bans, and they could observe her in their usual indiscreet manner.

'*Beignets, beignets – les meilleurs de toute la Côte d'Azur…*'

It wasn't a mere boast. It was a bellow, a very loud bellow, from a young man dragging a large red box on four wheels with chunky, grey, soft tyres, so made to travel easily on the beach without sinking into the sand. On the box were pictures of beignets, illustrating the various flavours available. On one of corners of the red box was a tall flagpole, with a large red flag flapping in the sea breeze. On the red flag was the word, Mascotte, in huge yellow letters, for all to see.

'*Mesdames, messieurs, les enfants…*'

'Jessica, what's that, what's going on?' Ellie had woken with a start. She wasn't asleep, merely drowsily daydreaming about how she and Julien would further their bonding. Considering that Ellie was a normal healthy sixteen-year-old girl, what she had in mind for furthering their bonding was best left unsaid.

'*Ce sont les plus savoureux…*'

'It's Kaled, the beignet boy.'

'Beignet?'

'*…et les plus gros…*'

'Doughnuts, he sells doughnuts. He's here every year. He shouts about them being tasty, the biggest, the best in France, and things like that. He's on *YouTube*.'

'*Seulement deux euros cinquante…*'

'Two and a half euros, who's going to pay that?'

'Does he shout all the time?'

'He only stops when someone buys one.

'*…les plus frais…*'

'Are they tasty?' Ellie was fat for a good reason. A ready supply of beignets on the beach in a variety of flavours was evidently very appealing.

'No.'

'*Je ne vous le direz pas deux fois, ce sont les meilleurs beignets de toute la France, − que dis-je − de toute l'Europe, enfin, j'exagère, peut-être, en tout cas de toute la France.*'

'Where's my purse.' Ellie decided she had better try one.

'**T**hey're cheats.'

Ewan was annoyed, having lost a football match on the beach to a gang of French boys. He and his two trusty pirate captains weren't doing too badly, considering they were outnumbered. When they were one goal behind, an adult came and told them to play elsewhere, because they were being a nuisance.

'I bet that man knew the others were one goal ahead,' Ewan added.

What Ewan actually meant was, that man was French, and the other boys were French, and that French man wanted the French boys to win, so they cheated, because everyone knows that's how the French win.

Hans had originally challenged the French boys to a penalty shootout. Knowing the German reputation for taking penalties, they refused. Hans concluded that their honour remained intact despite being a goal down. Ewan was happy to go along with that; honour was honour, after all.

'We should hunt for the treasure before someone else finds it,' said Hans, who was philosophical about losing the football match.

'We haven't explored around the rocks in the sea the other end of the beach,' said Noé, 'let's go.'

'I hope Grandad finds that treasure map,' added Ewan.

They grabbed their snorkels and masks then made their way to the other end of the beach. Once in the water they were easily distracted.

They found a shoal of sea bream that swam around and ate seaweed, and they were big ones. You had to be careful not to scare them because, if you did, they did a synchronised poo, which looked like little bits of seaweed. You didn't want to swim in poo, did you?

The three pirates weren't careful, were they?

Between them, they managed to find one octopus, and two hairy starfish. They also saw several shells with those little hermit crabs inside. If you held one, after a while the hermit crab would come out with claws held high, checking what was going on. When poked, they would immediately return into their shells and hide, which served them right.

After a while, they climbed onto the rocks and sat in the sun to warm up, discussing what they would buy when they found the pirate treasure.

Ewan wanted a real pirate watch, a real wooden pirate peg leg, a real pirate cutlass, and a real pirate parrot. Noé wanted to buy Monaco, be king, and drive racing cars. Hans was more practical and wanted to buy a few factories, like BMW, Mercedes Benz, and Porsche. Then he would build an underwater treasure-hunting digger and then find more treasure so he could buy a Harley Davison motorbike, because they were expensive.

'Then I'm going to buy a spaceship and fly everywhere, like in Star Wars,' added Ewan, who felt he lacked ambition after hearing what the other two had in mind.

'I could probably build you one if you like,' offered Hans generously, 'with a discount.'

'I'll probably get a Japanese one, they'll be more reliable,' countered Ewan casually.

'Who says?'

'My Mum.'

'What does she know?' Hans wasn't impressed with Ewan's source of information.

'I'd get a Chinese spaceship if I were you, they're cheaper.' Noé's suggestion was a good one. Everyone knew the Chinese were cheapest.

'Good point,' said Ewan.

Max was distracted and had had a mixed afternoon at Chez Claude. He got several orders wrong and felt the need to placate his customers with extra wine. He needn't have bothered, because his customers were similarly distracted.

Laetitia was only six and with all her lookout duties, doing over the enemy, pirating in general, swimming, and a few other things, was plumb tuckered out. Her black pirate face makeup was a mess and she had put on her black frilly tutu skirt, which had seen better days. She was hoping to join Hans and the others except they were playing football, which was boring, so she decided to keep lookout secretly. She then sat at Max's VIP table overlooking the beach and promptly fell sound asleep.

What Max and his customers saw was a tiny fallen black swan – ugly duckling would be nearer the truth – draped over the table in the prime location on the terrace. Before falling asleep, with heavy eyelids and a giant yawn, the last thing Laetitia saw was Max, and she really liked Max.

'Furcuff, Max.'

Lucy and the others had taken over Max's salon and laptop at the back of the terrace. Here he had soft, low, easy chairs and two sofas under shade where he usually guided his customers for aperitifs, and then took their orders. He had scented candles burning and long soft, silk drapes, which gently waved in the breeze. Customers liked Max's salon because it was très chic, a reminder of Saint-Tropez.

It wasn't available that day

Like Laetitia, Lucy took her responsibilities seriously except without falling asleep. Then again, Lucy hadn't done over the enemy, so perhaps Laetitia could be forgiven her derogation of duties. Lucy had responsibility for entertainment on *Black Pearl* and come hell or high water, entertainment she would provide.

Lucy was surprised how well provided pirates were for music, songs, and dance. Her favourite was the *Pirates of Penzance*, with a real pirate king, and a groovy song to match. All Ewan had to do was learn a few words, and that was him sorted. Lucy felt that the female songs in the *Pirates of Penzance* were a bit cissy. She would have to improvise.

She liked the pirates in the *Pirates of the Caribbean* except it didn't have songs. It had Blackbeard, so that was Grandad sorted, though she would have to do something with his hair. He didn't look like Blackbeard with that gross ponytail and scraggy beard. He would have to have a scar on his cheek. Jessica could arrange that, she was sure. All Grandad had to do was be killed by the pirate king and then pretend to be dead. That shouldn't be too difficult, even for him.

This was all new for Màx, with buccaneer beauties on his terrace, singing peculiar songs, and practicing dance steps. Since his customers found them delightful and entertaining, he took the opportunity to profit from what was going on. He normally played soft music on his sound system, nothing too modern or loud. Since that wasn't possible, he plugged his sound system into his laptop and gave Lucy a microphone.

'Thanks, Max, this'll make things easier.'

Lucy, while singing her version of 'I am a Pirate King', attracted many listeners from the beach allowing Max and his barman to take additional orders. He quickly added, Pirate's Punch, onto his chalkboard, and the barman improvised a lethal rum cocktail, which brought tears to your eyes; or was it the appeal of Lucy's singing?

Late afternoon was always hectic on the beach. The sun had lost its heat, and adults had had their afternoon siesta, along with the younger children.

Max was busy.

'*Qu'est il se passe?*' asked a customer.

'They're my pirates,' replied Max, with pride.

'Furcuff!' Laetitia had fleetingly woken, saw something amiss on the beach and shouted in the nasty sort of way, then promptly fell asleep again. On the other hand, she might have been dreaming and reliving her earlier triumphs. Who knows?

'*Quelle belle petite fille?*'

'*Oui,*' Max replied cautiously.

Initially, Max wasn't sure about his salon being taken over. Now he saw things in a different light. Lucy provided good family holiday entertainment attracting many customers.

'Lucy,' ventured Max in a quiet moment, 'You can rehearse here whenever you want, with one request.'

'What?'

'When you are ready, can you do a performance at Chez Claude?'

'Of course we can, Max, anytime, ace.'

'Does your show have a name?'

'Not yet.'

'What about, *Pirates of Provence*?'

'Ace, thanks.'

'That's settled then.'

Virginia did ballet classes, so became responsible for the dancing. Lucy was a bit worried about Virginia's pirate dances, particularly after she watched how they did it on *YouTube*. It didn't really matter what pirates did. The main thing, it appeared, pirates had to be drunk. She wouldn't tell her pirates that, especially Grandad, because she didn't want any problems.

'That's what pirates do,' declared Lucy.

'That's not proper dancing,' stated Virginia indignantly.

Lucy quite liked Kevin Kline's version of 'I am a Pirate King' because it involved things like swinging from the ships rigging, and walking the plank. They found another version on *YouTube*, by someone called Anthony Warlow, which was easier. All that was required was to stand on a beer barrel and prance around a bit.

Lucy and the others considered their options.

'When we do the show on your Grandad's pirate ship, then Ewan can swing on the rigging and walk the plank, like in the film,' explained Nina.

'Ewan can't swing on the rigging because he don't like heights. He can walk the plank. It's a pity there are no sharks.'

'Are you sure he's your brother?' queried Nina.

'Mum says he is. He's not properly recorded, so he might not be, not legally.'

'Noé can do the swinging and pretend to sing. With any luck he might slip.' What would you expect Nina to say? He was her brother, after all. 'Ewan can hide somewhere and sing from there.'

'Good idea,' agreed Lucy.

'When we do it at Max's place, Ewan and the others can do that dance on the beer barrels,' suggested Nina.

'We haven't got barrels,' protested Virginia, who was responsible for the dances. Prancing around on beer barrels didn't coincide with her artistic intentions and classical Italian ballet classes.

'We'll borrow some from Max.'

'Good idea,' agreed Lucy once more.

'What about Laetitia?'

'She's the pirate lookout, so she can do that. Best not get her too involved because she's swearing a lot these days.'

They got onto the more essential details, like how to make their costumes, and practice their fake fights, like in the *Perils of the Pirate Princess*. The website said, 'Kids, don't you be trying this at home.' What did they know? The best bit was the pirate pranks, which the buccaneer beauties did on the pirates. They'd keep them secret, they decided.

When Grandad had finished doing nothing, he decided to row the Zodiac ashore, go for a swim, and then go for a walk along the beach to see what was going on. His friends normally went to the beach late afternoon to have a swim, and then chat with each other; it was a social thing. He didn't need to keep a close eye on the youngsters because he had a theory that children never intentionally put themselves in real danger. Most children's accidents he put down to thoughtless parents who either pressurised their kids or fussed too much. Nevertheless, he still kept a cautionary eye on what they were doing.

Grandad saw Max who assured him that Lucy and her friends were not a bother. They both examined the fallen ugly duckling asleep on the VIP table, while enjoying a large pirate punch. A couple of Grandad's cronies joined them for an early aperitif, as that was their habit.

As the sun set over the hills, everyone drifted back to *Black Pearl*, mainly from hunger.

While they strolled back along the beach, Jessica and Ellie picked up the others. That might seem a mature action by Jessica and you might consider it to be out of character. It was. Jessica had an ulterior motive, as you would expect a teenage girl going through her awkward period to have. She wanted everyone back on *Black Pearl*, washed, fed, and the dishes done so that she and Ellie could return to the beach quickly.

'Jessica,' said Lucy, 'we need Julien's help with the music, urgently.'

'I'll see to it,' offered Ellie eagerly.

'We've got the songs and dances worked out. We need to sort out the music,' explained Lucy. 'That includes you, Ewan, because we've a real pirate king song for you.'

'A pirate king song?'

'It's called 'I am a Pirate King' and I've got the words written down.'

'Awesome.'

'Did you see Grandad on the beach?' enquired Lucy. 'He was pulling old biddies.' Lucy was only ten and any female over the age of thirty was definitely old.

'What, Grandad pulling on the beach?' This surprised Jessica. 'Are you sure, Lucy?'

Lucy was offended that Jessica, her cousin, could doubt her word. 'Then he kissed them. It was disgusting.'

'I'll deal with it.'

This illustrated an interesting contrast of how children of different ages understood what was said, assuming a sixteen-year-old girl going through her awkward period could be described as a child; young woman, perhaps.

In all her innocence, Lucy described exactly what she had seen. Where the sea waves lapped the beach, this occasionally caused a small, stony, steep slope making it difficult for elderly women to exit the sea. As Grandad walked down the beach, being a kind sort of chap, he would help the odd elderly woman out of the sea by offering his hand and pulling them gently out of the water. If a friend, exchanging kisses on both cheeks was only polite.

Jessica was sixteen and when a man pulled, the meaning was different. She knew this because boys at her school were preoccupied with pulling girls, rather than on examination results, a hormonal thing which, unfortunately, continued for decades.

'Grandad, what are we going to do with you,' mused Jessica to herself, 'you randy old goat.'

Chapter 7
Tea or supper

Moules marinières were a particular favourite.

Ellie was uncertain at first, though when she saw Laetitia tucking in, she decided she had better follow suit, or go hungry. The frites were good, and Grandad knew how to keep them warm and crisp. The moules, cooked in a sauce much like a soup, meant that baguette for dunking and spoons were required.

'Makeup?' enquired Jessica without menace, although you knew she was serious. 'Explain, and I want an unambiguous answer.'

'What's unam…, you know, that word?' asked Laetitia.

Grandad did his best to keep a low profile and ate his moules…

'It was me.' Lucy thought she had better own up. 'I definitely need it for my show.'

'Metoo, metoo.' Laetitia wasn't sure what the fuss was. One thing for sure, she needed that makeup to be a proper pirate lookout.

'Ask next time.' Jessica was making a point because she didn't want the others meddling with her things.

'Sorry.' Lucy knew she had done wrong.

Everyone sighed in relief and relaxed, particularly Ewan.

'Your show, Lucy, I'll help if you want,' added Jessica in conciliatory mood, 'but I'm not singing any of your pirate songs.'

'Can't you play your flute?' asked Lucy, not wanting to miss an opportunity. She needed a band and knew Jessica could play the flute.

'I didn't bring it.'

'I'm sure Julien can get hold of one, he's into music in a big way,' suggested Ellie, 'I'll ask him.'

'Thanks, Ellie,' said Lucy.

That wasn't what Jessica wanted to hear from her best friend, was it?

'Metoo, metoo.' Laetitia was making sure she didn't miss anything. She was more concerned with the manner Ellie was tucking into the moules, and she wanted her share.

'Grandad,' asked Ewan, 'what about my pirate treasure map, did you find it?'

'I've had a good look in all the obvious places,' Grandad explained. 'I haven't been in the chain locker because I'm too big and couldn't get in. It's a bit mucky and dark in there, so probably not a good place to hide a treasure map.'

Ewan reasoned that a mucky and dark chain locker where adults couldn't get in was clearly a good sneaky place to hide a treasure map. If he had a treasure map, he would get a little cabin boy to hide it, and then make him walk the plank to feed the sharks to keep it a secret.

'What's a chain locker?' asked Laetitia, for which Ewan was grateful, because he didn't know either. He didn't want to ask in case one of the others got ideas. If there was a treasure map on *Black Pearl*, then by rights, it belonged to him.

'It is a little store room near the crew accommodation where the anchor chain goes in,' clarified Grandad casually, 'and difficult to reach. There might be crabs in there.'

'Crabs?' Ewan wasn't afraid of crabs, not little ones anyway.

'They sometimes hang on to the chain when we up anchor. They live among all the muck and can grow quite big. You wouldn't catch me going in there. Who wants cheese?'

'Yes please, Mr err Charlie.'

'Metoo, metoo,' shouted Laetitia, with sauce from the moules dribbling down her chin, 'I'm starving.'

'*Eins, zwei, eins, zwei…*'

'She's batty,' remarked Ewan.

'She's nice, isn't she, Grandad,' added Laetitia.

'It's Gisela,' said Grandad. 'She's from Germany.'

Gisela was again wearing her distinctive blue bathing cap enjoying an evening swim, doing the backstroke. This was her favourite way to swim despite not being able to see where she was going, oblivious to being a danger to any boat that got in her way.

'She makes a lot of splash for an old biddy,' commented Lucy.

'She's a very interesting lady,' remarked Grandad, hoping she didn't tangle with his anchor chain.

'You know her?' asked Jessica while catching the eye of Ellie, who nodded back knowingly.

'Her father was an athlete, a runner, in the 1936 Berlin Olympic Games.'

'Did he win?' asked Ewan.

'I don't think so.'

'We did the 1936 Olympics in history,' commented Ellie, 'you know, Hitler and things.'

'She must be ancient,' added Ewan.

'She's not that old.' Grandad felt he had to defend his friend. 'Hitler saw the Olympic Games as an opportunity to promote his government and ideals of racial supremacy.'

'You mean he didn't like Jews or Blacks,' added Ellie.

'We had to read *Boy in the Striped Pyjamas*. It's a kid's book,' was Jessica's contribution to the conversation.

'I've read that,' added Lucy. 'But I didn't understand it all.'

'Metoo, metoo.' She didn't want to be left out, did she?

'No you haven't.'

'Initially, Hitler wouldn't allow German Jews to participate in the Olympics. When other nations threatened to boycott the Games, he relented and allowed one token Jew, a woman, I think.'

'That's wrong?' added Lucy, who could recognise unfairness when she came across one.

'You must have heard about Jessie Owen?' continued Grandad.

'I think so.' Ellie was being truthful because the name was familiar.

'He was a black American and he won four gold medals. Hitler refused to place the medals around his neck and shake his hand. Hitler said the Americans should be ashamed of themselves for letting negroes win their medals,' continued Grandad. 'He also said he would never allow himself to be photographed shaking hands with a negro.'

'Do you think Gisela's father would have run against Jessie Owen,' asked Ellie.

'I don't know. He might have, I suppose.'

Both Jessica and Ellie watched the woman in the sea wearing the blue bathing cap, doing the backstroke, making a big splash. Having artfully dodged Grandad's anchor chain she was now in danger of colliding with an incoming speedboat.

'That's not all,' added Grandad. 'During the Second World War, Gisela's father ended up on the Russian Front, was captured, and became a prisoner-of-war.'

'Awesome.' Ewan was impressed with anything to do with wars, and here we had Russians and prisoners.

'Gisela and her family lived in northern Germany, an area taken over by the Russians, which then became part of Poland. The Russian soldiers came along and told Gisela's family to leave their house immediately and go. All Gisela took with her was her doll – she was a small girl then. The family ended up in East Germany.'

'Only one doll?' cried Laetitia, horrified at the thought.

'What happened next?' Ewan asked.

'Gisela's father remained a prisoner, doing forced labour, for about eight years after the War ended. When he was released, he claimed all his family lived in West Germany and he was allowed to go there.'

'You said his family was in East Germany,' remarked Ellie.

'When he got to West Germany, he then managed to negotiate for his family to join him. Not many wanted to live in East Germany, not by choice, because it was under severe communist rule. He was lucky because things got more difficult after that.'

'All that from someone swimming in a blue hat,' was Jessica's concluding remark.

'More cheese, Jessica?' Grandad asked, 'and who's for pudding, *tarte au citron*, with *crème anglaise*.'

'Ace.'

'Awesome.'

'Metoo, metoo.'

'What's *crème anglaise*?' asked Ellie.

'Cold custard,' explained Jessica.

'*Hi*, Mum, it's me.' Laetitia was on the mobile.

'xxxx'

'Uh huh, I'm bein good and I'm a pirate lookout and done over the enemy who were teenagers, big, and French.'

'xxxx'

Dunno.'

'xxxx'

'Uh huh, Jessica's bein good and doing all the dishes and fings.'

'xxxx'

'Dishes.'

'xxxx'

'I am talkin proper.'

'xxxx'

Uh huh, Jessica's makin sure Ewan behaves or he's dead meat.'

'xxxx'

'Dunno.'

'xxxx'

'Jessica's busy so can't talk now.'

'xxxx'

'Grandad's busy in the chartroom, gotta go, furcuff.'

'xxxx xx—'

Jessica and Ellie steered the Zodiac to the beach and met up with Julien and his friend, Thierry.

While Julien was an outgoing sort of chap, Thierry was more reserved, more serious. Like Julien, he also had recently finished his bac and was going to study medicine at the Faculté de Médecine de Marseille. Julien and Thierry had been friends all their lives, and had been to the same schools. While Thierry wasn't tall, he was slim, athletic, not bad looking with a rugged sort of face and a scar across his nose from playing rugby.

'Hi, Julien,' greeted Ellie. 'Great, you've brought your guitar.'

'It might come in handy.'

'Who's your friend?'

'Thierry.'

'What's he carrying?'

'His bongo drums.'

'Oh!'

You need to remember they were two teenage French boys who had recently completed their bacs, and were hoping for some fun. They were meeting two English girls on the beach, and if playing a guitar and bongo drums didn't do it, then nothing would. If it was fun they were after, they were soon to find it in abundance.

Thierry shook hands with Jessica and Ellie by way of greeting.

English girls were new to him and he wasn't sure of English etiquette when meeting for the first time; and he was shy.

'Hi,' said Jessica, a little taken aback. She wasn't sure about Thierry, although she quite liked his shyness. Most boys she'd come across were in your face, rude, and made it abundantly clear what they were after, and it wasn't conversation.

They walked to the end of the beach where the old boathouse was, the opposite end to Chez Claude. They made small talk, exchanging basic information about each other, as teenagers would. Each was weighing the other up, age, education, likes and dislikes, taste in music, teenage things.

Ellie and Julien walked ahead, and their talk wasn't small, because they had met before, be it only a couple of times. Ellie had promised Lucy to pass information to Julien about her show and wanted to know when he was available for rehearsals.

'Rehearsals?' queried Julien.

'Afraid so.'

'A flute for Jessica?'

'Afraid so.'

'It's about pirates?'

'*Pirates of Provence.*'

'It sounds great.' Julien wasn't sure what he had agreed to, particularly when Ellie explained they were to give a live performance.

'Does Thierry play an instrument?' asked Ellie.

'Bongo drums, he's exceptionally good on those.'

'I'm sure Lucy will want bongo drums, you'll have to tell him.'

'I could ask—'

'No, tell him. I'm not sure Lucy does asking, it's not her style.' Ellie had an ulterior motive to wanting Thierry around. She was aware that in the pecking order, because of her being fat, most boys gravitate towards Jessica. Not that Jessica would steal Julien from her, because she would never do that. She just didn't trust boys.

'Tell him what?' Jessica asked, having overheard Ellie.

Ellie explained about the bongo drums. Thierry was all for it. Any chance to play his beloved bongo drums wasn't to be missed, and he'd always wanted to be a pirate.

71

'This Lucy,' queried Thierry, 'she must be your big sister?'

'Not quite,' Jessica replied mischievously, 'she's my little cousin.'

Jessica had never known anyone who played bongo drums before, and this one had a sexy French accent.

Thierry was confused. He quite fancied Jessica.

She was fair-haired, slim with pleasing proportions, as Max had noticed earlier that day. She was naturally athletically lean without being aggressively sportive. She was extremely good at skiing, swimming, diving, and jumping from high rocks.

The four teenagers settled down on the sand at the end of the beach with their backs to the rocks, gazing down the beach.

'This is what Lucy has in mind for you music lovers.' Jessica was online with her iPhone and held it for all to hear and see. She had the Kevin Kline version of 'I am a Pirate King' for the others to hear.

'That's good,' said Julien, who was already strumming along.

'We can change the beat slightly,' added Thierry while playing his bongo drums.

'I like it,' agreed Julien.

Jessica had noticed that with the French, their taste in music needed serious maintenance. And as to their dancing, that was genuinely embarrassing.

'Who wants a beer?' Jessica managed to take a few from *Black Pearl* without Grandad knowing. The bottles were those with a screw cap, which was fortunate because she had forgotten to bring a bottle opener.

The four teenagers sat in a line, guzzling warm beer, with Ellie and Julien so close that their bodies touched, which wasn't difficult considering they were both fat. They were bonding, though not as intimately as Ellie had hoped, not yet anyway.

It was a warm, balmy evening with a clear, cloudless sky. It was difficult not to gaze at the stars and constellations and wonder their names. Far on the horizon, a large passenger ship headed towards Toulon. In the bay, *Black Pearl's* anchor light swayed slowly back and forth in the slight swell. Flying down the coast in an easterly direction, at regular intervals, were the navigation lights of aeroplanes making their final approach to Nice airport.

To the south was a flashing light.

'Where's that?' asked Ellie.

'Phare du Titan. It's a lighthouse on one of the islands, Le Levant,' Thierry explained.

'What's that?' Ellie was pointing low in the sky.

'A shooting star, we see loads here,' answered Jessica. 'When you see one you have to make a wish.'

Ellie did.

It was August and the time of the year when each night there was a meteor shower associated with the comet Swift-Tuttle. Fireballs as bright as Jupiter and Venus flashed fleetingly, sometimes up to sixty an hour, sometimes even more.

It was a spectacle to watch as Ellie soon found out. Her fingers accidently touched Julien's, who responded by holding her hand. She searched for more shooting stars, wanting more wishes.

It was a thrilling evening for Ellie, on the beach, sipping warm beer, holding hands with the sexiest boy she had ever known. She decided she liked Pramousquier and while there, the rest of the world no longer existed. What was going on beyond the beach she didn't want to know.

It had always been a magical place for Jessica, who had spent every summer in Pramousquier since she was born. It never failed to get to her. As far as she was concerned, she would spend every summer in Pramousquier. She was on a cool party boat. It wasn't yet a party boat, more a pirate ship. As you would expect, she had plans to rectify that matter.

The beach wasn't visible from the road and it was difficult to reach unless you knew where the two footpaths were. Between the coast road and beach, hidden among the trees, were villas and apartments, with direct access to the beach. It was an idyllic place and the two boys knew it.

'Julien, did you manage to get some?' asked Jessica.

'*C'est fait.*'

Julien extracted something from his pocket. It was crumpled and he pressed it into its proper shape, put it between his lips, and lit it. The smell was distinctive. Even if you had never smelt it before you could guess what it was.

'Good one, Julien.'

'A joint, cool,' Ellie remarked. 'Good one, Jessica.'

Jessica and Ellie had experimented with smoking joints back home. It was always a clandestine activity and they were never comfortable doing it. Julien passed the joint around the others, who took tentative pulls, unsure what to do. Likewise, the two boys were novices. It was summer and they were alone on the beach in an idyllic location, so what the hell, why not. Thierry coughed a little and didn't really like it.

'Do you remember the doughnut man, he was a scream,' commented Ellie, all girlie and giggling, 'he was here, shouting his shout.'

'You mean beignet boy,' replied Jessica, '*les meilleurs de tout la fucking Côte d'Azur*. Two and a half euros each, who'd pay that?'

'People were actually buying them,' added Ellie. 'They tasted okay, I tried one.'

'Is that how much beignets are on the beach?' asked Julien, who also was giggling, along with Ellie.

'We need a way to get more cash,' commented Jessica, who appeared to be more experienced in sharing a joint, 'any ideas, anyone?'

'Why?' asked Ellie, who was worried that Jessica wanted to buy more joints, or whatever the French call them. The occasional one was okay, a distraction on holiday. Regular smoking was not her scene. She wanted to enjoy Julien on planet Earth, not planet Zog.

'I'll explain later.'

'Okay.'

'I have a summer job at Carrefour,' said Thierry. 'I think I can help.'

'Carfor?' queried Ellie.

'It's one of the supermarkets in Le Lavandou,' explained Jessica.

'I help in inventory control,' added Thierry.

'How can Carrefour help?' Jessica asked.

'It sells beignets.'

'I'm listening.'

'We never sell them all, but we keep getting more each day, so we sell them off at half price the next day. We end up having to dump loads. I think I can get them even cheaper if I made an offer for the whole lot. You can then sell them on the beach much cheaper than beignet boy, and offer different flavours and sizes.'

'That's a great idea.' Jessica recognised a good idea when she saw one. 'They only sell one size on the beach and the younger kids can't manage them.'

'Beignet boy is good at selling them,' argued Ellie, 'with all that shouting he does.'

'When it comes to making a racket on the beach, we have a secret weapon,' explained Jessica. 'We've got Laetitia, Lucy, and Ewan.'

It was best to leave the group of hormonal teenagers on the beach, because, being candid, it was impossible to describe the influence of warm beer, marijuana, and the occasional shooting star on the experimenting adolescents. Yes, they giggled a lot as you would expect, and everything seemed hilarious, particularly their plans for selling beignets. They discussed cash flows and marketing plans in considerable detail, which was remarkable considering their state. It was all harmless high spirits. Ellie forgot about her earlier plans she had in mind with Julien, although they did hold hands in a very bonding way.

Julien strummed to the tune of 'I am a Pirate King' while Thierry drummed the beat on his bongo drums, much to the bemusement of Jessica.

'Give us a break.'

Grandad was still awake, reading in his hammock and sipping an agreeable single malt whisky, when Jessica and Ellie arrived back on board *Black Pearl*. The two girls were later than promised, though not enough to concern Grandad. He could hear and see where they were, but not what they were doing.

'Sorry we're late, Grandad, the Zodiac wouldn't go straight,' apologised a giggling Jessica.

'We had a good time, Mr err Charlie.'

'Who wants a drink?' enquired Grandad. 'That warm beer you had must have tasted of camel urine. Best take cold beers next time.'

'Thanks, Grandad.'

Chapter 8
Next morning

Grandad got up earlier than normal.

He woke to the soft caterwauling tones of Ewan practicing his songs from the crew accommodation. Surprisingly, Ewan kept his volume down, remembering being done over by Jessica the previous morning, and he didn't want to risk that happening again.

Grandad peered out to sea, trying to estimate the wind direction. The sea was almost calm, with little ripples disturbing the surface. The atmosphere was dry because the horizon was remarkably clear, with the Maures Hills seemingly closer, and the cloudless sky very blue. The wind would increase in an hour or so. It would be a perfect day for sailing. He knew by early afternoon the wind would be too strong for sailing with novices, so the quicker they got going, the better it would be.

'Breakfast is nearly ready,' called Grandad.

'Help, help…'

'Grandad, Laetitia's seen that ghost again.'

'Where's my bikini.'

'Jessica, can I borrow your makeup again?'

'No.'

'Thanks.'

Ellie arrived on deck first, hungry as a horse, and eager to go. She was wearing a pair of tight cut-off jeans and a white t-shirt with 'Big Ones are Best' plastered across her chest. 'Do you like my sailing outfit?'

Ellie gave a twirl. Grandad didn't know what to think, but he enjoyed the effort being made by everyone with what they wore. Under the circumstances, he couldn't disagree with the motif.

'It's just the thing, Ellie.'

'Grandad, why's Laetitia so smelly, it's disgusting.' Lucy was next on deck for breakfast and she wasn't dressed as a pirate princess. She wore only a bikini and a large pair of familiar looking spectacles perched precariously on the end of her little sunburnt nose. She held her notebook open and busily wrote down critical things, such as alterations to her *Pirates of Provence* script. Likewise, she was ready to write things that Grandad might tell her to tell her Mum next time she saw her. In fact, Lucy had added one or two of her own things she was going to tell her Mum, things like, it wasn't proper for girls to have to keep their bedrooms tidy or clean their shoes for school, all fully attributed to Grandad, of course.

That little girl definitely had a creative side that bodes well for her future. 'I'm a producer, how do I look?'

'Just like a producer, Lucy, but mind you don't break my glasses.'

'They're mine now.'

'Oh!'

'I heard you, Lucy, I'm not smelly, you're smelly.' Laetitia arrived on deck in Jessica's bedraggled black frilly tutu skirt hanging from her neck and a different face-paint arrangement.

'Scrote,' added Lucy, thus ending that particular conversation.

'Ellie did my makeup.' Today's pirate lookout facial decoration involved a pale purple background, a scarlet red skull on each cheek, and black crossbones under her nose. From a distance, her face appeared a mess while closer inspection revealed an artistic composition easily missed. 'How do I look?'

'Like the best pirate lookout I've ever seen,' Grandad affably agreed.

Laetitia then started to climb the mainmast, which wasn't an easy task in her bedraggled outfit. 'I'll have a quick peek around before breakfast just to make sure we aren't being attacked by the enemy.'

'I feel like death.' Jessica certainly didn't look like death because she was stunning in her bikini bottoms and white t-shirt with 'Little Ones are more Juicy' across her chest. She had her straw-coloured hair casually tied behind her head, and no makeup. 'Do you like my sailing outfit, Grandad?'

'Yes, I do.'

He struggled with his emotions because the t-shirt had once belonged to his wife who had often worn it at the villa, be it a long time ago. He had forgotten about the t-shirt and it still held fond memories. It was a bigger fit on Jessica and the motif didn't accurately describe what the t-shirt was hiding. He was pleased Jessica wanted to wear it.

'Where did you get the t-shirt?'

'Aunty Marina gave it me. She was going to throw it until I came to the rescue. Retro, don't you think.'

'Retro?'

'Kind of old-fashioned,' explained Jessica. 'It's going to be sunny all day. The wind is from the east and will reach eight to ten knots by mid-afternoon. That's good isn't it?'

'Excellent weather for sailing,' agreed Grandad, 'how do you know all that?'

'iPhone,' answered Jessica, waving said gadget in her hand. 'Christ Grandad, where do you get your weather forecasts? No, don't answer because you'll tell me you sniff the seaweed or something.'

'Leave some for me.' Ewan was the last to arrive on deck, and he looked guilty. He was wearing his swimming shorts, the ones he wore yesterday and for bed. The shorts were now grubby, with muddy smears here and there for additional decoration. In fact, he had muddy smears on his knees, arms, legs, chest, and face.

'What have you been up to?' Lucy was the first to notice her grubby twin brother. 'No wonder they didn't record you properly, being like that. Haven't you heard of a shower?'

'Nuffin, I've done nuffin.' If you had successfully completed a secret mission, like Ewan, then you would expect a little bit of mud here and there, but he couldn't tell Lucy that, could he?

'What did I tell you about not wanting smelly little boys on my klipper?'

'It's Grandad's klipper,' argued Ewan bravely. 'It's only a bit of mud, and it don't smell, not much anyway.'

'I'm sure it'll wash off, so eat your breakfast.' Grandad made a mental note to wash out his chain locker when he had time.

'What we doing today, Grandad?' Lucy enquired.

'We're going sailing.'

'Ace.'

'Metoo, metoo.'

'That's not fair,' protested Ewan. 'I've got important things to do.'

'There'll be plenty of time for that later,' added Grandad.

Ellie had done her homework, because Grandad found her useful when weighing anchor. He decided to use the engine leaving Pramousquier bay before hoisting the sails. He hadn't used the sails before, and wanted to be far away from land and other boats.

Grandad went to the chartroom and started the engine. At the helm was Jessica, who quite liked her role as pilot, even though see wasn't sure what to do.

'How do you steer this thing,' Jessica asked.

'Remember there is a delay between turning the helm and *Black Pearl* responding.' Grandad could see that Jessica was puzzled by this. 'Think of it this way, if your Mum tells you to do something, do you do it straight away? No! You do it, but not immediately.'

'Got it.'

'Steer towards the islands.'

'Which one?'

'Port Cros. Sail due south on the compass.'

'Got it,' declared Jessica, examining her iPhone.

Grandad was curious and therefore scrutinised Jessica's iPhone more closely. He saw the coastline and all the islands clearly on the screen. Because of the aspect from *Black Pearl*, the islands of Port Cros and Le Levant, visually to the eye, appeared to be one. Port Cros was the smaller to the west, clearly visible on the iPhone. He saw the position of *Black Pearl*, just south of la Pointe du Souffre.

'I downloaded Google Maps, it's free.'

'Useful gadget that,' said Grandad.

'iPhone, Grandad, iPhone 6s.'

Ellie, having finished her anchor duties, was inspecting the sails and rigging with Lucy, figuring out how they worked and what to do. Jessica was getting the hang of steering *Black Pearl*. Laetitia was half way up the main mast doing her pirate lookout duties, shouting this and that. Ewan was at the bows with his pretend parrot on his shoulder, straddling the bowsprit, and yelling pirate things like, 'Shiver me timbers,' and, 'We'll keel-haul ya, ya yellow-bellied mutinous swine,' and other useful threats.

'Grandad?'

'Yes, Ewan.'

'What's a keel?'

'It's the bottom of the boat.'

'Grandad?'

'Yes, Laetitia.'

'Land ho.'

'Thank you, pirate lookout,

'Grandad, steering this thing isn't easy.'

'You're doing fine.'

'Mr err Charlie?'

'Yes, Ellie.'

'Shall we set and trim the sails? I think I've worked out what to do.'

'Excellent.' Grandad was pleased because sailing wasn't one of his strengths. They didn't have sails on supertankers.

'Head to wind,' ordered Ellie.

'What?' Jessica replied.

'Steer into the wind,' explained Grandad. 'You'll know when that is when the flag is flying dead astern and the wind feels the same on both cheeks. It is east on your compass.'

'Got it.'

'Mr err Charlie, stop the engine.'

'Okay.'

'Laetitia, down you get.'

'Okay.'

'All hands haul the ropes, and that means you as well, Ewan.'

'Metoo, metoo.'

Up went the mainsail, followed by the mizzen, both easily handled with the combined exertion of Grandad, Ellie, Lucy, and Ewan. Laetitia was ever so helpful by tugging her own ropes – well away from the others, thankfully. Setting the outer foresail was tricky. *Black Pearl* actually had three headsails. Neither Grandad nor Ellie felt confident enough to set all three, some other time, perhaps.

'Jessica, bring her around to the south again,' shouted Grandad.

At first, *Black Pearl* was reluctant to turn, so Grandad briefly turned on the engine to provide some forward movement and steerage. As *Black Pearl* slowly changed direction, the wind filled the sails. Everyone watched in awe as the klipper took on the shape of a real ship, with sails and stays tight, leaning away from the wind.

Grandad checked to see if Jessica was coping; she was.

'Keep Port Cros on the port bow and the wind will be just right for sailing.'

'Got it.'

Grandad and Ellie trimmed the sails as best they could. There was no getting away from it; *Black Pearl* was a remarkable sight.

Unbeknown to those on *Black Pearl*, several pairs of binoculars belonging to those perched on the cliff tops of Cap Nègre were following their progress with admiration. Who wouldn't envy the chance to sail an old Dutch klipper around the Mediterranean coastline. One middle-age man, slight height and build, and prominent nose, viewed the nautical scene with a smile, wishing he were on board so he could escape the pressures of responsibility. He saw the black skull and crossbones flag, high on *Black Pearl's* mizzenmast, flying gallantly downwind and this reminded him of his recent professional years. The only small but irritating flaw in what he saw was the large Red Ensign in full display proudly announcing *Black Pearl's* nationality.

'*Ou est Hull?*' he idly commented.

'Is it dinnertime yet?' Laetitia was hungry.

'It's lunch, actually. Mum said only working class people calls it dinner.' Lucy was perhaps being a little unfair.

'We call it dinner at school,' argued Laetitia, hurt by what her cousin said because it sounded like a putdown. 'Don't you have dinnertime at your school? It is dinner isn't it Grandad.'

'Dinner is the name of the main meal of the day,' explained Grandad. 'Historically, it refers to the first meal of the day, eaten around midday. I'm not sure when we'll get back tonight, because it depends on the weather, so today our main meal, dinner, will be around midday. Other days, when we have a help-yourself lunch, then we call that lunch, because our main meal will be in the evening.'

'Sorry, Laetitia, I didn't know,' apologised Lucy while scribbling in her notebook. 'Mum never explained that to me.'

'That's okay.' Laetitia loved her Grandad and it is not difficult to realise why.

'Next time you see your mother,' added Grandad patiently, 'tell her from me, in your own words, all about dinner. Don't forget to add that since she lacks a classical education she ought not to promulgate to her unfortunate offspring snobbish tendencies unbecoming of a daughter of mine.'

'Christ, Grandad, that's a lot to write down.' Lucy, who also loved her Grandad, took time to file Grandad's words of wisdom accurately in her notebook, because she didn't want any unbecoming snobbish tendencies. She also added that girls must never eat cabbage or sprouts for dinner because they smelt horrible, although it was okay for boys to eat them, especially Ewan.

'Dinner will be a couple of hours yet,' Grandad informed Laetitia. 'After all that hard work, we could all do with a snack.' Grandad went to the galley and did two things. Firstly, he decided what to have for ~~lunch~~ dinner – barbecue. Secondly, he prepared a morning snack for everyone, toasted baguette with melted cheese, some chilli dips and nachos, a giant bag of crisps, and plenty of cold drinks. He also grabbed a couple of packets of biscuits, just to make sure. These he placed on the deck table for all to nibble, at leisure.

'How fast are we going, Grandad?' enquired Lucy.

'About five knots.'

'Is that fast?'

'Six miles an hour, like a decent jogging pace,' explained Grandad.

'Are we nearly there yet?' asked Laetitia, through a mouthful of baguette.

'Not quite…'

'How far is it?' Lucy wanted to know.

'About ten miles.'

'So it'll take two hours.'

'Yes, about that.'

'Ace,' stated Lucy. 'We've got plenty of time for rehearsals, and I need everyone.'

Grandad took the hint. 'I'll give Jessica a break on the helm.'

The next couple of hours were spent in idyllic pirate paradise. Jessica and Ellie also had an enjoyable time, although if asked, they'd never admit it. Between them all, they sorted out their songs, and two productions, one for *Black Pearl*, and one for Chez Claude. They also sorted out the roles for the others, including Noé's swinging sequence from *Black Pearl's* rigging. Lucy was ambitious with what she had in mind for Noé. The acid test was, if Laetitia could do it, then so could Noé, which seemed reasonable. Maybe not from Noé's point-of-view, but he wasn't there to argue otherwise.

That wasn't all…

Jessica had other things on her mind. If she and Ellie were to become successful beignet sellers on the beach, they needed a welcome distraction from beignet boy, who was already successful and firmly established on the beach.

'I can't sing Lady Gaga songs, no way,' Ewan argued.

For any adult taking an interest, the delicate negotiations and agreements that took place on the deck of *Black Pearl* that morning would have been a lesson for all to learn. Grandad took no notice because he was too busy steering *Black Pearl*, yanking this rope, poking that sail, and glancing wistfully into the sky to check for signs of the weather changing. No one fell overboard, not even Laetitia when she did one of her rehearsal swings on the rigging. If they were happy with whatever they were up to, then he also was happy.

Between songs, and pirate dances, the youngsters were sitting around the table, heads close together, involved with clandestine negotiations, thick as pirates, up to no good. Everyone had a point-of-view, and wanted something, except Laetitia, who merely wanted to demonstrate her backward swing on the rigging.

Take Ewan, for example…

What others often described as a caterwauling singing voice was now, for Ewan, a commodity in demand by both Lucy and Jessica. They often say that there was always a deal to be done, and this was a good example.

If Lucy were to declare that Ewan was properly recorded and not to utter otherwise to her friends, then Ewan would sing in Lucy's shows. In fact, Ewan had some tremendous ideas about what he and his two pirate captain friends could do to liven things up. After spitting on their palms, they shook on the deal. Rest assured, once her shows were over Lucy would again openly declare Ewan not properly recorded, nothing Ewan wouldn't expect. Since Lucy was the older of the twins, she would continue to remind Ewan of that fact, and anyone willing to listen, because that wasn't part of the deal.

'Metoo, metoo.'

'Yep, and you,' agreed Lucy.

Ewan's negotiations with Jessica were more delicate, because you didn't mess with Jessica.

If Jessica refrained from giving Ewan Chinese burns, and duckings, then Ewan would sing pirate songs on the beach at a place and time determined by Jessica. Ewan categorically refused to sing Lady Gaga songs, and he would happily have had Chinese burns as punishment. When Ewan asked why he had to sing on the beach, Jessica informed him that it was none of his business and he would find out soon enough and he had better be ready. Ewan was allowed to bring his two friends along to do pirate things, but nothing frightening, or else.

Jessica refused to seal the deal with the spitting habit despite being informed by both Lucy and Ewan that was what proper pirates did. Rest assured, once Ewan had outlived his usefulness, Jessica would inflict on him a Chinese burn to remember and any amount of duckings, nothing Ewan wouldn't expect.

'Metoo, metoo.'

'Yes, you as well.'

Negotiations between Jessica, Lucy, and to a lesser extent Ellie, were amiable and to everyone's advantage, whatever they were. We'll never know what those advantages were, because they were girls. Rest assured that the future fate of poor Ewan was high on their agenda.

Grandad was getting worried because *Black Pearl* was slowly approaching the island of Port Cros, and apart from a copy of the local tourist map, he had no charts to help him. On the positive side, he had a copy, in English, of the boating, fishing, and diving regulations and limits for Port Cros. He studied his printouts from Google Earth, which did provide some assistance.

He saw the channel between Levant, a prohibited military area, and Port Cros, a gap of about two thirds of a mile. On the north-east corner of Port Cros was a narrow bay, Baie de Port Man, about three hundred yards wide, and half a mile long. It was a perfect place for a barbecue.

'Lost, Grandad?' Jessica was standing next to him with her iPhone in hand. 'Want to have a look?'

'Useful gadget that.'

'iPhone, Grandad, iPhone 6s, like I said before.'

Grandad estimated he had less than two miles to go and he needed to adjust his course accordingly. It meant putting the wind slightly forward of his beam, not a good thing for novice sailors. He decided to drop sails and manoeuvre into the bay using his engine.

'Can you see the entrance to the bay?' Grandad indicated on Jessica's iPhone. 'Steer towards the middle.'

'Okay.'

Grandad got his novice crew together and they quickly dropped all sails, outer foresail first, followed by mainsail, and lastly the mizzen. Ellie did most of the work and coordination because Grandad was trying too hard to remember all the correct nautical terms and things like that. By contrast, Ellie's thinking was different, sails had to come down and ropes released, and that, according to Ellie, was that.

'Ewan, untie that rope and let go slowly, not that one, the other one, good one Ewan, you're a little dream. Lucy, slip that rope around that bendy bit and let it out slowly, and I'll tidy the sail as it drops, you're a love, Lucy…'

Now Laetitia would tell you an entirely different story, because the ropes she pulled and untied certainly did the trick unknown to all the others who didn't know a thing. She certainly saved the day and she knew it wasn't worth the bother to explain that to the others. Yes, that was the fate of a lowly six-year-old pirate lookout and she knew that if Hans were present, then he would know and fully appreciate her heroic acts, which saved the day.

'Well done everyone,' said Grandad, while starting the engine.

'Metoo, metoo.'

'Especially you, Laetitia.' Grandad knew about her heroic acts, obviously.

Grandad then remembered to start the echo sounder. The water appeared deep enough but best to be sure. He had everything under control with tourist map, echo sounder, Jessica's gadget, and a lively crew. What more did he need?

'Watch this Grandad, you can change the scale on the screen,' explained Jessica while giving a demonstration.

'You stroked the screen?'

'Cool, don't you think?'

'It's also a phone?'

'Yes.'

'It goes on the internet?'

'Yes.'

'Useful gadget—'

'iPhone… yes, useful gadget that, like you said.'

There were other boats already anchored in the bay, not many, but none as large as *Black Pearl*. With Jessica on the helm, Grandad chose his spot to anchor. As they entered the bay, on the left hand side, Grandad saw an old fort on la Pointe de Port Man. Behind the wall of the fort there appeared to be a renovated building but he couldn't make out what it was. The bay was calm and the water crystal clear.

Jessica sailed *Black Pearl* into Baie de Port Man like a seasoned sailor. Grandad and Ellie prepared the anchor. He explained that they weren't to drop the anchor. Ellie was to let it out slowly. The island was a national park and maritime protection zone, and any damage to the seabed was prohibited. He stopped the engine and briefly put it into reverse to stop any forward movement. *Black Pearl* drifted astern while Ellie slowly let out the anchor under Grandad's direction.

Because of its isolation, there were other boats at anchor in the Baie hoping for seclusion. Unfortunately, it was a popular place for boats but despite that, it still had an element of remoteness and adventure. The coastline was rugged and rocky, with small wild beaches full of driftwood and seaweed. The seabed was covered with seaweed, giving the sea a dark green colour rather than the turquoise blue you get with a sandy seabed.

'Is it dinnertime now?' Being a busy pirate lookout sure makes you hungry. While Ellie was also hungry, she relied upon Laetitia being hungry. Because of her size, Ellie didn't like drawing attention to being preoccupied about when the next meal was.

'Soon,' replied Grandad, 'why don't you all go for a swim while I get things ready.'

'Wow, this place is awesome,' exclaimed Ewan. 'Can I go exploring in the kayak because I've got important things to do.'

'After dinner,' replied Grandad.

'I've got import—' argued Ewan before being interrupted.

'Why don't you have a swim around *Black Pearl* to check for any damage? You can't be too careful.' That'll keep his mind off hidden treasure, Grandad thought, even if only for a short while, because that treasure map must be burning a large hole wherever he'd hidden it.

'Okay.' Ewan didn't want to sink on a pirate ship, not yet anyway, because he had important things to do before sinking.

'What are we having for lunch, Grandad?' asked Jessica.

'Dinner!' the two small girls aged six and ten answered in unison.

'We're having a barbecue with a salad.'

'I'll do the salad,' offered Ellie. 'I'm good at that. When we do food technology at school, they always make me do salads. It's supposed to be some kind of subtle subliminal message because I'm fat. The teacher must think I'm thick.'

'Why don't you go for a swim while I rig up the barbecue?'

'Okay.'

'You both did an excellent job sailing *Black Pearl* to the island. I couldn't have done it without you.'

Jessica and Ellie were thrilled.

They loved sailing *Black Pearl* and saw all sorts of possibilities for the summer. Saint-Tropez would be their immediate destination. As far as they were concerned, if it wasn't for them, Grandad would still be sailing half way to Africa looking for the island. Jessica saw the need for having nautical charts, despite what Grandad said.

Grandad had one of those special barbecues that you attach to the klipper's rail with it hanging over the water. He also kept a pile of driftwood he had collected from the beach.

Grandad had three types of sausages, homemade special-recipe steak haché, spare ribs, and chicken legs. Ellie was good at making salad. She managed to rustle up three different types, while Jessica laid the table and prepared a tangy, savoury, couscous. With a few dips and nachos to start, cheese and melon de Cavaillon to finish, it was another enjoyable meal on the deck of *Black Pearl*.

Everyone sat around the deck table in the sheltered clear waters of Baie de Port Man on as near a Robinson Crusoe deserted tropical island as you could get in the northern Mediterranean. Grandad, Jessica, and Ellie casually sipped chilled local rosé wine with ice cubes, while the rest enjoyed Orangina. It was a local custom to have ice cubes in rosé wine so not to get intoxicated because people had to work in the afternoon.

'I can't see any sign of life on the island,' commented Ellie, who still couldn't believe her luck being on *Black Pearl*.

'There is a small village and a hotel at the other end of the island. Being a national park, further development and cars aren't allowed,' explained Grandad. 'Between the wars, the island was a haunt for artists and authors. There was a German garrison on the island during the last war, which would have been a good posting, until the allies arrived in 1944. If you want to escape, then this is the place to come, except it is a favourite place in the summer for yachts and boats.'

Ewan was impatient to get away. 'Can I go in the kayak now?'

'Yes, of course you can.'

'Can I go as well?' Lucy wasn't going to be left behind.

'Of course you can, there's plenty of room.'

'That's not fair, I bagged the kayak first.'

'I'm older than you and—'

'I'm taller than you—'

'The kayak goes faster with two paddling,' offered Grandad as conciliation.

'I suppose…' agreed Ewan grudgingly.

'Metoo, metoo.'

'Yes, I'm sure there's room for you, you'll need a pirate lookout, won't you Ewan,' suggested Grandad.

'I suppose…'

'Barbary pirates used to attack this island for hundreds of years. You saw the fort as we entered the bay. That was built so that islanders could defend themselves against pirates.'

Ewan's mind was in a spin. Pirates, real pirates, hundreds of years. There must be loads of treasure on this island. 'What's a Barbary pirate?'

'North African Arabs from places like Tunis, Tripoli, and Algiers. They were after Christian slaves, and plundering treasure, of course.'

'Do you think they did plundering at Pramousquier?'

'They must have. It's a good bay for pirates to anchor in.'

Ewan saw the advantage of having two others with him. He would secretly hunt for treasure and get Lucy and Laetitia to help without them knowing. He'd tell them they were hunting for snakes, or lucky stones, or something like that. He would mark places where the treasure was and come back later to collect it with Hans and Noé. They could paddle back in the kayak, in secret. Maybe not Hans, because he was getting too bossy, wasn't he.

After thinking about it, he wasn't sure about paddling back because it was a long way. He might be a brave pirate king, but he wasn't that brave, not yet anyway. He'd have to come back when he was braver. These were serious decisions and considerations for Ewan to make, something parents never understood.

What followed was a scramble to gather snorkels, masks, and spades.

'Laetitia, don't forget your water wings.'

'I won't, and it's pirate lookout, remember.'

'Don't leave the bay.' Grandad had a good view of the bay and could keep a cautious eye on the three intrepid explorers.

'Furcuff.' Laetitia was happy.

'If you both help me clear the table, then you can do whatever you want. I'll do the dishes.'

'Okay.' Jessica and Ellie were pleased they could help.

'Do you have any plans this afternoon?' asked Grandad.

'We'll do a bit of swimming and snorkelling,' Jessica said, 'then a bit of serious chilling out.'

Grandad was pleased the two older girls didn't want to use the Zodiac, because he wanted it near at hand in case the others got into difficulty.

After washing the dishes, Grandad treated himself to a calvados, with plenty of ice, and retired to his hammock with a novel and a pair of binoculars so he could keep an eye on the youngsters.

'If I fall asleep, Jessica, can you keep an eye on the others?'

Grandad was in no hurry to return to Pramousquier because where he had anchored the sea was calm. Out at sea the wind had increased in strength, although that was normal in the afternoon. Later, he knew, the wind would drop and he would sail *Black Pearl* back to Pramousquier.

According to Jessica and Ellie, they were in full control of *Black Pearl*, and it was best to humour Grandad as best they could and not hurt his feelings. After reading his old nautical books, they now knew a thing or two.

According to Laetitia, she was in total control of *Black Pearl* and was exasperated with the antics of the others. Only she knew which rope to pull, which button to push, what to throw, and what to untie, all the essential things. The others didn't realise, and no one listened to her, all because she was little. She dearly loved her Grandad who needed looking after, and that was hard work. She had to cope with the antics of Ewan, although Lucy was okay, most of the time anyway. Her big sister Jessica and Ellie were plainly getting too big for their boots with all that meddling around steering and pulling sails. What did they know?

According to Grandad, getting from A to B in one piece was all that mattered.

*A*s we expected Grandad promptly fell asleep in his hammock. Jessica gently lifted the empty glass from his fingers before it dropped.

'What was in it?' asked Ellie.

'It smells revolting,' Jessica whispered, sniffing the glass. 'Ellie, have you got a pair of scissors so we can get rid of that gross ponytail.'

'You can't do that!'

'Quick, get a pair.'

'Where from?' Ellie was worried, because she liked the ponytail.

'I don't know?'

'Do it another time, when we're more organised.'

'You're right. He always has a siesta in the afternoon.'

Jessica gave Ellie lessons on how to snorkel, although things didn't go according to plan, Ellie kept breathing in while wearing her mask, which promptly filled with seawater, causing Ellie to have that drowning sensation, and as a consequence, she was not at all enamoured with all that underwater swimming nonsense.

'Ellie, you breathe through your snorkel, not your nose.'

That didn't work and Ellie still didn't like drowning, no matter how clear or warm the water.

'Let's do a few jumps from the deck of *Black Pearl*?'

'Good idea,' agreed Jessica, 'and we'll practice our dives.'

Grandad was vaguely aware of hearing the shrieks of delight from the two teenagers, one evidently taking time out from being awkward, jumping, and diving from the bow of his klipper.

Now and then, they went into the chartroom and studied Grandad's old nautical books, planning teenage mischief. Other times they laid on the sunbeds, fiddling with the iPhone and, despite poor coverage, contacted Thierry about the deal he had done with Carrefour over the beignets. Jessica committed up to fifty euros for their initial purchase, all the cash she had for the summer, and planned to hit the beach selling them the next afternoon.

Jessica was true to her word and kept an eye on the others.

She could see Ewan digging holes here and there, and Lucy and Laetitia leaping about, ignoring Ewan as best they could.

Lucy and Laetitia adamantly refused to dig holes and they definitely didn't want to find snakes. Ewan regretted mentioning the snakes. Was this a useful lesson learnt when handling females? Probably not because Ewan was only a boy, remember, and you can't expect too much!

Lucy elected to try out a few buccaneer beauty steps with her eager-to-please young cousin. It's a pity that dancing wasn't one of Lucy's strong points, and she had many as we well know. Still, both girls had a thoroughly enjoyable time, particularly as Ewan was finding their dancing irksome.

Lucy hadn't forgotten that Virginia was responsible for the dancing. She did ballet classes and that seemed as good a qualification as any. If you were a producer and director, like Lucy, then you took your responsibilities seriously, and found things to worry about. For example, Virginia was Italian and that was a worry. Lucy wasn't sure if Italian ballet was the same as English ballet, and she based her concern on Italian food being different to English food. It stands to reason that ballet must be different, doesn't it?

After much leaping around an irked Ewan, who kept digging holes for no reason, Lucy deduced that since she liked Parmigiano-Reggiano, and prosciutto di Parma, and pizzas, and they came from Italy, then Italian ballet was probably okay. She was a sophisticated girl, was Lucy!

With a late afternoon on-shore wind, *Black Pearl* made excellent time on the return journey. During the trip, Grandad checked his water tanks, which surprisingly, were in good order. He disliked discharging sewage into the sea from his black water tanks, and where possible discharged ashore when in port. Unfortunately, Port du Lavandou didn't have any facilities for this. His tanks were large, and despite the best endeavours of the others, there was ample room for more. When mid-way between the mainland and islands, he took the opportunity to discharge water from his grey water tanks, waste from sinks and showers. He still had, surprisingly, plenty of fresh water.

Grandad anchored in Pramousquier bay in more or less the same position as before, sheltered from the mistral if it were to blow. The sun was setting over the Maures Hills, and the wind had dropped with the sea almost calm with odd ripples shimmering in the evening light.

Laetitia had fallen asleep when *Black Pearl* arrived and missed all the excitement and activity. When Jessica had shouted, drop anchor, Laetitia woke up with a start, and immediately started tugging the first rope that came to hand, the downhaul for the mizzen sail, which the rest had already lowered and neatly stowed, so no damage done. She was confused and didn't know how the others had managed without her. Grandad must have covered for her, because he must know what to do, although she had her doubts about that.

'Is it teatime yet?' Laetitia was hungry.

'Soon.'

'Fresh baguette?' called Julien from a small dinghy he had borrowed from Max.

Grandad gazed over the side and saw Julien, Thierry, a brown bag with baguettes poking out the end, a guitar, and drum-like things. 'I'll drop the ladder.'

'*Ciao*, Julien, furcuff.' Laetitia liked Julien. She had also been listening to Virginia, who was Italian.

After passing up the baguettes, guitar, bongo drums, and other things, Julien and Thierry climbed aboard and greeted everyone.

'This is Thierry,' Julien explained to Grandad.

'Can I play your guitar, Julien?' asked Ewan, 'I'll be careful, honest.'

'Sure.'

'Is it teatime now?'

'Laetitia, you can help me lay the table. You boys are welcome to stay for tea. We haven't much, mainly leftovers from our meal earlier.'

'Tea?' Julien knew the English drank a lot of tea…

'Food, supper, things to eat,' Jessica whispered. 'We have to be careful what we say when Lucy's around, otherwise we end up in her little black book.'

'*Merci beaucoup.*'

Tea did indeed consist of a lot left over from the barbecue with sausages, spare ribs marinated in a chilli dip, and chicken legs garnished with pepper and grey sea-salt. They combined Ellie's salads to make one big salad, with feta cheese. Grandad had also baked two camembert de Normandie, with crushed garlic cloves. He slashed open the round, fat, camembert with a cross, and the warm creamy cheese oozed out giving an enticing aroma difficult to resist. With all that and other leftovers, there was no shortage of food.

'Get stuck in everyone,' said Grandad, while dribbling the warm cheese with extra-virgin olive oil.

Laetitia dipped a chunk of baguette into the melted cheese and attacked it hungrily. 'That's how you eat it, Ellie.'

Ellie didn't need showing twice.

Ewan made a giant hot-dog with two sausages, feta cheese salad, and topped the lot with tomato relish. Everyone ate well. The best Grandad could muster up for dessert was some fresh stoned apricots, dribbled with melted chocolate, which were scrumptious.

Feeding hungry children was easy, Grandad concluded. Just provide good food and let them get on with it. Unfortunately, most parents do not abide by Grandad's maxim and restrict their children's diet to a few ill-chosen boring ingredients and a reminder about the poor starving unfortunates who populate regions of Africa. The teenagers washed down their food with cold beer, while the younger children settled for orange juice with orange juice ice cubes. Grandad kept to his rosé wine.

'Good meal, Grandad,' complimented Jessica. 'It's my turn to do the dishes? Come on Thierry, give me a hand.'

'The rest of you come with me for rehearsals, and that also means you, Ewan,' ordered Lucy.

'I've got important things to do,' argued Ewan.

'What's more important than *Pirates of Provence*?'

'That's not fair—'

'Listen, I've got one rule.' Lucy didn't want any misunderstanding.

'What's that?'

'You do things my way.'

'That's not fair—'

'Bring your guitar, Julien.'

'Okay.'

'Metoo, metoo.'

'Ellie, if you borrow Jessica's iPhone, then we can listen to the songs once more.'

'That's still not fair.'

For Grandad, it was a delightful evening. He settled down in his hammock with a bottle of rosé wine at hand, bright stars shining overhead, and the pleasant noise of the boisterous children on deck, absorbed with their rehearsals.

Initially, Jessica had a difficult time with the flute Julien had brought along, mainly because it was slightly different to her own. She soon got the hang of it. She had a good ear and managed to join in with the Black Pearl Band. Lucy had given them that name.

Ellie took on the role of assistant to Lucy, taking notes, gently suggesting this and that without undermining Lucy's authority. Ewan tended to behave with Ellie helping little Lucy, and anyway, he was allowed to sing 'I am a Pirate King', which was his current favourite. What Ewan found distracting was Laetitia joining in the singing with him. She had quite a loud tuneless voice, like a wail. Perhaps the tunes will come with time; she was still only six.

When not rehearsing, everyone sat around the table, heads close together, whispering. Laetitia gave the game away by glancing across to Grandad with a guilty look. They were definitely up to no good.

Max paused from his duties in Chez Claude, sat on the beach with a glass of wine, and glanced over towards *Black Pearl*. What those on board didn't realise was how sound travelled across still water in an enclosed bay, with a backdrop of hills.

Julien's guitar notes didn't travel far, unlike the beat of the bongo drums and the caterwauling voice of Ewan. His voice couldn't be described as not being tuneful, perhaps a semitone flat, but that was his style. It was definitely an acquired taste. The clear pitch of the flute also carried across the bay, as did Lucy's cries of, action, and, cut. The odd tuneless wailing noise Max couldn't quite place!

There were four others on the beach, two girls, two boys, standing not far from where Max was sitting, staring out to sea, trying to work out how they could get to *Black Pearl*. When they got to the beach earlier that morning, they saw with horror that the pirate ship and its crew had disappeared, without warning. They were greatly relieved when *Black Pearl* returned that evening.

'Can you take us across, Max,' asked Virginia, 'I think they'll need us. I've got to teach them my dance steps.'

'We've been practicing all day,' added Nina.

'We've got real important business to do,' stated Hans.

'And it can't wait,' added Noé.

Ewan had texted Hans earlier that morning with the message, 'Found secret pirate treasure map, tell no one.' They had assumed Ewan had sailed away with his secret map to find the treasure without them, which wasn't proper, was it, because they were a gang, one for all, all for one, and all that.

'They'll still be there in the morning,' said Max kindly.

'You sure?'

'*Oui.*'

Max recognised the tunes as those belonging to *Pirates of Provence*, and saw an opportunity to promote Chez Claude. When he returned to serving his customers, he absently nodded out to sea in the direction of *Black Pearl*. 'They're rehearsing a musical they're going to perform here, keep an eye out for the notice.'

'What musical is that?'

'*Pirates of Provence.*'

Chapter 9
Trouble brewing

'**Has** he fucking phoned?' asked Mother from Hell, while on the phone to her sister-in-law, Marina.

Others may know Mother from Hell as, Jo, or Auntie Jo, or in the case of Laetitia, simply as Mum.

Jo never did get along with Grandad and things got worse when Laetitia was born. While she was still in hospital, recovering, her husband had celebrated with friends. Grandad took the drunken husband, his son Dominic, to register the birth because Jo had some silly names in mind. History had confirmed that Dominic signed the registry book thus verifying the dirty deed, although he could never remember doing so. While Grandad considered Laetitia an enchanting name, Jo thought otherwise. She never forgave Grandad.

She believed her father-in-law to be reckless and irresponsible. Apart from the naming of Laetitia fiasco, she based her opinion on how her father-in-law dressed, which usually comprised of an un-ironed grandad linen shirt, tatty jeans in need of burning, and grubby sandals. The sandals were expensive ones, because Grandad said they were the only things in contact with the ground and it was best to be safe than sorry.

'He's a Grandad, that's why he wears a grandad shirt,' argued her husband, Dominic.

'But he isn't some aging hippy pop-star, is he?' countered Jo.

'He was wearing them before aging hippy pop-stars were invented.'

Grandad also refused to wear socks until the frost and snow arrived. He then wore an old pair of manky, beige, suede dessert boots, which according to Jo, were unsuitable for wet and cold weather. She also regarded suede boots as unhygienic, particularly Grandad's, who never cleaned his.

It is as well she hadn't yet seen his ponytail and beard...

Her own father was boring. He wore corduroy trousers, a neatly ironed shirt, tie, smart tweed jacket, and sensible, polished, oxford brogues. He also didn't know what to do with grandchildren, or unsurprisingly, his own daughter, Jo, when she was a child.

Mother from Hell didn't like visiting Provence, because it was hot, sand got into everything, she couldn't speak a word of French, and her reckless and irresponsible father-in-law was there.

Neither did she like her daughters wandering around on their own, nor the jumping and diving from rocks tomfoolery. Apart from anything else, it was dangerous. Mother from Hell couldn't swim and had a fear of the sea. Her own father had instilled in her that water was hazardous, with tides that dragged everyone out to sea, and had nasty creatures that attacked you. Dominic explained that the sea at Pramousquier was safe and he had survived without any harm. She had seen people stung by jellyfish, so there was no argument about the sea being safe. It wasn't.

'Children rarely get stung, they're not that careless,' Dominic argued.

'Our children, for Christ's sake, we've got to protect them.'

'We can't keep them wrapped in cotton wool all their lives.'

'What about those treacherous back dives? They must be bad for your ears and surely, you'll hit the rocks. Your father is a bad influence. He's reckless.'

Dominic could never do back dives, unlike his sister, Marina. He wasn't against back dives. He had fond memories of Pramousquier, and still maintained friends from his childhood days. One friend lived in Paris, and he and Jo visited him and his wife regularly, because Jo could happily cope with Paris, but not Pramousquier.

You might ask, why did Mother from Hell allow her two daughters to stay with her evil father-in-law?

Expedience.

Her parents didn't do grandchildren. They had a busy social calendar and couldn't possibly squeeze them in. In any case, their bungalow was not the place for tiresome grandchildren, with everything just so and not to be meddled with under any circumstances. You had to feed them and how inconsiderate was that? Children were too distracting and they would interfere with their uninspired dull lives.

While both Jo and Dominic had busy careers, and despite being able to afford it, they didn't want to pay for a full time child minder. It was to Pramousquier that Jessica and Laetitia went each summer.

Mother from Hell gave Grandad clear and inappropriate instructions on how to look after her children, and preached to poor Jessica and Laetitia on what they could and couldn't do. Of course, no one paid the least bit of attention.

'*H*as he?' demanded Mother from Hell once more.

'Lucy did phone and everything is fine,' replied Marina evasively. 'She and Ewan seem to be enjoying themselves. They were having pizzas.'

'See, he can't even give them proper food.'

'Hasn't anybody phoned you?' queried Marina.

'Laetitia did, and said she had a fight with some big boys. I ask you, your father allowing big boys to beat up poor Laetitia.'

'I'm sure she is exaggerating, she's only little, you know.' Marina knew her father and he would never intentionally allow anyone to get into serious danger. A bit of danger maybe! That's how you learnt about things, he claimed. He gave you space and freedom. She knew that from experience. He always kept a watchful eye on you.

'Laetitia was covering up about something, I could tell. She said Jessica was washing the dishes and that's a lie. Jessica and dishes don't fucking go together.'

'Dad can be very persuasive when he wants.'

'Don't talk to me about Jessica. She's a lazy conniving shitbag who never lifts a finger to help.'

'No wonder, if that's how you talk to her.'

Marina didn't much like her sister-in-law, and considered her spineless and insipid. She also thought her ungrateful, because Grandad, and Gran when she was alive, had had Jessica and Laetitia every summer. No wonder Jessica called her Mother from Hell – she was.

'What about Laetitia's language? I am sure she told me to, fuck off, my own daughter, and she's only six.'

'You must have misheard, or perhaps she's copying someone else.' Unfortunately, the sarcasm was lost on Mother from Hell.

'Laetitia mentioned something about your father being in a chartroom. What's that about?'

'It's probably Dad reminiscing about his tanker days. You know how he likes to tell stories.'

'Perhaps,' conceded Mother from Hell reluctantly. 'How did Lucy sound on the phone?'

'Lucy told me not to be a pain. I was fussing about being careful not to burn, and to keep a lookout for jellyfish, so perhaps I was being a bit anal.'

'Jellyfish, they can kill you.'

'There aren't any jellyfish as far as I could make out. They don't kill because I should know, I've been stung plenty of times.'

'You think that's acceptable, do you?'

'It's only a gentle tingle.'

'I keep telling Dominic about skin cancer. He won't listen. Pramousquier is a dreadful place, why did I let them go.'

'Because you find it convenient, that's why, so don't kid yourself.' Marina couldn't hold back her irritation.

'No need to take that attitude,' snapped Mother from Hell.

'Silly bitch!' Marina mumbled while putting the phone down.

Chapter 10
Serious business

Jessica and Ellie got up early.

The night before, Jessica had mentioned to Grandad that she and Ellie had things to do in Le Lavandou, and could they take the Zodiac. Grandad knew not to ask why, because if he were supposed to know, then they would tell him.

Grandad had breakfast ready for the two teenagers, which they ate with hearty appetites.

'If you get the opportunity, can you buy a few things for me?'

'No problem,' said Jessica. 'I think we're having lunch at Julien's place.'

'You'll enjoy that.'

Julien's parents had a couple of tables outside, serving sandwiches, quiches, gâteaux, tartes, drinks, and other delights. It was a fine place for lunch because Grandad occasionally went there when in Le Lavandou.

The boulangerie was a family affair, with everything baked on the premises. People these days more often relied upon the supermarket because they were more convenient and much cheaper. Other boulangeries relied upon deliveries from a factory, again keeping down costs, thus providing a homogenous dreary range of products. Some places offered, baguette maison, freshly baked on the premises. More often than not, these were frozen, bought in quantity, and kept in the freezer before a final bake. The younger generation didn't want to follow their parents' example, working hard and struggling only just to make ends meet. The days of the traditional family boulangerie were numbered. Julien was a good example.

'I've got one or two things to do before we go,' Jessica informed Grandad.

She went forward to the crew accommodation, and gently opened Ewan's door, and bellowed, 'Oggie, oggie, oggie, and don't forget what I said, little boy.' It was a shout in vain, because Ewan was fast asleep, and didn't hear a thing.'

She went below deck and stood outside Lucy and Laetitia's cabin.

'Help, help...' whispered Jessica.

'Grandad, quick, Laetitia's seen that ghost again.'

Jessica then returned on deck.

'I feel a lot better for that,' she explained. 'I've got to go, Grandad.'

Grandad smiled; she hadn't sworn once.

*M*ax often queried his awareness of the fairer sex...

When Lucy, Laetitia, Virginia, and Nina turned up to practice their buccaneer beauty dances, he took a long, deep breath. Max greeted them with a kiss on the cheek, as this was his custom. Nina and Virginia were fine, but when he did this with Lucy, she simulated being sick. Laetitia happily accepted hers and then promptly told him to, furcuff, admittedly, in a pleasant kind of way.

...because girls and women, whatever their age, were still a mystery.

Mornings were quiet at Chez Claude, so Lucy and the others taking over his laptop, salon, rearranging the tables on the terrace, wasn't too much of a disruption.

For the sake of information, Laetitia was wearing her much-dishevelled pirate lookout outfit, with a different face decoration. This she had had to do herself because Jessica and Ellie had left early that morning while she was still fast asleep, which wasn't right, was it. She went for the green effect, with girlie pink stripes radiating from her nose. Possibly, she forgot about being a pirate and simply went for the feminine touch!

With Jessica not around to do Laetitia's hair, Lucy had a go. Laetitia wanted a ponytail. Lucy was in a creative mood and followed a theme in keeping with pirates. Laetitia was delighted to end up with a ponytail that protruded upwards from the top of her head, looking like a single palm tree on a small deserted island. At some earlier time, Jessica probably stole Grandad's black bandana and gave it to Laetitia to wear. That morning Laetitia was proudly wearing it, with palm tree poking above. When Grandad saw it, he counted to five, slowly, and then informed Laetitia she was a beautiful pirate lookout, the best ever.

Virginia, who was responsible for the dances in *Pirates of Provence*, was having a difficult time with Lucy and Laetitia. What would you expect with them having spent all day practicing on a deserted pirate island full of murderous Arabs who kidnapped Christians, plundered, and did other horrid things? Clearly, they picked up a thing or two about pirate dancing, particularly with Laetitia's rhythmic gym input, except it didn't coincide with Virginia's Italian ballet moves. In truth, Lucy was confusing her dances. Despite preferring pirate dances, she was a buccaneer beauty, and they danced differently, according to Virginia.

'You said I'm responsible for the dancing,' stated a very indignant Virginia.

'I meant only for the buccaneer beauties,' said Lucy, remembering their difference of opinion a couple of days ago. 'Pirates don't do ballet, do they?'

'Boys do,' argued Virginia. 'I've seen them.'

'Not pirates though, you haven't seen pirates do ballet.'

She hadn't.

When summoned to adjudicate, Max didn't know what to say.

After witnessing the alternatives, he saw merit in both dances, which wasn't what either Lucy or Virginia wanted to hear. Put it this way, while Lucy's pirate dance had savageness most becoming for pillaging pirates, Virginia's definitely had a certain artistic quality truly befitting buccaneer beauties. He needed more time to think.

'Well?' demanded Lucy.

'I can see merit—'

'Do you know how pirates dance?'

'*Mais oui*,' replied Max. The moment he said it, he knew it was a mistake. How had he managed once more to get himself into one of these predicaments? He never learnt.

'Prove it,' demanded Virginia.

'Yep, if you're so clever...' added Lucy.

'Go on Max, you show them,' encouraged Nina, who, being French, didn't doubt for one second that, Max, who was also French, couldn't do a decent pirate dance.

They all stared at Max, Lucy with her hands menacingly on her hips, waiting in anticipation.

Even Chef, who was behind the bar enjoying a late morning double espresso, watched in anticipation. '*Ce sera intéressant,*' he said to himself.

What else could Max do?

Admittedly, he tried his best...

'That's not a pirate dance, that's what red Indians do.' Sadly, for Max, Virginia was correct in her assertion.

'Yep, you're hopeless,' agreed Lucy.

'I thought it was good, Max.' What else could Nina say, being French?

'Metoo, metoo.'

Laetitia believed it was a terrific dance. She even joined in with Max, because it was easy, not like the other dances. She saw the benefit in doing those silly rhythmic gym classes because, at last, they came in handy. She liked the, 'Wa-woo-woo-hoo,' war cry, which she was extremely good at doing. It was then that Max recognised the origins of the strange wailing noises he heard coming from *Black Pearl* the previous evening. It wasn't an engine problem after all!

Chef witnessed the odd contribution to Lucy's dancing repertoire with bewilderment, because he agreed with Lucy, Max was hopeless. He sighed, shook his head, and sipped his espresso.

'Let's go for lunch,' said Virginia.

'Metoo, metoo,' agreed Laetitia, who was always hungry.

'What are we going to do for Jessica, I promised her a pirate dance this afternoon,' pleaded Lucy, 'she'll go mad.'

'Best do Max's dance,' suggested Nina, 'I think we can all do that.'

'We've got no choice,' Lucy conceded.

'Metoo, metoo,' because she could do it real good.

See, reasoned Nina smugly to herself, these foreigners don't know anything, not like us French.

Ewan was on the beach with his two trusty pirate captains, Hans and Noé, even if one was a bit too bossy for his liking. They were sitting on the rocks at the end of the beach, not far from Chez Claude, huddled over something nobody else was supposed to see.

It was Ewan's pirate treasure map.

'Are you sure it's real?' Hans queried in a rather haughty manner.

'Yeah, I had to scare away a giant crab, and it was in a proper dangerous hiding place where no one would dare to go in. It's got blood stains and it's got the burnt bits.' Ewan's description of the crab was a bit of an exaggeration, because the multi-legged sea creature in question was not only dead, but also quite small. It was the best Grandad could find at the time.

'It looks real to me,' agreed Noé. 'You can see the slash marks made by the pirate cutlasses when they were fighting and things. It's all brown, so it must be old.'

'It's a bit faint like you'd expect for an old pirate treasure map, and it's in code.' Ewan wanted to make his point.

'Isn't it in French?'

'Lots of the pirates around here were Arabs.'

'How do you know that?'

'Because I was on a pirate island yesterday and they had Arabs.'

While the others couldn't argue with that because they weren't there, it didn't solve their problem. They had a coded treasure map.

'We gotta figure out this code,' added Ewan.

'You found the treasure map on an English ship?' Hans was German and therefore logical in his thinking.

'Yeah…' Ewan neglected to mention it was an old Dutch klipper. Grandad was English, definitely, so that made it an English ship.

'The pirate captain must have been English, and the crew all Arab. It's normal to recruit cheap foreign labour, everyone does it,' said Hans.

'We're in France, so it must be in a French code,' argued Noé.

'I don't think so,' Hans answered, with a patronising tone. 'It must be an English code so that the Arabs and French couldn't read it.'

'Maybe…' That's as close to a yes that Noé was going to admit, because finding an English treasure map on a French beach was definitely wrong, wasn't it.

'I'll do some asking around,' said Ewan, meaning he'd ask Grandad.

They had been examining the map for ages but it still didn't make any sense. They could see the bay, with the coastline marked, dotted lines all over, a couple of crosses, and some trees, rocks, and things.

'It's an old map, isn't it?' said Hans.

'Yeah.'

'So any trees on the map must now be very old.'

'Yeah.'

'So let's go and check all the old trees and then sort out the writing and other things later.'

'Okay,' agreed Ewan reluctantly, because it was his map, and he should be in charge, not bossy Hans, and given time, he would have said that.

'We should be able to find the rocks,' said Noé, 'they'll be the same.'

'I was going to say that.' It certainly wasn't Ewan's day.

They studied the map a little longer, and then they did some searching around. They found old trees. To their dismay, there were lots of them. The Maures Hills were densely forested with cork oaks, pine trees, mimosas, and the typical garrigue scrubland, which scratched your legs as you walked through it. Nearer the beach, where the villas and apartments were, the landscape was modern, with palm trees, and other fancy trees, which were not old. Even they could see that.

Rocks were difficult to see because of all the new trees, which were higher than most of the rocks.

'I'm hungry,' declared Ewan, who then invited his two friends aboard *Black Pearl*, mainly to show them the chain locker, where he had found his secret map. There might be some other clues he had missed and his friends might see something. After Hans and Noé had informed their grandparents where they were going, they all swam out to *Black Pearl*.

'What's for lunch?' Ewan asked Grandad.

'It's on the table.'

'Where're the others?'

'Jessica and Ellie had things to do in Le Lavandou and Lucy and Laetitia are having lunch with Virginia and Nina.'

Grandad continued with his tasks, washing down the teak decking, tidying up the ropes, checking the tanks, and other such remedial nautical tasks. He also cleaned through the inside accommodation, excluding the cabins of the youngsters. He briefly glanced into their cabins and witnessed an unbelievable mess, like after a frantic jumble sale in the local village hall. On the other hand, the youngsters consider they were doing a good job keeping their cabins clean and tidy, as per rule six. Everything was where they wanted it to be, close to hand and feet, all within sight so you couldn't lose it, because parents don't know how to keep a cabin tidy, not properly anyway. The beds they kept unmade so that it was easier to get back into at night. Everyone knows that, except parents of course.

Ewan judged that it was a good time to inform his two friends of their other pirate duties they had to perform over the coming days, and err… that afternoon.

Participating in Lucy's *Pirates of Provence* show wasn't too hard a sell. As expected, Noé wasn't happy about swinging from the ships rigging. He glumly gazed up at the rigging of the mainmast, and didn't find it a comforting sight. He liked swimming under the water, not swinging in the air. If he were meant to fly, he would have wings, which he didn't.

'Swinging?' queried Noé.

'Yeah, it's easy. Laetitia does it all the time, just like how I taught her. You're not scared, are you?'

'No.' He would never admit that he was and wouldn't be outdone by a girl, especially not a little one, like Laetitia. He still wasn't happy.

Hans wasn't happy either. Noé had his swinging bit. Ewan had his walking the plank tricks and singing. So what was he supposed to do?

Quick thinking, Ewan said the swinging and walking the plank things were for the *Black Pearl* show, not the performance at Chez Claude. The Chez Claude production required Hans to organise the dancing on beer barrels. Everyone knew Germans were best at that.

'Max will probably give us free drinks,' said Ewan, 'because doing pirate things can be thirsty work.'

'Isn't dancing on beer barrels dangerous?' probed Hans.

'It's easy.' Secretly, Ewan agreed with Hans because he had to sing while dancing on the beer barrels, and how daft was that.

Convincing Hans and Noé of their other duties wasn't so easy…

'This afternoon?' queried Hans. 'Selling *beignets*?'

'If we don't go, Jessica said we're all dead meat.' Ewan had unjustly emphasised the plural, because he wanted to grab the attention of his two friends. Even they knew they weren't a match for Jessica.

'What about the treasure?' Noé asked.

'We can secretly hunt at the same time. All we have to do is make lots of noise,' Ewan explained.

'What kind of noise?' Hans asked with suspicion, and rightly so. While everyone knew they were good at making lots of noise, surely selling beignets required a special kind of noise. If Jessica was involved, then it definitely would.

'I've got to sing and you've got to do the chorus.'

'We don't know any chorus.'

'We've got an hour to practice.'

'You didn't tell us that.'

'Just did.'

Jessica and Ellie returned to *Black Pearl* from Le Lavandou with their shopping. Grandad could see things in the Zodiac concealed with an old towel. That was their business, not his. After quickly changing into bikinis, and with an unusually large bag, the two teenage girls took the Zodiac to the beach, the old boathouse end. They looked guilty and were up to no good, Grandad could see that.

By three in the afternoon, the sun was setting towards the west, and the heat of the midday sun weakened. It was time for everyone to return to the beach. In fact, the beach was busiest from mid-afternoon onwards, which was the favourite time of the day. Parents had done their shopping in the morning. Those who decided that a trip out doing tourist things might be a good idea now realised it wasn't. Children were happiest left to their own devices, whatever their age, a simple concept parents failed to grasp.

By about four in the afternoon, everyone on the beach got peckish, probably because they were not used to the fresh sea air and all the exercise. That was when the beignet seller strikes, and Jessica was aware of that.

Thierry had purchased a splendid selection of beignets. They had maxi beignets, mini beignets, beignets fourré, all kinds with a variety of fillings. Some were coated in chocolate or icing sugar with hundreds and thousands. Others were filled with vanilla custard or one of several flavours of jam. And let's not forget the traditional beignet, covered in sugar, which were irresistible to children.

There were big ones for teenagers and adults, and little ones for the children. The beignets were not out-of-date, only a day or so old, and difficult to sell to the fickle French in the supermarket. One thing for sure, they tasted better on the beach. They carefully removed any reference to Carrefour.

The traditional beach beignet seller keeps their beignets in a sweaty tin box that's been in the sun all day. They have to cut them open, spread the insides with a filling from some grotty jar, and dust them with icing sugar to make them appear attractive. They're too big for the smaller children, and after being dropped in the sand and handled by small mucky hands, parents reluctantly had to finish them.

What would you eat?

From a commercial point-of-view, Jessica had hit upon a good idea and had planned her enterprise carefully.

She had Ewan and his two trusty pirate captains take over part of the beach near the old boathouse, the opposite end to Chez Claude. They were to be four yards from the water's edge so as not to be soaked by rogue waves. They had to do this before everyone returned to the beach after their afternoon siesta.

When Jessica and Ellie arrived, they placed two of Grandad's spare blankets over the sand with a clean, white tablecloth on top – no, he didn't know – and set up shop. Julien loaned them some spare large cake trays from his parent's boulangerie – no, they didn't know either. They had borrowed two of Max's beach parasols, to provide much needed shade for the beignets – yes, he did know, but only when he saw them disappearing down the beach with the buccaneer beauties. 'Thanks, Max,' Lucy had shouted.

Jessica laid out her beignets, large ones on the right and smaller ones to the left, and with her artistic flair, ensured a tempting impression on the eye. She dusted the beignets with icing sugar, not wanting to miss a trick. They were ready and had already attracted a small crowd of onlookers. Ellie sat by the beignets, her large stature appearing motherly and welcoming, ready to serve her customers. A simple sign stated that large beignets were one euro, and small ones fifty centimes. This undercut beignet boy by more than half, and was more than double the cost Jessica had to pay, thus ensuring a sizeable profit.

The next phase was for Ewan to sing 'I am a Pirate King'

accompanied by Hans and Noé. That wasn't particularly a success, because, along with Laetitia doing her version of Max's pirate dance like some gothic devil creature, it frightened some of the smaller children. Luckily, it did attract the attention of the parents, and they were the ones who held the purse strings, so nothing lost.

The sign of a good entrepreneur was how quickly they could adapt to changing market conditions, and, despite what Mother from Hell might have thought, Jessica was no idiot. She quickly got Lucy to sing 'Walking in the Air' from *The Snowman*, which she accompanied with her flute. With her pleasing voice, Lucy held her notes to perfection, complemented by the tender tones of the flute.

Nina joined Laetitia in her dance, having recognised it as the one Max did earlier. The three boys agreed the dance was a good one because it wasn't cissy, and joined in, adding a bit of grit to the procedures. Virginia wasn't going to be left out, though pride wouldn't allow her to do Max's dance. She did her ballet, exactly as taught in her classes. She hadn't been to many classes. Did that matter?

Lucy decided that Ewan, Hans, and Noé needed some practice dancing on beer barrels. She drew three circles in the sand, in a line, and ordered them to, 'Get at it, *tout de suite.*'

Grandad could hear the flute playing from his hammock on *Black Pearl* and recognised it as one of Jessica's practice pieces from way back. He glanced towards the beach and saw nothing untoward. He was pleased that his grandchildren were enjoying themselves.

Those on the beach enjoyed the animation offered by Jessica and her helpers. Animation refers to some kind of cultural entertainment much loved by the French, where the cultural link isn't obligatory.

A useful little detail, suggested by Ellie, was to wash the hands of children with soapy water from a spray gun, and then dry them with one of Grandad's clean white towels. Beignets taste so much better when not eaten with mucky hands, explained Ellie, remembering her own experience from a few days ago. Virginia and Nina helped with the hand washing. With a box of white tissues used for handling, they sold each beignet in a clean and hygienic manner. Who could possibly complain?

They couldn't go wrong.

Ewan, the two pirate captains, and Laetitia danced down the beach la-la-ing to the tune of 'Walking in the Air' thus attracting more attention. As you would expect, Ewan and his two trusty pirate captains were quite happy to roam the beach, hunting here and there for you know what, and had a genuine excuse to do so. It didn't get much better than that.

When Lucy had finished her singing, much to her dismay she watched the others doing their version of the pirate dance. She made a few comments in her notebook and left it at that for the time being. She could see the others were enjoying themselves.

Jessica continued playing her flute without feeling self-conscious. She was enjoying herself and felt relaxed. She had been having a difficult time before arriving at Pramousquier, with continual bickering and arguments with Mother from Hell and her teachers at school. The whole world was against her and nobody understood. She wanted to do things, her things. Would they listen, least of all that inane student counsellor person, or whatever she called herself? All she said was, but how do you feel about that, and wanted to give her hugs, which didn't help matters. Jessica wanted to tell her to shut the fuck up.

In Pramousquier, nobody got onto her, telling her to do this, that, and the other. Things were different.

'Jessica,' prompted Ellie, while gazing down the beach.

'I've seen him.'

What they had seen was a very disgruntled beignet boy who couldn't sell a beignet if his life depended on it. He was fifty yards down the beach, staring at Jessica and her efficient team, with his mobile to his ear, telling someone all about what was going on. As you would expect, he wasn't a happy beignet boy, nor was his controller, who was at the other end of the mobile. After finishing his call, beignet boy wandered down to the other end of the beach where there was less competition.

Unknown to Jessica were two plagistes, the ones nearest to the old boathouse, planning what to do about the new competition. They didn't sell beignets. They sold crêpes, with a variety of fillings. While they didn't sell many, mainly because they were overpriced, they barely tolerated beignet boy wandering up and down the beach. More competition was a different matter.

Les plagistes, with their beach restaurants, like beignet boy, had a very short season to make money. They needed to make enough profit to keep them going for the rest of the year. Around that part of France, there were few alternative job opportunities, particularly during the winter months. Both agreed that what they saw was bad for them, because business was business, after all. In the end they let it go, just that once.

'You're English?' inquired a man with a well-spoken English voice. He had been hanging around, enjoying the animation. He was wearing one of those Panama hats you buy at the market, a neat pink shirt, smart cream linen trousers, and bare feet. His bare feet were his contribution to being laid-back on the beach under a parasol, feeling uncomfortable.

'Most of us are,' answered Ellie cheerily.

'Are you on holiday?'

'We're here for the summer living on that fabulous old klipper in the bay,' explained Ellie, pointing at *Black Pearl*. 'What about you?'

'I'm retired now and have a villa further inland. We're here for the day to see friends and they insisted we go to the beach. Unfortunately, my wife isn't a beach person, but what could we do.'

He directed his gaze to the back of the beach where his wife, dressed prim, proper, and very unsuitable for the beach, was with another couple. The man sat under the parasol wearing his retro shorts and short sleeve shirt with the buttons undone, reading a book, and looked hot and uncomfortable. His large attractive wife, by contrast, was enjoying the sun.

'I do like to see a bit of initiative,' the man continued. 'My daughter once spent a summer selling doughnuts on the beach. She told me all about it.'

'Oh?' queried Ellie.

'It is all controlled by the Marseille mafia, at least, that was what my daughter told me,' said the man as he walked to join his wife and friends at the back of the beach.

'Jessica, did you hear that,' whispered Ellie, slightly worried, 'mafia.'

'I heard,' replied Jessica. 'If any mafia come near us, they'll regret it. I'll set Laetitia onto them, and then they'll be sorry.'

'Or we'll get Ewan to sing.'

'That'll do the trick,' and they both laughed.

'*I* hope the children aren't a problem?' Grandad had paddled to the beach in the kayak and was enjoying a beer with Max at Chez Claude.

'No, not really,' replied Max. 'I need to get into their rhythm, their thinking, their…their…'

'I know what you mean,' consoled Grandad, which wasn't much of a consolation.

'They are always one step ahead of me. As for Laetitia…'

'They are all fond of you,' Grandad explained. 'You're like a big brother who is always looking out for them.'

'Mmm…'

Grandad walked up the beach, though not as far as the youngsters. He didn't want to pry, and he could see they were up to something. It was a social time of day and most of his friends were on the beach enjoying the late afternoon sun, swimming, and catching up with the gossip. Grandad noticed that beignet boy, who was normally high-spirited, seemed a bit glum. Then one of the plagistes who had observed Jessica earlier, didn't wave as usual; but he always was a bit temperamental.

Jessica sent Lucy up the beach to ward off Grandad in case he came too close. She stood on the waterline, with her hands placed menacingly on her hips, daring him to get closer, which he didn't. He was too busy talking with his friends, helping the occasional elderly woman out of the water and exchanging kisses on both cheeks with those he knew.

'Disgusting,' said Lucy.

The evening meal on *Black Pearl* was a happy and sociable affair.

Jessica had more than doubled her initial investment of fifty euros. The whole enterprise had exceeded her expectations and everyone had helped and had a good time. She realised that with some determination and teamwork, she could achieve things, like generating additional cash to buy unmentionable items she wanted to keep secret.

Ellie loved every second of everything that was happening. She had Julien to think about, her sexy French boy who was quite different to all the other boys she knew. She was a teenager, away from home, in the south of France, and living on an amazing old Dutch klipper. Best of all was Jessica's Grandad and all the others, who were welcoming and loveable, even Ewan. She was having the happiest time of her life.

Children, when happy, can be quite positive.

For example, Lucy didn't get dejected over Ewan and his two friend's disastrous endeavours at singing. Ewan's rendition wasn't too bad if you liked that kind of caterwauling noise, and it wasn't his fault two small children started to cry. The other two pirates, Ewan's friends, needed working on. Be it begrudgingly, Lucy saw merit in Max's pirate dance, which appeared authentic, particularly with Laetitia's fervent help. Lucy was slowly coming to terms with Virginia's Italian ballet for the buccaneer beauties, mainly because of the positive response she received on the beach. As any reputable director will tell you, you can't argue with a happy audience. All things considered, Lucy was pleased.

You might think Ewan begrudged missing precious treasure hunting time. He didn't. Under cover of the pirate dance, he and his two trusty pirate captains, despite one being a bit too bossy for his liking, had managed to explore that end of the beach. Nothing doing there, they had concluded.

Ewan made an astonishing discovery when he returned to *Black Pearl*. When he glanced back at the beach and wave to his two friends, what do you think he saw?

Rocks!

Trees, some higher than others!

Ewan deduced that on a treasure map, rocks and trees would only be visible from a pirate ship out at sea, not on land. Bossy Hans hadn't considered that, nor had clever-dick Noé.

As for Laetitia, she was living in paradise, pure and utter paradise, with not a concern in the whole world. You might think a child so small would miss her parents, particularly her mother. She hadn't given them a second thought.

There was continuous bickering at home, particularly between her big sister, Jessica, and her mother. This rubbed off on to her father, who tried not to take sides but in doing so, received the wrath from both. He couldn't win. Home wasn't a happy place. Thankfully, most of the antagonism went way over Laetitia's head.

Laetitia didn't even mind having to wash her face before tea because her pirate makeup was getting into a terrible state. Laetitia's attempt at washing her face, even with soap, wasn't the success Grandad had hoped.

Everyone loved Laetitia, particularly her big sister Jessica, despite the odd nasty furcuff now and then. That's what you said to younger siblings, wasn't it? No malice intended.

Grandad had prepared one of his famous bath meals, his signature dish so to speak, one he devised years ago with leftovers. Pork cutlets with baked courgettes covered with bleu d'Auvergne cheese. For starters, he had the usual dips. Jessica had used her initiative and had bought some hummus, and Grandad had dressed this with olive oil and a sprinkling of paprika, to give it more bite. He even baked some pita bread, well, his own version anyway. It was warm, and all you had to do was tear it into pieces and dip.

There were no parents to moan about manners, or whine about keeping your elbows off the table, or telling you not to speak with your mouth full, and other silly instructions all made to make life difficult. Parents were the bane of a child's life. That didn't include Grandad of course, because he was a blessing for any child.

'So what did you all do today?' asked Grandad, more out of form because he knew the answer.

'Nuffin.'

'Yep, not much.'

'I did some lookout for Hans, and a pirate dance, and—'

'We had a quiet day, didn't we Ellie.'

'Oh yes, Mr err Charlie, very quiet. You were right; Julien's parents gave us a good lunch.'

Following the cheese, Grandad had baked a tarte tatin, like an upside-down apple pie, accompanied by his own version of egg custard.

'*Eins, zwei, eins, zwei…*'

'It's Gisela, furcuff,' greeted Laetitia with delight, because she had bought a maxi beignet from them that afternoon.

'Charlie,' Gisela spluttered from under her distinctive blue bathing cap, 'what delightful grandchildren you have—'

'Hi, have a lovely swim,' shouted Jessica, then in a whisper to the others said, 'keep talking to the old bag in case she tells Grandad what we've been up to.'

'Watch out for the méduses, we've seen lots today.' Lucy was quite clever with that because, like most elderly people on the beach, Gisela feared meeting the dreaded méduses.

'Oh, oh, oh dear…'

'Good one, Lucy,' whispered Jessica.

'I can't see any at the moment, be careful, that's all,' added Lucy because she could see Gisela was in distress and felt guilty about frightening her.

'Oh, oh, *danke, danke*…' and off she went back towards the beach, doing her backstroke with additional fervour, though not moving much faster than normal.

'Isn't she a lovely lady,' said Ellie.

'Come on, let's clear the table,' said Grandad.

Clearing the table wasn't a problem because they all helped. Lucy and Ewan were racking their brains whether-or-not they had heard Jessica swear that day, because they didn't want to do the dishes. Jessica soon put them out of their misery…

'Don't worry you two morons; I'll do the effing dishes.'

…problem solved.

'*It*'s me, Mum, the pirate king.' Ewan was on the mobile.

'xxxx'

'It's me, the pirate king, Ewan, y'know, your son, the one bigger than Lucy.'

'xxxx xxxx'

'I'm not being rude.'

'xxxx'

'Grandad said so.'

'xxxx'

'Don't do behavin now I'm pirate king.'

'xxxx'

'We sailed to a pirate island yesterday and it was awesome and we had a barbecue on the pirate ship and I'm the star and I'm the pirate king and I have to walk the plank and do all the tricks all by myself and I'm the star and Hans is dead bossy and Jessica does all the dishes because she keeps swearing and we help her sell beignets on the beach and it's awesome here and—'

'xxxx xxxx'

'Ship – I think Grandad borrowed it from a friend.'

'xxxx'

'How do I know?'

'xxxx'

'Grandad's busy.'

'xxxx'

'I meant eating, not selling beignets. They taste dead good.'

'xxxx'

'Nuffin.'

'xxxx'

'Nuffin, honest, gotta go, bye.'

It was getting dark and the three younger children were fighting sleep despite being tired. They didn't want to go to bed, not yet anyway.

'Can we have a story, Grandad,' asked Laetitia.

'One about the war,' begged Ewan.

'One about pirates, pleeease,' pleaded Laetitia.

'Yep, definitely pirates.'

Laetitia climbed onto the hammock with Grandad, and cuddled up. Lucy and Ewan sat on the padded bench in front of the chartroom. With their legs overlapping, the twins engaged in a short bout of rivalry kicking, more out of habit than anything. They soon found their space and settled down quietly.

Grandad sipped his calvados and began…

'Off the French coast in the Mediterranean is a small rocky island, used by Barbary pirates for plundering and other murderous deeds. The island was known as Middle Island to the ancient Greeks, but that was a long time ago.'

'There must have been other islands if they called it Middle Island,' said Lucy, who, as we know, was a clever young girl.

'The island had a cross-shaped small port used by pirates because it offered good protection for their ships.'

'Did the pirates have a name for the island?' asked Lucy.

'I don't know,' replied Grandad.

Ewan remained quiet, but he was listening. Intently! He knew. It was called Port Cros, the island with a cross-shaped port. It was in the middle of other islands, wasn't it? They'd been there the day before. There was definitely treasure somewhere, definitely.

'During those days, pirates were always fighting among themselves and sinking each other's ships, which can be a nuisance if you're a pirate. During the summer, several hundred years ago, there were four notorious pirate gangs. They met on Middle Island and made a pact never to attack each other so they could spend more time doing proper pirate things like plundering and treasure hunting.'

'Did they have a pirate king?' asked Lucy.

'I think they did. He was old and wiser than the others and he had a hook on one arm and a black patch over one eye.'

'What was wrong with his eye?' asked the enquiring Lucy.

'What...'

'You said he had a black patch over one eye.' Lucy was thinking about the costumes for her *Pirates of Provence* and wanted to get things right.

'You remember he had a hook on one arm? He lost his hand in a fierce battle when plundering. Soon after he had his hook fitted, he had an itch on his nose and when he went to scratch it, he forgot about his new hook and...'

'Ha, ha, very witty.'

'Did he have a parrot,' asked Ewan.

'All pirate ships had parrots, so he must have,' improvised Grandad, aware of Ewan always talking to his imaginary parrot.

'Why did pirates have parrots?' Ewan was trying not to fall to sleep and found talking helped.

'As a pet on a ship, they were convenient and easier to keep than a monkey or a dog. They didn't need much looking after and they were too small to eat if the crew were starving.'

'Yuck...' Laetitia didn't fancy roast parrot, despite her healthy appetite.

'Also, when pirates went ashore getting drunk, fighting, and chasing women, they often ran out of money. With a parrot on your shoulder, they could sell it, because parrots were exotic, rare, and valuable.'

'You mean I could sell my parrot for lots of money,' asked Ewan.

'Only if it was real,' argued Lucy.

'It is real, everyone plays with it.' You couldn't argue with that because everyone did.

'As an act of good faith,' continued Grandad, 'each pirate captain buried their treasure and if any of them were killed, their treasure was to be divided between the others. Each pirate captain drew a map showing the location of their treasure and gave a copy to the others.

'Not very long after the meeting on Middle Island, all the pirate captains were either killed in battle or captured by the authorities and hanged. No one knew where the treasure maps were hidden, so the treasure was lost forever and the story became folklore and myth, only told in the local bars after drinking lots of rum and pastis.'

'Is that how you found out about the story, Grandad, in a bar?' asked Lucy, who clearly doubted the validity of the whole pirate story.

'It was,' confirmed Grandad. 'I don't think we should trust pirate stories told in bars though.'

'What happened next?' asked someone who did trust such stories. The thought of four lots of hidden treasure was irresistible.

'Two hundred years later, while tending his goats in the hills, a young boy found an old leather pouch hidden in the rocks, and inside were three old parchments. He took them to his father who identified them as pirate treasure maps. The fourth map was missing. Over the next year or so, the goat boy and his father went on expeditions to find the hidden treasure. They climbed hills, crossed dried up river beds and eventually found the location of the hidden treasure, which were in rotten wooden boxes. When they opened each box, they found that the fiendish pirates had cheated each other and filled the boxes with stones. The fourth map, the one belonging to the pirate king, is still missing to this day, or so the story goes.'

'Do you think the pirate king was a cheat like the others?'

'Some pirates, while plunderers and murderers, were honourable people.'

'Do you know his name?'

'It could have been Redbeard, who was a famous Barbary pirate.'

'Redbeard?' queried Lucy, 'you're making it up.'

'You can check it out on Max's laptop. I think he was Turkish. He conquered Libya and Tunisia over five hundred years ago. As far as I know, he did a bit of ravaging in most of the towns and villages around here, including Toulon, which isn't far.'

'So Redbeard was real,' marvelled Ewan.

'He certainly was.'

'Where's Libya and Tunisia?'

Grandad pointed to the south. 'If you go that way, and dodge the islands, and keep going, that's where.'

'Why did they call him Redbeard?' asked Lucy, who now believed Grandad, because she knew that Grandad would know she would check it out on Max's laptop.

'They called him Barbarossa, which was Italian for red beard. As far as I know, he had a big bushy red beard and wore a turban.'

Laetitia, who had fallen asleep, missed the end of the story. Grandad carefully carried her to her cabin and put her to bed. He noticed she smelt a bit and her face still had the remains of several days painting. Why worry? She was absorbed in her own world and was happy. He'd make sure she had a good swim the next morning.

Lucy began corrections to her script.

She had a dilemma because she wanted both Redbeard and Blackbeard in her story and that wasn't easy. If she had them early in the story, they could have a fight with cutlasses, one could kill the other, and that would solve the problem. She could have Max as Redbeard and Grandad as Blackbeard. Grandad could kill Max, and then Ewan, who was the pirate king, could kill Grandad, because she needed Ewan to sing some of the songs and everyone knew Grandad couldn't sing.

It wouldn't be proper if Ewan killed Grandad, so she would have Hans play the pirate king for the fight with Blackbeard, because Hans was taller than Ewan. That made sense, because she had already planned Noé doing the swinging because Ewan didn't like heights. The less you saw of Ewan the better, because he was younger than she was. In fact, Ewan was useless. It was unfortunate he could sing. Yep, despite Ewan, her script was coming along quite nicely.

Ewan was quiet, contemplating his situation. He had suffered a setback. He should have known about pirates being deceitful where hidden treasure was concerned. If he were a real pirate with treasure, he reckoned he would make fake treasure maps to put others off the scent, and he would have a secret code, only known to him. Yes, he would definitely lie if he were a pirate. He had a lot to think about…

Jessica and Ellie had taken the Zodiac ashore and met up with Julien and Thierry. They were on the beach, the end where the old boathouse was, smoking what they shouldn't be smoking and enjoying their successful venture at selling beignets. Jessica knew exactly what she wanted to do with her profits and, together with her friends, planned further mischief and exploits.

Grandad retired to his hammock with a generous slug of calvados and congratulated himself on one more successful day minding his grandchildren. There were no broken bones, no blood, no arguments, or fights, nobody was ever hungry, everyone was happy doing whatever they were doing, and he was extremely happy looking after them.

It had been said that for some, life was one hell of a job. For Grandad, life was easy, and very, very, good.

Chapter 11
Teenagers bearing gifts

According to some, there was a lot to be said for having a routine, though for Grandad, life was too short for such mundane matters. It was best simply to wake up each morning and take it from there.

If you were Jessica, you woke up and wondered why everyone was getting up at midnight and making such an awful noise. Eventually she had to get up because she had many plans and not much time. She had a beignet business to run generating much needed cash for things best left unsaid. She had other mischievous plans only known to her and Ellie. Things required planning and that needed time. If Jessica was half as industrious at school as she was that summer in Pramousquier, she would have straight *A* grades in all her examinations and would be head girl without any difficulty, and Mother from Hell would definitely not be on her back all the time.

Jessica didn't know that, did she?

If you were Ellie, you woke up and wondered what was going to materialise that day because, for her, life was now one long adventure. Not only that, she and Julien had been bonding closely. Not too closely, because she was a good girl and as boys went, Julien was a good boy. But you can only be good for so long.

If you were Ewan, you woke up with secrets and plans, but everything everyone else said, did, or suggested, got in his way. Nobody understood his predicament and because it was all secret, he couldn't explain. He wasn't greedy, because when he found the secret pirate treasure he would give a little bit to Grandad so he could do some repairs on *Black Pearl*, like get a proper toaster and make it easy to take off the flippers so that he could use them as pirate landing crafts, and other useful things like that.

If you were Lucy, you also woke up with a mission. It was a different mission to her younger and, thankfully, not identical twin, because being identical would have been too much for her. As with creative types, she went straight to her notes and made adjustments and corrections. She would then tell Laetitia there were no ghosts on *Black Pearl*, which she reckoned was unfortunate. Being artistic, she believed seeing the odd ghost on a pirate ship essential to her creativity. Laetitia had given her too many false alarms to be a reliable source of information more's the pity.

If you were Laetitia, you woke up bursting for a wee and your cousin telling you there were no ghosts. What did she know?

Laetitia had several secret friendly ghosts, the same variety as Ewan's parrot.

When she clambered up the ratline for her pirate lookout duties, a friendly ghost taught her what to do. That's why she was so good at it. Then there was the ghost who played with her and her dolls and got her into trouble for not being a good lookout. She could live with the disgrace because she had redeemed herself by doing over the enemy on the beach, who were teenagers, big, and French. Then there was the ghost who taught her how to sail *Black Pearl*, except no one listened to her, so she had to do it all by herself. Her best friend ghost was the one she talked to when she went to the loo and kept her company. She knew a thing or two about ghosts did Laetitia.

'*P*orridge?' queried Jessica.

It was breakfast time and Grandad believed it was time for a change.

'Yes,' explained Grandad, 'it's got slow release energy and that's what you need when you're on the beach.'

'Get a life, Grandad.'

'You can have it with honey or sliced fresh figs.'

They were all hungry, particularly Laetitia and Ellie, who were always hungry, but despite all the original moans and groans, not a drop of porridge was left; and he had made plenty.

'Have I got a wonderful surprise for you all,' said Jessica, handing over four tickets.

'What are they?' asked Lucy, because she liked surprises.

'Tickets for *Gigi*, great, don't you think?'

Grandad had a closer look at the four tickets and they were for a performance of *Gigi* that evening at the local salle des fêtes.

'Thank heaven for little girls,' sang Jessica. 'It's a musical, Maurice Chevalier and all that, so you four will enjoy it. It starts at nine tonight. Best leave in plenty of time so you get good seats. I've arranged for you all to have pizzas at Olivier's after.'

Jessica was definitely aiming her marketing pitch at the three younger ones, because Grandad didn't seem too keen.

'A musical,' said Lucy, who loved musicals, and she might get some tips for her own show, 'ace.'

'Awesome,' added Ewan, who also loved musicals, and it shouldn't interfere with his treasure hunting.

'Metoo, metoo.'

'That seems to be a vote of confidence, Jessica, thank you very much.' Grandad was pleased Jessica had planned a night out for everyone. He could see Ellie wasn't particularly comfortable, perhaps the porridge hadn't agreed with her. 'What about you and Ellie?'

'There weren't enough tickets,' answered Jessica vaguely. 'We'll keep watch on *Black Pearl*, won't we Ellie.'

'That's very considerate of you,' said Grandad.

'We'll have Julien and Thierry on board so we can practice our pirate tunes, if that's okay.'

'That's fine.'

Grandad wasn't completely naïve, not yet anyway.

Having had two children of his own, he knew what mischief teenagers got up to when left to their own devices. He also was once a teenager and could still remember some of the antics he got up to unbeknown to his parents.

You had to know the right question to ask.

If you interrogated your teenage children, or granddaughter, with a batch of questions, they felt either threatened or indignant because of the implied mistrust. Either way, that would result in immediate hostility of said teenager and probably a mouthful of abuse, thus achieving nothing.

Grandad sensed Jessica was up to no good, though nothing he could put his finger on. What the hell, Jessica and Ellie were over sixteen and he trusted them not to do anything too silly.

Thinking about it, perhaps Grandad was a bit naïve!

'I'm taking *Black Pearl* to Le Lavandou this morning,' explained Grandad. 'I've got a few things to do.'

'Metoo, metoo.'

'Yes, I'll need a good lookout.'

'No way am I going,' protested Ewan, 'I'm too busy.'

'I can't go either,' added Lucy. 'I've got creative things to sort.'

'That's okay. I've already asked Noé and Nina's grandparents to keep an eye on you both.'

'Ace.'

'Awesome.'

'When will you be back?' asked Jessica.

'I'll be using the engine, so should be back for lunch. Although we have plenty, I want to top up with fresh water and fuel. I'll be doing some shopping as well.'

'We're coming too. We'll do the navigating and steering,' Jessica informed Grandad.

'Can we?' pleaded Ellie.

'That's fine,' agreed Grandad.

'That's settled then,' said Jessica, quite pleased because, with all her careful planning, everything was carefully falling into place.

'We need the practice,' added Ellie.

Grandad was impressed with the nautical abilities of Jessica and Ellie.

They did a close encounter with la Pointe du Cap Nègre, mainly to see if Carla was at home. Whoever was at home gave *Black Pearl* a wave and watched the old Dutch klipper sail majestically past.

'I can't believe you jumped off that rock, Jessica,' said Ellie with admiration while sailing past the Pointe.

'I'll get you to jump before the end of the holiday,' replied Jessica. 'If you go on *YouTube* you'll see others doing it.'

'Never, and that's definite.'

'Useful gadget that,' remarked Grandad as Jessica glanced at her iPhone.

When they arrived at Port du Lavandou, Grandad manoeuvred *Black Pearl* to the station carburants, and moored alongside. He organised the filling of fresh water and fuel for the engine, and then went into town to do his shopping. One of his stops was at the brocante, because he had some pirate treasure to collect.

Julien met Jessica and Ellie and they disappeared. Up to no good, concluded Grandad, much like himself.

Ewan was convinced he had the map for finding Redbeard's treasure. He got into a huddle with his two friends at one end of the beach, well away of any potential listener. He explained all about the Barbary pirates and Redbeard. Admittedly, Ewan's version of was slightly different to Grandad's, and Pramousquier bay featured high on Redbeard's pursuits.

While Ewan might not appreciate it, he was lucky to have Hans as a friend, because he was methodical and efficient in his approach. Even Noé was worth his weight in treasure because he was an excellent swimmer and he was helpful when in the mood. If only they used their skills to best advantage, they would have made a formidable team.

Ewan wanted to find the treasure because he was an avid collector of odd things, not dead frogs or anything because they eventually started to smell and made Mum mad. He collected interesting things, like a hair from a lion's mane, a crocodile tooth, and a stud from Wayne Rooney's football boots. While these treasures were real to Ewan and carefully hidden among his underpants, their authenticity and provenance were, at best, dubious.

'We gotta go out to sea to work out the treasure map,' explained Ewan.

'We'll go in the kayak,' proposed Noé.

'We can't take the map with us because we can't risk it getting wet,' said Hans sensibly. 'It must be very fragile.'

'We'll make a copy.' Noé was good at ideas.

'We haven't got time.' Until then, Ewan hadn't considered about the safety of his map, but knowing about the treachery of pirates, you had to be careful, didn't you? He had carefully hidden his treasure map on board *Black Pearl*. No one would ever want to investigate Ewan's dirty underpants; that's for sure.

'We'll go out in the kayak and make a map of what we can see, and then we can compare it with Redbeard's,' added Ewan carefully.

*L*ucy was under pressure.

She still had several creative matters to resolve, like too many elderly pirates, a useless pirate king who didn't like heights, Laetitia demanding to be the star, dances to arrange, Blackbeard's fight to sort, swinging to organise, and many other things she had written in her notebook. It was all getting in a muddle, especially with Grandad's facts she had written down and had to tell to her Mum next time she saw her.

She and her two friends took up their usual position at Max's and got down to some serious work. Things were going fine until Max came along with a carafe of chilled water and a dish of olives.

'Lucy, can you manage Saturday for the show?'

'Saturday?' Lucy was in a panic, she didn't like deadlines. Normally she did a performance when she was ready; and she certainly wasn't ready.

'It's a good time for me.'

'What day is it today?'

'Thursday.'

'Thursday!'

'Is Saturday a problem?'

'That'll be okay, Max,' answered Nina primly, much to Lucy's annoyance, *'pas de problème.'*

'Good,' said Max. 'I'll put a notice up to let people know. I am excited about seeing your show and so is everyone else.'

Max needed to discuss with Chef a new children's menu with a pirate theme. He also wanted a barbecue on the beach, like real pirates, and additional tables making room for more customers. He had to order plenty of rum, definitely. There were lots to organise and little time. First, he had an important task to do.

'Why did you say that,' whispered Lucy, 'because it's not okay.'

'It is now,' said Nina.

'I think I'm going to have a migraine,' sighed Lucy, with eyed closed, arm resting on her forehead, head tilted upwards, in classical Shakespearean manner. It was quite a performance.

'Glaces pour les jeunes filles.' Max knew how to win the hearts of the buccaneer beauties.

'Thanks Max,' all disagreements and migraine forgotten.

*F*or Laetitia, every day was a perfect day.

She had many likes, although they were not all the same. She liked having Grandad about because she loved him, and his cooking was better than Mum's; and she always felt safe with Grandad. That was her essential number one like.

She liked to keep pirate lookout for Hans, who she knew appreciated her bravery and skills. Yet she liked playing with her dolls, which can make things awkward when she was doing lookout. She liked talking French to everyone. Unfortunately, nobody understood her French, which she found strange because French people were supposed to understand. She liked ice cream, and Max, and wearing her new pirate lookout outfit with pretty frills, and putting on pirate makeup, and eating, and swinging, and doing over the enemy, and swimming, and she could swim for real now. These weren't essential likes, but they all add up to perfect days for Laetitia.

Finally, a recent favourite like was going to the toilet because she didn't have to flush it, not like at home where Mum always shouted at her when she didn't flush it, which wasn't right, was it, because she was only little, and she always played with her dolls on the toilet so how was she supposed to remember.

'*A*re you listening to me, Max said Saturday?'

Black Pearl was back in Pramousquier bay, and everyone was ravenous and tucking into lunch.

'I know my song, so what's the problem.' As far as Ewan was concerned, he was the star, and so long as he knew his words then everything was fine.

'You don't know the dance routines.'

'We'll do more practicing on the beach when Jessica is sell—'

'Thank you Ewan,' said daughter who was going through her awkward period in a menacing manner, 'sewing costumes, remember.'

'Sewing costumes?' Ewan wasn't always the quickest. 'Ouch, oh yeah, costumes, that's right. No need to kick me, that hurt.'

'What about the music?'

'That's all in order,' said Ellie. 'Julien, Thierry, and Jessica have it in hand. We need to know about your dances and you did mention some other songs. Let us know what they are and we'll listen to them on the iPhone and take it from there.'

'Blackbeard's got to kill Redbeard and then the pirate king kills Blackbeard and then sings a song,' Lucy spluttered, 'it's all a muddle.'

'Metoo, metoo.'

Everyone glanced at Laetitia with surprise at this new twist in the plot. Who does she kill? Lucy wouldn't let her sing, surely. Laetitia, having staked her claim to this killing business, because she was good at that wasn't she, helped herself to one more plate of yummy food.

'Tell us all about it and I'm sure we can sort it out,' said Ellie kindly.

'Okay.' Lucy explained her plot, and after a few creative wrangles, things were more or less agreed.

The disputes were minor ones, although Ewan would argue otherwise. He didn't take kindly to Hans killing Blackbeard because he wanted to do that.

'How will the audience be able to hear you sing if you're busy doing all the killing,' coaxed Ellie. 'It wouldn't be considerate on the audience, would it?'

'We're going to have to get a black wig for Grandad, cos his hair is grey,' said Lucy, who was slowly getting used to the idea that her show would take place on Saturday. 'We can't have Blackbeard with grey hair.'

'Not sure we can get a wig,' Jessica said. 'A little bit of makeup should do the trick?'

'Does Max know about his role as Redbeard?' asked Ellie.

'I forgot to tell him.'

'I'll talk to him later,' said Grandad, 'and we'll sort out the fighting and killing bits.'

'When do I sing and who can I kill?' asked Laetitia. Nobody had told her what to do and that wasn't right was it.

'Not this time, Laetitia,' explained Lucy carefully. 'You're the pirate lookout and you're dancing, so you'll be too busy to sing and kill.'

After the success of the previous day, Jessica had increased her budget for her beignet business.

When she and the others arrived on the beach, disgruntled beignet boy was straight away on his mobile, phoning his controller. His takings

128

the previous day were down and his controller wasn't pleased, nor was he, because his own income was a percentage of his sales. There was room on Pramousquier beach for only one beignet seller, and that was he, not them.

Beignet selling that afternoon was more or less a re-enactment of the previous day, except more professional. On the advice of Julien, they decided not to advertise prices for the beignets because, legally, to sell beignets on the beach you needed a licence. They simply left a box with a sign for voluntary donations.

'I've checked with my father,' Julien had explained. 'So long as we don't sell the beignets, then we don't need a licence. We give them away and if people make donations then that's their business.'

With all the singing and dancing, Jessica and the others were a happy gang. Lucy, with surreptitious help and support from Ellie, directed her cast with confidence. Jessica had a good ear for tunes and easily mastered the music on her flute. Even the dancing improved, and nothing a couple more rehearsals couldn't sort.

The beer barrel dance was a different matter.

Since three barrels in the sand wasn't the success she hoped, Lucy experimented with four barrels, hoping it would make things easier. That only confused the three prancing pirates, which wasn't unusual, because they were only boys!

Jessica had two extra visitors and no, they weren't ~~buying~~ donating. They had walked down the beach purposefully and with a mission.

'*Qu'est-ce que tu fais?*' asked one of the two plagistes.

'I don't understand,' lied Jessica. Her French was almost perfect.

'You can't sell beignets here, you need a licence,' said the other man.

'I'm not selling anything.'

'Don't you be clever with me? I can see money in the box.'

'Donations only,' explained Jessica innocently, indicating her sign. 'Can't you read?'

'We'll see about that,' said the man and they both stomped back from whence they came. They received a few jeers from those on the beach that were enjoying the animation and splendid beignets, which were much tastier than those offered by beignet boy.

'What about costumes?' Lucy asked.

'I've got mine,' said Laetitia, 'and I'm wearing it.' In case you were wondering, Laetitia had deliberated not wearing it that afternoon, because she found it difficult to walk in, although you wouldn't believe that if you saw her. With all the talking over lunch about production matters and feeling a little cheated about not being allowed to sing or do any killing, which wasn't right, she wanted to make her point, her point being she was ready, even if nobody else was. She wasn't going to be left out, that's for sure.

'Are there any charity shops nearby?' asked Ellie.

'No, they don't appear to have them in France,' answered Jessica. 'We can wear rolled up jeans and pirate-looking t-shirts. A few headscarves will help, black for the boys and pink for the girls.

'I've got a long black cotton skirt we could cut up,' offered Ellie, 'it's too hot to wear here.' Ellie wore black a lot.

Ellie felt at home at Pramousquier. She loved it there. Being an only child with no brothers and sisters, she also loved being with the others. Aboard *Black Pearl*, she could be herself and felt comfortable and it agreed with her easy-going nature. Despite knowing Jessica could be a handful and more than a little mischievous, she didn't mind, because Jessica's heart was in the right place.

'I've got a black t-shirt that's a bit too tight now. Someone can wear that,' added Jessica.

'I'll tell Grandad to make some pirate hats,' said Lucy.

~~Sales~~ Donations were good, rehearsals were fine, and even Ewan and the boys were enjoying themselves, despite losing precious treasure hunting time. The only problem they had was sand on some of the beignets when Noé got too intense during one of the dances. Nobody seemed to mind.

'Trouble,' whispered Ellie.

Laetitia was dismayed because, despite being pirate lookout, she hadn't noticed trouble, unlike Ellie. She felt she had let Hans down.

Down the beach was beignet boy pointing in their direction and next to him was an agitated man, bickering with exaggerated arm movements. His demeanour was menacing, with dark slicked-back hair and long sideburns that reached his chin. He wore dark blue jeans that had seen better days, a shirt and nondescript pullover, and heavy boots, all incongruous with being on a hot Mediterranean beach, and he was smoking the stub of a cigarette. He stopped bickering with poor beignet boy and then took a few steps towards Jessica and gang to see what was going on. He stared at Jessica through dark, narrow eyes, and having thrown his stub into the sea, lit another cigarette.

'Mafia man,' whispered Ellie quietly, hoping only Jessica could hear.

'If he takes one more step in our direction, he'll regret it.' Jessica meant it, as well.

Adults often speak to each other in low, quiet tones, assuming young children can't hear. Unknown to them, young children have acute, sensitive hearing, are attentive, and despite seemingly playing with their dolls, or whatever, hear every word spoken. Usually it didn't matter, because adults never have anything interesting to say and were exceedingly boring.

Laetitia was a good case in question. She was always around but nobody saw her. Despite giving her best energetic rendering of Max's pirate dance, and banned from singing and killing, they took her for granted. If you were Laetitia, and smarting from your derogation of lookout duties, wanting to impress Hans, and hearing the words, he'll regret it, you didn't need telling once, never mind twice.

'Charrrrge…'

Everyone on the beach stopped to watch the little six-year-old girl, green face with pink stripes, and black tutu skirt around her neck with very drooping frills, run down the beach, armed with a beignet, shouting…

'Kill the muffee man, this is our beach, furcuff,' and other such pirate lookout expletives.

'Charr—'

If being unkind, you might expect a little six-year-old girl running down the beach to trip over her black tutu skirt with very drooping frills. She did.

Her beignet fell into the sea, which hurt her feeling because she felt she had let Jessica down. That plucky little girl with a heart of the bravest pirate lookout, stood up, and picked up her soggy beignet. She forced back her tears, and continued her advance on the muffee man.

'—rrge.'

131

She splashed muffee man, the one with dark slicked-back hair and long sideburns that reached his chin, letting him know who was in charge of that particular part of the beach. Then she threw her soggy beignet at him as hard as she could – which wasn't hard, as you would expect. It landed full on his right boot, appearing unsightly.

Laetitia didn't have a snorkel to wiggle under his nose like with the six teenage boys, so she wiggled her finger in a threatening manner, which we know is possible from this particular brave six-year-old girl.

'Furcuff or I'll slice you in half with my faithful cutlass.' That was one of Ewan's lines in the show, without the furcuff, and Laetitia delivered it with far more emotion and aplomb than Ewan ever could.

The man with the dark slicked-back hair and long sideburns that reached his chin justifiably lost heart. After kicking the soggy beignet on his right boot into the sea, he turned round and walked away, scowling at poor beignet boy as he walked past.

Laetitia only hoped Hans was watching her heroic act although didn't expect him to join her in her annihilation of the nasty muffee man. From her limited experience, boys seemingly didn't do such things. She turned round, and proudly marched back, head held high. Others nearby on the beach applauded Laetitia because they believed it was all part of the beach animation.

'Good one, Laetitia,' said Jessica, 'you're a little star.'

Laetitia knew that, didn't she? It was Lucy who didn't know...

Ellie gave Laetitia a huge cuddly hug. This mafia business was an unforeseen turn of events. She didn't doubt they could deal with it.

The three boys had watched not knowing what was expected of them. They were only little pirates, weren't they? What could they do? Whatever the problem was, Laetitia sorted it out without their help. If Laetitia were in difficulty with her muffee man, the three brave boys would have rushed to her rescue, saving the day – but possibly not.

Ewan might have. Laetitia was his cousin, after all, and despite what you might think, he was fond of her.

'You've wasted a whole beignet,' was all Lucy said.

Ewan watched the controller warily. 'I bet his family were Barbary pirates who did the plundering and things,' Ewan whispered to his two pirate captains. 'He must have found out about our treasure map.'

'Are you sure it's suitable?' Max asked, while Grandad examined one of his fliers.

> Saturday night musical extravaganza
> *At*
> **– Chez Claude –**
> Performed by the
> ***Pirates of Black Pearl***
> *In*
> The **WORLD** premiere of
> **'PIRATES OF PROVENCE'**
> (Booking essential)

'It'll be fine,' said Grandad.

Grandad had a hard time convincing Max he was to be Redbeard, and he, Grandad, while playing Blackbeard, was to kill him in a pirate feud over hidden treasure.

'Why does Redbeard get killed?' Max asked. 'He died of old age in his palace near Constantinople.'

'It's in Lucy's script,' answered Grandad, 'and if she says Redbeard gets killed, then Redbeard gets killed.'

'I'm not sure about this.'

'It'll be good for business, Max. You will already be dressed as a pirate, and our little piece won't take longer than a minute or so. Your customers will love it.'

'I'll have to take your word on that.'

'You'll need a cutlass.'

'Cutlass!'

'I keep telling you, it's in Lucy's script. And don't forget, Redbeard was a Turk, so you'll need a turban.'

'Turban!'

When they all returned to *Black Pearl*, they were in good spirits, happy, and contented. The younger ones were excited because they were going to see *Gigi*, and then eating out. Strangely, Jessica and Ellie were also excited. They weren't going anywhere, apparently.

Jessica was happy because her takings for the afternoon were almost double the previous day. With only having an honesty box, people on the beach were generous. Unbeknown to Jessica, people on the beach assumed the beignets were part of the animation. They enjoyed the singing and dancing and this had kept their children captivated for most of the afternoon.

Lucy's rehearsals had gone well and she appreciated Ellie's assistance. While still a little worried, like most directors she hoped things would be fine on the night.

Ewan now had a clearer picture of the layout of Pramousquier bay and was eager to crack Redbeard's coded treasure map. He was a little worried about the Barbary pirate with dark slicked-back hair and long sideburns that reached his chin, the one he'd seen on the beach. He had the treasure map so was one-step ahead. In any case, if Laetitia could see him off so easily then he couldn't be a problem, could he?

Ellie was getting to know Julien better and she liked what she saw. He wasn't pushy and never made comments about her size. He was quite a size himself, so wasn't in a position to comment, was he?

While Jessica and Ellie were a little worried about mafia man, their logic was similar to that of Ewan. If Laetitia could see him off so easily then there wasn't much to concern them, was there?

Laetitia, she was always happy, why wouldn't she be?

'What have you all been doing this afternoon,' asked Grandad. He had heard the singing and music at the other end of the beach, and he was particularly pleased that everyone got on well together.

'Nuffin.'

'Yep, nuffin.'

'Metoo, metoo.'

What did you expect them to say?

'We'll have a light tea to keep us going, because we want to have room for our pizzas later, don't we,' said Grandad.

Light tea consisted of a selection of mezzes Grandad had bought earlier that morning from an Algerian restaurant in the backstreets of Le Lavandou. Outside the restaurant were two tables with chairs on the narrow footpath where the owner and his friends gathered each day to drink coffee and pass the time of day. They were always there. Grandad concluded their wives must be happy to have the men out from under their feet all day, knowing where they were. Grandad frequently ate there because it was cheap and the food good.

Grandad served a traditional Berber flatbread, with a selection of salads and dips with names he couldn't remember. One was a couscous salad, and he dribbled olive oil over the dips. There were cold spicy lamb sausages, and to finish, he had two plates of honey-based pastries. It was a healthy, well-balanced meal, thought Grandad!

'Jessica, can you give Laetitia a bath and use plenty of soap,' asked Grandad, 'she's beginning to smell a bit.'

'Of course I can, she's my little star.'

'I don't smell, do I Jessica?'

'It is boys that smell, you know, slugs and snails and all that,' which was a clever answer by Jessica. She didn't deny Laetitia smelt because that would have been a difficult thing to do, under the circumstances.

'See, Grandad,' declared Laetitia, pride restored.

Everyone scrubbed up fine. Grandad had put on a pair of long trousers, a clean white shirt, and a pullover casually over his shoulders. While it was the middle of summer in the south of France, and the weather was hot, why you might ask, would Grandad want to wear a pullover in the evening?

It's what the locals did to indicate to the tourists that they were local, used to the heat, and therefore needed a pullover in the evenings. Grandad was aware of that.

'Laetitia, do you have to wear that black frilly thing around your neck?' queried Grandad gently.

'Uh huh.' Laetitia still wanted to impress Lucy, who had first and final say in who does what in the pirate play. It wasn't right she didn't have a singing part. She's going to practice and that'll teach Lucy.

'Let's go,' Grandad sighed, having completed a tour of *Black Pearl* and confirming all was in order.

He took the Zodiac, paddled it ashore, and pulled it above the waterline on the beach in front of Chez Claude so Max could keep an eye on it. They had to walk to the salle des fêtes along the old railway track. Grandad remembered to bring along a couple of torches for their return journey, when it would be dark. They arrived in plenty of time and the children sat in the front row, which was normal in France.

Grandad saw Gisela with two of her friends at the back, so he went to see them and catch up with the local gossip.

'Grandad's kissing old biddies again,' Lucy remarked. 'It's disgusting. Wait until I tell Jessica.'

While there weren't many other children there, those that were joined Lucy, Ewan, and Laetitia in the front row. Grandad made sure everyone went to the toilet before the start, so not to disturb the performance. When nine o'clock arrived, nothing much happened. Things never started on time in France. Grandad sat at the back with Gisela and the others.

'It is very brave of you bringing the children to see *Gigi*,' said Gisela. 'I hope they enjoy it.'

'I'm sure they will.'

Someone at the front clapped their hands and everyone took their seats. Proceedings started with the local mayor giving a speech thanking everyone for doing whatever they did, and there were many to thank. The actors who were to do the musical were an amateur troupe from Cavalaire, a small tourist town a few miles to the east.

The lights dimmed and the curtains opened. Grandad was immediately worried because he knew that musicals required music, and music required a band, at the very least, a piano.

It was a play, with no songs whatsoever!

While Grandad's grasp of French wasn't fluent, he knew the plot of *Gigi* and he sensed something was wrong. Gigi herself was supposed to be a young Parisian girl, and the actress playing the part was some middle-aged woman pretending to be young, except it didn't work. Perhaps this interpretation of *Gigi* was a parody, a satire, a travesty of the original plot where Gigi was an older woman and the older rich playboy was to be a young man. That was the sort of thing the French did. No, the rich playboy was indeed old. Cavalaire, Grandad concluded, was evidently devoid of young women wanting to be members of that particular amateur troupe.

Lucy glared at Grandad from the front row and looked daggers, mouthing what about the songs. What could he do, it wasn't his fault. He couldn't march up to the front row, grab his grandchildren, say sorry, and then leave the salle to its fate. He decided to brave it out and then do a runner at the intermission, praying there was one.

Fortunately, there was…

As soon as the intermission curtain came down, Lucy marched up the centre aisle with a face of thunder to find Grandad, who was with his friends at the back.

'We're going,' said Grandad, who got in first. 'Get the others.'

Ewan was talking to one of the other boys in the front row, swopping words like, ennuyeux, nul, merde, rubbish, and so on, all adjectives which seem reasonable if you were a ten-year-old expecting a sing-along musical.

As for Laetitia, she was fast asleep like a ragdoll flopped over her chair. What would you expect after her adventurous and exhausting day? Grandad carefully lifted her, laid her over his shoulder, and carried her out.

'Oh good, it's finished then,' commented Ewan.

Pizz'Olive was nothing flash, only a van, owned by Olivier, parked on the old railway track near the church in Le Canadel. His pizzas were the best in the area using recipes individually created with the help of his mother. He made his own base and the toppings were the best, with fresh spinach, artichokes, tomatoes, onions, crème fraîche, tasty cheese, all sorts of things. The walk to the van took a few minutes, and when they arrived, the delicious smell woke Laetitia.

'Metoo, metoo.'

Olivier served Grandad with a generous glass of Jack Daniel's while waiting for the pizzas. To the side of the serving hatch were two photographs, one of Olivier with Nicholas Sarkozy, who often jogged past the van, and the other was Olivier with Roger Taylor.

'What's this with Roger Taylor?' asked Grandad. 'Isn't he the drummer for the rock band, Queen?'

'Great band,' replied Olivier. 'He was best man at a wedding nearby a few months ago, and I provided the pizzas for the reception.'

'Whose wedding was it?' asked Grandad.

'Bob Geldof,' replied Olivier with a shrug. 'I don't know who he is.'

Ewan got a pizza to himself, which he named Pizza Pirate, made to his own recipe, a bit of everything. Grandad ordered two others, which was barely enough, because Laetitia almost managed a whole one to herself. Luckily, Ewan couldn't quite manage all his, so Grandad helped him out.

Grandad and his young grandchildren were in good spirits and played hide-and-seek along the old railway line and made ghostly shadows with Grandad's torch. It was dark, with a clear sky and almost full Moon. Parts of the old railway track had high banks, excluding all artificial light and the stars above stood out despite the bright Moon.

'That's the North Star, Polaris,' identified Lucy.

Grandad had been pointing out some of the stars and constellations from *Black Pearl*. He hadn't realised anybody had taken notice.

'That's the plough, Ursula Minor.' It was Ewan, not wanting to be outdone by his twin sister, because everyone knew the North Star.

'Ursa, you thicko.'

'Grandad, the Moon.' There was no way Laetitia was going to be left out of the celestial spotting!

'Deneb, right above our heads,' added Lucy.

'Arcturus, over there.'

'That one's Aquarius.'

'Where?' Grandad asked. They had come to where the old railway line ran along the cliff edge, with clear views out to sea.

'There,' said Lucy, pointing low on the horizon, out to sea towards the islands.

'I think you're right.'

"Aquarius', that's from *Hair*, awesome song,' Ewan added and began quietly singing it to himself, which was unusual – not singing, because he's always doing that. It was singing quietly which was unusual.

'Where's Laetitia?'

'Boo! You couldn't find me. It's my turn to hide again.'

They arrived at the beach and began walking towards Chez Claude and Grandad immediately knew all was not as it should be. He could hear Thierry's bongo drums, even Jessica's flute, despite the shouting and laughter coming from *Black Pearl*. At the stern of *Black Pearl* was an armada of small craft, like ducklings around their mother.

Party boat!

Grandad had arrived back earlier than planned, having skipped the second half of *Gigi*. He wasn't supposed to arrive back early, was he?

Grandad had suspected something was up when Jessica offered tickets for *Gigi*. Not only that, when Jessica and Ellie went shopping in Le Lavandou that morning they returned with bags full of mysterious things, which they surreptitiously hid in their cabin.

'What's going on?' demanded Lucy.

'Jessica, with a few friends,' answered Grandad pleasantly. 'If you listen carefully I think they are practicing your pirate songs.'

'Ace.'

'Who wants ice cream at Max's?'

'Yeah,' replied Ewan, 'can I have two flavours.'

'Yep,' added Lucy, 'two flavours please.'

'Metoo, metoo.'

'Cognac, a large one,' was Grandad's preferred choice.

Chapter 12
Beignet war

It was early morning and Grandad and Ewan were having a quiet cup of tea on deck, y'know, serious male bonding, while the girls remained fast asleep below decks.

'Grandad, if you were a pirate and you had to bury treasure, where would you bury it?'

'That's a difficult question,' said Grandad.

'Yeah, I know...'

'I can't see how pirates could have buried treasure in deep water, because they didn't have proper diving gear in those days.'

'Yeah, good thinking.'

'The problem with burying treasure on the beach is that with storms and things it can move. You've seen how the sand and rocks move around on the beach.'

'Yeah, you're right.' This wasn't what Ewan wanted to hear.

Ewan was getting worried because what use was a treasure map if your treasure moved. Grandad decided he had better help. His hastily drawn treasure map he had hidden in the chain locker, while finely executed and looked genuine to a ten-year-old, wasn't necessarily that helpful. Grandad hadn't realised treasure hunting would become Ewan's passion. Normally, his attention span was a couple of hours at best.

Living on a pirate ship, sailing to pirate infested islands, owning a pretend parrot, and being a pirate king did have an influence on the imagination of Ewan, something Grandad failed to take into account.

'Shallow water seems a good place to hide treasure, that's where I would hide it,' said Grandad. 'The Chez Claude end of the beach would be the best place, because it is protected by Cap Nègre.'

That made sense to Ewan. His treasure map indicated that end somewhere. 'Grandad, what do you know about secret pirate codes?'

'Pirates were mostly an illiterate lot, so they wouldn't know anything about secret codes. Pirate captains were cleverer, and I would imagine they'd use their own language.'

'Awesome.'

'Why are you so interested in pirate treasure?' asked Grandad with a mischievous twinkle in his eye.

'Just asking,' replied Ewan most unconvincingly.

'Pirates used wooden chests and they would have disintegrated over time, and treasure would have scattered all over the seabed, so I shouldn't think there would be much gold and things left now.'

'If I was hunting for treasure, I wouldn't want to find gold,' said Ewan. 'It would only be taken away, so that's no use. I would want pirate things I can keep.'

'Help, help…'

'Laetitia's really seen a ghost this time, cos I heard her talking to it on the loo,' shouted Lucy.

'It sounds like the girls are getting up,' said Grandad.

Everyone loved breakfast.

They came on deck in dribs and drabs, dopey, in pyjamas or swimsuits. It was an informal sort of affair. It was just one more day for getting up to mischief without parents bothering you. They were all in high spirits with the anticipation of what lay ahead, because they all had plans.

Even Laetitia had plans because she had been speaking to one of her friendly ghosts who agreed with her that Hans did think she was a good pirate lookout, so she was going to do some good looking out and spot the nasty muffee man before anybody else. That wasn't until the afternoon when Jessica was selling her beignets. That morning she wanted some quality time with her dolls. She still felt a little bit tired because she didn't get to bed until late, and didn't want to be tired in the afternoon when she was doing her looking and things.

'Sorry about last night, Grandad,' apologised Jessica. 'I couldn't help it, what with living on a cool party boat.'

'It's okay,' said Grandad, who had learned patience from many years of having to be so. 'Just ask if you want a party. In fact, let's have a pirate party and invite all our friends.'

'Metoo, metoo.'

'We'll have a *Pirates of Provence* party, with a few pirate songs and things. We'll combine it with Lucy's show. You can sort it, can't you Lucy?'

'Have a *Pirates of Provence* party, with a few pirate songs!' exclaimed the producer, director and scriptwriter, although we simply call her, Lucy, who feigned in the best theatrical tradition, with arm to forehead. 'I'm going to have a nervous breakdown.'

Jessica was confused.

She fully expected to be done good and proper, or grounded, or both; that's what Mother from Hell would have done. She hadn't realised *Gigi* wasn't a musical, so her timings were all out, not that she didn't think she wouldn't get caught red handed, so to speak, not so blatantly anyway. She had planned that *Gigi* would end about eleven, then allowed half an hour to eat, half an hour walking back, which would give her till midnight. She wasn't to know Grandad would turn up shortly before eleven.

'Leave the party arrangements to me,' said Jessica. 'You keep charge of the entertainment side of things, Lucy, because you're good at that.'

When they all got back from *Gigi* the precious evening, Grandad, Max, and a couple of the others enjoyed a bottle of cognac. Lucy insisted Grandad and Max gave her a rehearsal of their pirate fight where Blackbeard kills poor Redbeard. She gave up in disgust because the two protagonists in question already had had a couple of cognacs too many and weren't getting it right. There was definitely a difference of opinion between actors and director. Lucy then joined Ewan, who was playing around with Max's laptop at the VIP table overlooking the bay.

What made Ewan contact his mother on Skype was puzzling. Things often were with Ewan. He saw her online and the opportunity was there, that's all. He's a boy, and they can do foolish things, can't they.

Laetitia had crawled onto a chair and had gone to sleep, complete with happy and memorable dreams – that's a guess, but how could her dreams be otherwise.

Spot on midnight, the armada of small boats, paddle contraptions, and other floating things, drifted away from *Black Pearl* and headed back to the beach.

After waiting a tactful few minutes, Grandad paddled the Zodiac back to *Black Pearl*.

Once aboard, ignoring the disarray on deck, Grandad put Laetitia to bed. Ewan didn't seem to notice that anything was amiss and went to bed himself. He wanted it to be morning because he had important things to do and the quickest way to get to the morning was to go to sleep.

After putting Laetitia to bed and having had a few cognacs too many, Grandad hung up his hammock and went to sleep. 'Goodnight everyone,' he slurred happily, 'don't forget to clean your teeth.'

Lucy, being more aware of things, informed Jessica they had all been at Max's for an hour or so while she had her party, and next time, she could at least have the courtesy of inviting her and her friends along rather than being conned into watching some dismal French musical without any songs. They were cousins, after all.

'Sorry, Lucy, I won't do it again.'

'Another thing,' added Lucy, 'I heard you playing my pirate music with a hip-hop beat and that's not how it's supposed to be.'

'Christ Lucy, not hip-hop, it was kind of like French *Yé-yé*. Tarantino loves it and he's a cool director.'

'*Yé-yé*?'

'You know, like Vintage French. It's definitely the *LBD* of international popular music, and Julien thinks it's going to go viral.'

'I'll think about it.' Although not knowing what *Yé-yé* or *LBD* meant, Lucy liked to think she was a progressive director. And if it was going to go viral! She wasn't sure who Tarantino was, but she would definitely do a search on Max's laptop and find out and while doing so, she would check out *Yé-yé* and *LBD*. With honour restored, Lucy went to bed.

'Do you think we got away with it?' Jessica asked.

'Only just,' replied Ellie, 'what's *Yé-yé*?'

'Some French sixties stuff.'

'Can we borrow the kayak this morning, Grandad, we want to explore Cap Nègre and have a closer look at the commemorative plaque,' Jessica asked. 'I've checked the weather on my iPhone and it is okay.'

'I'm not jumping from any rock,' protested Ellie, 'never.'

'That's fine.' Grandad knew that local weather conditions always created an onshore wind in the afternoon. Mornings were okay. 'Useful gadget that.'

'I'm still not jumping.'

Having clarified her position regarding jumping, Ellie was looking forward to her journey in the kayak, climbing up la Pointe du Cap Nègre and other rocks en route, swimming in the deep, crystal clear water, completely isolated and undisturbed. Ellie woke each morning and still had to pinch herself, not believing her luck being on *Black Pearl*, meeting Julien, and all the things she had done; and Charlie was the best.

No need to explain what Ewan was up to, nor Lucy either, who was getting butterflies in her stomach over the opening of her latest production, *Pirates of Provence*, at Max's on Saturday.

'Grandad?'

'Yes, Lucy.'

'We'll need pirate hats.'

'Pirate hats?'

'Yep, and we need them before tomorrow night. Can you manage that?'

'I'll see what I can do.'

'That's not the answer I wanted to hear.'

'Pirate hats it is.'

'Thanks, Grandad, I knew you would.'

This left Grandad and Laetitia to have a quiet morning on *Black Pearl*. Laetitia happily played with her dolls while Grandad did his usual daily nautical tasks cleaning this and that, and food preparation. Laetitia wanted to help Grandad with his tasks and was quite a Little Miss Helpful for all of ten minutes before returning to her dolls. She even practiced her singing, hoping it might improve, because it wasn't right, her not being allowed to sing, despite doing over the six teenage boys, and sorting out the nasty muffee man. She did a re-enactment of doing over the six boys with the help of Grandad's flip-flops because she didn't have enough dolls for that.

'Grandad, do you like my singing?'

'Singing!' The wailing he had put down as, justifiably, a dreadful racket youngsters make now and then.

Laetitia wasn't silly.

Despite loving him lots, she recognised the query in Grandad's reply and therefore continued her practicing with vigour. Grandad sighed, because the infernal racket she was making only aggravated his headache. You also would have had a headache after enjoying the amount of cognac he had had the previous evening. He abandoned braving it out and fell back on taking some aspirin and ibuprofen, because the dreadful noise Laetitia was making was definitely harmful to his health.

'Laetitia, is that one of my flip-flops floating in the sea?'

Jessica and Ellie were getting quite good at paddling the red kayak. Whereas Jessica was an experienced kayaker, Ellie was as strong as an ox

As they rounded la Pointe du Souffre, the sea was rougher. They paddled in a southwest direction, following the high cliffs of Cap Nègre. They were alone apart from the large seagulls, which colonised the cliffs. The sea was deep and clear. Half way along Cap Nègre were some rocks joined to the cliff by a shallow shelf, where Jessica beached the kayak. The two girls climbed the rocks and gazed into the sea from a height of about eight feet.

'This is a good place to dive from,' declared Jessica.

'Not me,' declared Ellie. Jumping from *Black Pearl* was bad enough, but from the rocks, with rocks below the water was another matter.

'It's easy,' said Jessica, before executing a perfect dive into the sea. She dived deep and slowly came to the surface in one smooth movement. When she broke water, she flipped her hair back and cleared her nose.

'Jump,' urged Jessica, 'the water's deep and it's safe. I'll count three, and then jump.'

'One.'

'Not me...'

'Two.'

'Never...'

'Three.'

'Arrrrr…'

Ellie jumped.

She didn't have time to think about it. She pinched her nose, and jumped. She came to the surface, spluttering, stomach full of butterflies, spitting out water.

'Let's do it again,' shouted Ellie.

They jumped a few more times and eventually, Jessica coaxed Ellie to dive. She did it once. It wasn't a pretty attempt, with legs flapping, a big splash, and she swallowed some water.

The red kayak continued its journey along the base of the cliffs and they paused at the Commandos d'Afrique commemorative plaque.

'Grandad has told you about that already.'

As they approached la Pointe du Cap Nègre, Jessica glanced up at the Bruni residence. Below the villa, on the cliff footpath was a man watching them through binoculars.

'What's that man staring at us for?' Ellie asked.

'Probably a secret service agent, a bit like MI5,' explained Jessica. 'It means that the Sarkozys are probably around.'

Two people from the terrace glanced down and waved, one being male and short in stature, the other an attractive female. Jessica and Ellie waved back. To be honest, Ellie wasn't into French politics and hadn't a clue who Sarkozy was.

They rounded the Pointe to where they could beach the kayak and then climb to its peak where the views along the coast were good.

The agent followed them through his binoculars, watching from below the villa. He spoke into his walky-talky, or whatever they're called, then sat down on a rock in the shade, watching. From his demeanour, he appeared irritated.

'How far have we paddled the kayak since leaving *Black Pearl*?' asked Ellie with pride, having never done such a thing before.

'About a mile.'

'It's high up here.'

'Ellie, you don't have to tell me that.'

'You're not going to jump, are you, it's too risky.'

'Don't say that, because when people say, don't jump, I jump.'

'Jessica, what's with all this jumping?'

'Because it's there,' explained Jessica, 'and the boys never dared to jump, not from here. They call it tombstoning now, although if you ask me, it's a ridiculous name.'

The small man, the one who waved earlier, came from the villa to talk to the agent, and both watched Jessica and Ellie. The man climbed down the steps from the villa, crossed the causeway, and climbed up to the Pointe and approached the girls.

'Who is he?' whispered Ellie, 'aren't we supposed to be here?'

'It's Sarko,' Jessica replied. 'This is public land and Grandad's been bringing me here since I could walk.'

'*Bonjour Mr err Sarko*,' Ellie said to the diminutive figure in front of her, not knowing who he was.

'*Ah, les deux Anglaises*, have you come to jump?' He peered tentatively down the cliff to the waves breaking over the rocks, white spray glistening in the bright sun. 'It is dangerous and only brave French men jump from here.'

'Not you as well,' said Jessica. 'Here's the deal. I'll jump if you jump. You being a brave French man, that shouldn't be a problem, should it?'

Jessica hadn't come to do any jumping, simply only to enjoy the view and do a bit of exploration with Ellie. Besides, it was an isolated and tranquil part of the coastline, apart from the irritating diminutive French man alleging he was brave.

'This is your English sense of humour, I think.'

Meeting a French example of the wimpy male fraternity on that rock once more, mocking her bravery was too much for Jessica, so she did what she did best.

She jumped.

Did the brave diminutive French man jump?

No.

Knowing he wasn't going to jump, Jessica pretended to be injured and floated face down in the water, motionless.

As you would expect, all hell broke loose.

The not so brave diminutive French man got into a panic and shouted to the agent, who spoke sharply into his walky-talky and ran towards the Pointe. Sarko ran here and there, frantic, and when he once more searched the water where Jessica lay, she wasn't there. More shouting followed, accompanied by spirited gesticulations in all directions, and the agent once more spoke into his walky-talky with a sense of urgency. They were isolated with no help nearby.

Ellie was mortified, her best friend having committed, as far as she was concerned, suicide. Jessica's body had disappeared under the water. What would she tell the others? How could she explain that she didn't know Jessica was going to jump? Why hadn't she stopped her? She was to blame. She was in too much shock to cry.

In the meantime, Jessica came from behind the rocks at the base of the Pointe where she had hid and shouted up to Ellie. 'Quick, jump, and let's get out of here.'

Ellie turned round and saw the agent fast approaching, with a gun in his hand, aggressive and serious. The other man was in hysterics, and then the lady who he was with earlier came running down the steps towards the Pointe to see what all the fuss was.

'Jump,' shouted Jessica, 'quick, before it's too late.'

What could Ellie do? The French MI5 chap, gun in hand, was approaching fast. She didn't want to die, or be arrested.

So she did it…

No, she didn't jump, that was a jump too high for Ellie.

She did what any sensible teenage girl would do in a tight corner. She sat down on top of la Pointe du Cap Nègre, and cried, and I mean cried, loud sobs, like the end of the world sobs. Did she cry with relief that Jessica was still alive, or from the fright that some French MI5 chap was threatening to shoot her, or both?

'Don't worry, Ellie, I'm coming…'

'*H*e still hasn't phoned,' stated Mother from Hell, once again on the phone to her sister-in-law, Marina.

'Have the children phoned?' Marina asked, trying to be reasonable.

'Only Laetitia and she didn't say much. Jessica hasn't bothered to phone. She wouldn't though, despite having one of those expensive phones. I wouldn't have bought it myself, except Dominic weakened. You know what a conniving shitbag Jessica is.'

'I don't think you should be calling Jessica things like that.' Marina knew teenagers could be difficult, because in her time, none came more difficult than she did. Parents have to put up with it. It comes with the job.

'Jessica is my fucking daughter, so I'll call her what I like.'

'They're all having a good time by the sounds of it,' Marina said.

'Are they now...'

'Yes, I was talking to the twins on Skype last night.'

'I didn't know your father was on Skype,' said Mother from Hell, ignoring the fact that the person in question was also her father-in-law.

'I don't think he is. Ewan was using the laptop at Chez Claude. They had been to see a play apparently, although nobody was impressed. They had pizzas.'

'See what I mean, he feeds them junk food every day. What time was this?'

'It must have been around ten or so.'

'Eleven o'clock their time, what kind of time is that?'

'They are on holiday.'

'So where was Jessica?'

'Oh, she was with Ellie at a party on one of those big boats in the bay. I saw it on Skype.'

'Whose boat was that?'

'I don't know because Ewan was a little vague about that. He quickly turned the video onto the terrace and guess what I saw?'

'What?'

'Dad appeared to be fighting. Max, who runs Chez Claude, was wearing a tea towel around his head and had Dad in a headlock. Lucy was trying to break them up.' Marina regretted saying that, because it didn't sound like a good thing for her father to be doing.

'You think that's amusing do you, your father brawling in a bar in front of the children.'

'I think they were only clowning around.'

'I'm not happy with this at all. I knew it was a bad idea allowing my children to spend their summer holiday with your father all by himself. He is totally unpredictable since his wife died.'

'Then get a baby sitter if you can afford one. You're treading on thin ice because you are talking about my Dad. Don't forget he is doing you a favour. You can at least pretend to be grateful, even if you're not.'

'Where was Laetitia while all this was going on,' asked Mother from Hell, ignoring Marina's last comment.

'She was asleep in a chair.'

'Just left alone to go to sleep in a bar?'

'She seemed comfortable enough. She had Jessica's black frilly skirt draped around her neck looking very cute. You know what she's like?'

'She was wearing Jessica's best party skirt? Do you know how much that thing cost?'

'What are you trying to say, Jo?'

'I knew I shouldn't have let them go. I've a good mind to fly out and bring them back.'

'What, and employ a full-time baby sitter?' said Marina, who found her sister-in-law irritating. 'You're too mean to do that.'

'Why do you always take that attitude with me?' barked Mother from Hell. 'I care for the wellbeing of my children, even if you don't.'

'Silly bitch!' We know who mumbled that after slamming down the phone.

A few weeks earlier, Mother from Hell had arranged a meeting with the student counsellor at Jessica's school. She was worried about Jessica's schoolwork, which appeared to be going downhill. Jessica never did any work at home, not like before.

'Jessica is just a normal healthy sixteen-year-old,' advised the counsellor.

'She isn't,' stated Mother from Hell forcefully.

'Is she happy at home?'

'She's happy making my life a misery.'

'Are you sure this is about Jessica,' offered the counsellor. 'You clearly have issues bothering you.'

'I don't want any of that talking therapy crap. I want to know what the school is going to do.'

'I can empathise with your feelings, of course—'

'I don't think you can, not without having a teenage daughter who's a little shitbag.'

'Come here and I'll give you a hug.'

'I don't want a fucking hug.'

'I find it helps.'

'It doesn't.'

'All girls that age can be a little challenging. She'll grow out of it, eventually. They usually do.'

'Your supercilious, patronising, and crass fucking comments don't help matters, do they…' was the last thing said by Mother from Hell, before flaunting out of the office, slamming the door, with far more attitude than Jessica.

It wasn't the best meeting.

The two trusty pirate captains listened intensely to Ewan as he related his findings about pirate treasure. He neglected to mention that he got his new information from Grandad. Both Hans and Noé regarded Ewan with greater respect.

'We can't read Turkish?'

'Grandad can.'

'Can he?' Noé was impressed, though not surprised, because Ewan's Grandad never ceased to amaze him.

'You didn't let him see the map, did you?' asked Hans.

'I covered it so he could only see the writing bits. It said things like, treasure map, beach, high rock, and old tree. The important thing on the map was the message. Grandad wrote it down for me.'

> 'Whoever finds this map must follow their nose because that is where the waste doth flow. Then look to the Cap where pirates might jump. Examine the map for lines to cross because that is where you will find the plunder. But beware of serpents.'

'What does it mean?' asked Hans.

'How do I know?' said Ewan.

'It don't even rhyme,' said Noé.

'Most pirates were pretty thick.'

'What's plunder?' asked Noé.

'That's pirate treasure.' Ewan knew that.

'What's waste?' asked Noé.

'How do I know,' replied Ewan, who was a bit fed up with all these silly questions he couldn't answer. 'Jessica is always talking about getting wasted, so why don't you go ask her.'

That wasn't going to happen, was it.

'Don't you English talk about toilet waste?' said Hans, who was recovering his superiority after Ewan's initial burst of information.

'You mean poo,' stated Ewan.

'Calling it toilet waste is more polite,' explained arrogant Hans. 'You are English and should know that.'

'Pirates aren't polite,' Ewan protested. 'Don't you know anything?'

The conversation between the three intrepid pirate treasure hunters went on in a similar manner for most of the morning, so no need to repeat everything. If anyone else were listening to this detailed and engaging conversation, they would have discovered that the Germans actually learnt English correctly in school, with adverbs, pronouns, prepositions, and such like, while the poor English have to pick it up as they go along. As for the French, well...

Noé couldn't grasp why pirates doing their pirating in France didn't do it in French, because that would have made sense and then he could have easily understood the secret pirate treasure map and code. It goes deeper than that with Noé, because the French as a nation failed to comprehend why the rest of the world hasn't already chosen French as their mother tongue, a language rich in... in... best ask them. Despite that, Noé's English was quite good, because it had to be. All his friends on the beach spoke English, and as we all know, that is the fate of the poor French and their language!

Ewan and his two trusty pirate captains managed to make some progress on Grandad's cryptic message on the treasure map. On a positive note, they did work out that a serpent might be a sea snake. The closest thing to that in Pramousquier bay were conger eels and, like Jessica, you didn't mess with them, although if pushed, they would much rather mess with conger eels than Jessica.

If Grandad had had more time, he might have come up with a better message. Being cryptic wasn't one of his things, particularly when in a hurry. It was the best he could do.

*L*ucy and the others had a fruitful and fulfilling morning on the terrace of Chez Claude. Max, who was suffering from a terrible hangover, didn't have the heart to argue. He did as he was told. Lucy wanted to inspect his beer barrels, the ones her pirates were to dance on, like the ones she saw on *YouTube*.

'They're metal,' said Lucy. 'Pirate beer barrels are made of wood.'

'That's how they are these days.'

'Then disguise them,' ordered Lucy, while adding that to her list of things to check in her notebook.

What had he got himself into, Max thought?

'Another thing,' Lucy barked unkindly. 'You better die properly next time, not like last night.'

'*Oui*, Lucy, of course.'

'Or you're dead meat.' Like all good directors, Lucy wasn't beyond stealing the lines of others.

Lucy's production was coming together as she planned.

She had even managed to get Max to hang a rope from the old tree on the terrace so she could get the swinging bits in. She wasn't sure how to get that in yet, and she made a note of it in her notebook.

Despite the hangover and the unfair bullying from Lucy, Max was pleased. Saturday night was a sell-out. He had arranged for extra tables on the beach so he could double his sittings. Having a fixed menu made things easier, particularly with having a barbecue. He was planning to have pirate kebabs on long skewers so that customers could roast their own over the flames, in true pirate style. Health and Safety hadn't caught up with that part of France.

*G*randad had prepared a splendid lunch.

They all did justice to Grandad's lunch, and ate the lot, with Laetitia and Ellie happily having an encore – that's second helpings if French isn't your thing.

'Done much this morning?' Grandad enquired.

'Nuffin much,' offered Ewan.

'You better kill Max properly, Grandad, I'm telling you,' threatened Lucy in director mode. 'I've had words with Max.'

'Yes, Lucy, I'll try.'

153

'That's not the answer I wanted to hear, Grandad.'

'I promise to kill Max properly.'

'You better remember.'

'Was the kayak okay,' Grandad asked Jessica and Ellie. He was a little concerned earlier when he saw a helicopter hovering around Cap Nègre and was relieved when the two teenagers had returned unharmed and in good spirits. 'No mishaps?'

'Jessica jumped off the big rock,' Ellie replied, 'and then we had tea with an attractive lady—'

Ellie didn't continue because she received the look from Jessica, which said, don't go there, and don't say a thing.

'Ouch!' The kick was just to make sure.

For those interested to know what occurred earlier that morning on la Pointe du Cap Nègre, it was as Ellie described, with a few details missing.

While Ellie sat and sobbed, the lady arrived and gave the man, and the gun wielding French MI5 chap, a scolding to remember. What she actually said we don't know, because it was delivered in fast Italian. With certainty, the parenthood of both men was unfairly questioned, and both accused of being lecherous perverts leering at young teenage girls who were doing nothing wrong except minding their own business. She decided that a cup of sweet tea was necessary to calm poor Ellie and invited the two girls onto her parents' terrace by the swimming pool.

'My middle name is, Gilberta,' the lady said, 'but my English friends sometimes call me, Gigi. They do it to tease me.'

'Gigi!' exclaimed Ellie. 'What a coincidence. That play was at Canadel the other evening. We didn't go, but the others went.'

'It was a bit of a disaster,' added Jessica. 'It was supposed to be a musical.'

Jessica provided an edited version of what happened that night. 'So it was you who had the party on the extraordinary boat anchored at Pramousquier,' said Gigi. 'It was quite a party, I heard.'

'It wasn't bad,' agreed Jessica with modesty. What was pleasing to Jessica was that others had heard about her party. 'Grandad didn't seem to mind, either.'

154

'It was absolutely fabulous,' said Ellie.

'Are you living on the boat?'

'Yes,' confirmed Jessica.

'It's a klipper and belongs to Jessica's Grandad, and his name is Charlie,' added Ellie.

While Jessica took the opportunity to practice her back dives in the pool, Ellie gave Gigi a demonstration of Jessica's iPhone. She was suitably impressed, particularly when shown a clip of 'I am a Pirate King' on *YouTube*.

'What is that?' asked Gigi, who was intrigued. So would you be if you had a sudden rendition of Anthony Warlow's pirate king routine? Ellie proudly described Lucy's coming production at Chez Claude.

Jessica couldn't help overhearing the conversation and this got her thinking. 'Yes, and you're welcome to come.'

Perhaps she could fix up Grandad with this super-sophisticated lady. Thinking about it more, fixing Grandad up with someone called Gigi, especially after that disastrous night, was something Jessica couldn't pass over. How could she?

While playing with the iPhone they listened to the Rolling Stones singing 'Ruby Tuesday', their original version from the '60s. This was a favourite of Jessica's, mainly because she could play the background flute melody rather well.

'Flute?' queried Gigi, 'I think it was Brian Jones using a recorder.'

'A recorder?'

'I think so.'

'Wait until I see Grandad, he told me it was a flute. It took me ages to learn.' said Jessica. 'We're doing 'Ruby Tuesday' tomorrow night.'

'It's not in Lucy's play list,' cautioned Ellie.

'It is now, and it's one of Grandad's favourites.'

'Mick Jagger, he's revolting,' said Ellie.

'Perhaps,' said Gigi reflectively.

'Some say Mick Jagger is a bit like Grandad,' added Jessica.

'I think you are fond of your Grandad.'

'He's the best. I think you'll like him. He's about the same age as Mick Jagger but looks a bit younger.'

'You will come tomorrow night, won't you?' Ellie pleaded.

*A*s soon as lunch was over, the youngsters were away as quick as a flash. Whatever they were up to, deemed Grandad, wasn't worthy enough to miss lunch. If you saw the meals Grandad prepared on *Black Pearl*, believe me, hell would freeze over before you would miss such a treat.

'Thanks Grandad,' they shouted as they all disappeared from whence they came.

'Are you sure you want to take all your dolls, Laetitia,' shouted Grandad, 'they'll get wet.'

'I'll only take one.'

Although mildly puzzled by the pre-occupation of the children, Grandad shrugged. He knew Lucy and Ewan had plenty to think about, what with all that directing and treasure hunting. There were no visible broken bones and Laetitia didn't smell so much now. Lucy hadn't lost or broken his her spectacles. He had also noticed Jessica wasn't swearing so much. Was Ellie losing weight, he pondered, while climbing onto his hammock for his afternoon siesta? All was well, was Grandad's last thought before slipping into that never-never land of an alcohol induced sleep.

*B*efore joining Jessica on the beach, Ewan and his two trusty pirate captains visited Chez Claude. They were going to have a very private and confidential conference meeting with Max, because they trusted him. As they stood on the terrace waiting for a convenient moment, because Max was busy serving, they gazed out to sea and dreamt about their treasure. Sure as sure can be, they would find it, of that, Ewan were certain.

'Look,' said Hans, pointing at the sea.

Ewan and Noé looked...

Then Noé slapped his forehead. 'Why didn't I remember?' We know the answer to that question. He's a boy!

'What?' Ewan asked, 'what?'

'The pipes,' said Hans.

The sea was clear, warm, and inviting. Swimmers were swimming. Children were playing. Fathers were digging holes and making sand castles. Mothers were chatting with their friends, ignoring husbands and children. Everyone was happy.

Amidst this, was something unnoticed by those on the beach? To the left of Chez Claude were two parallel lines going out to sea.

The pipes.

Some years they were covered by sand and other years completely exposed, depending upon the weather over the winter. The reason Noé kept slapping his forehead was he occasionally tied his rubber dingy to one of the pipes. That year the pipes were partially exposed and barely visible. You had to know they were there.

'The pipes,' repeated Ewan slowly, 'good one Hans.'

The pipes were a leftover from bygone days when the original coastal manoirs, lovely manor houses, existed and their sewage and water drained to sea. In those days, people didn't think much of the beach. It was more of a dumping ground. Having been demolished, pseudo-Provençal style villas replaced the original manoirs. The new villas weren't ugly as such, merely lacking the character of the original buildings. The pipes remained on the surface of the seabed, now unused, quite well preserved for their age despite the odd crack, and extended to about one hundred yards out to sea.

'Let's read that secret message again,' said Hans, all thoughts of talking with Max forgotten.

Ewan dug around his things, found the message, and read it aloud. 'Whoever finds this map must follow their nose…'

'That makes sense,' said Hans. 'The pipe would have had toilet waste in it so would have smelt horrid. We follow the pipe to the end.'

'And look to where the pirates jump,' Noé prompted, 'where's that?'

'That's definitely the jumping cliff,' answered Ewan.

'That means the treasure is hidden somewhere between the end of the pipes and the jumping cliff,' added Noé.

'Where's that map we drew on the kayak?' Hans asked.

'It's on *Black Pearl*,' replied Ewan. It wasn't that he didn't trust his two friends, but you couldn't be too careful. 'We'll check it later.'

After Ewan had seen that man on the beach yesterday, the one with the dark slicked-back hair and long sideburns that reached his chin, he was being particularly cautious. He therefore hid everything on *Black Pearl*, in his usual special place, safe in the knowledge that no one ever got past Grandad, not even Jessica.

Ewan wanted to check all his maps and secret messages alone. He wanted to think things through at his own pace. Whenever he was planning, Hans always came up with smart-arse ideas, which confused him. Ewan was the pirate king and they had to do what he said, not the other way round. He wanted to be the one who found the treasure.

He was also worried about Noé's underwater swimming ability and not being afraid of conger eels. It didn't make sense, did it, not being afraid of conger eels. What if Noé started to search in holes and things without him knowing, not that he would because Noé wasn't like that. What if that man on the beach, the one with long sideburns that reached his chin, captured Noé, tortured him, and then made him check all the holes and underwater caves for the hidden pirate treasure, what then?

Ewan hadn't realised hunting for hidden pirate treasure was such a precarious business.

He also had to deal with Jessica and her beignet business, and learn songs for Lucy. On top of all that, he had to learn how to dance on beer barrels, which was plain daft. Every man knew how to dance on beer barrels, because it's kind of instinctive. Lucy wouldn't listen, would she?

'Let's go,' said Ewan, 'because if we're late, Jessica will go mad, and we don't want that, do we?'

They certainly didn't.

Julien had managed to get the afternoon off and had brought his guitar to the beach. As far as Lucy was concerned, Julien was there to help her with her preparations, and who was he to argue. As far as Ellie was concerned, Julien was there because he wanted to be with her, which he did. Jessica didn't mind why Julien was there, because his being there made the others happy. She wanted happy beignet sellers, didn't she!

Donations into the beignet honesty box were coming in fast.

Lucy loved that time of day because she had the attention of all the key players in her show, and she made the most of it. She measured out three imaginary beer barrels in the sand and got Ewan and his two trusty captains to practice their barrel dance, because they were still useless.

'You better get your act together, or there'll be trouble, won't there Jessica,' added Lucy, and yes, it was a threat.

What was confusing the boys was the number of barrels, one day three, next day four, then three again. Sand wasn't easy to jump on, not like proper wooden beer barrels.

'That's your job, Hans, you're to blame,' hissed Ewan, quite unfairly.

Poor Hans didn't know what was expected of him. Lucy hadn't briefed him, had she? How could he choreograph a beer barrel dance without a correct and proper briefing from the director, preferably in writing with an agreed protocol? Lucy didn't know that her twin brother, Ewan, had given Hans that responsibility, did she?

The dance of the buccaneer beauties was quite good and the one where the pirates joined in, the Max pirate dance, was also coming along well, despite the over energetic portrayal by Laetitia. The songs and music weren't a problem. Then again, she didn't know about the addition of 'Ruby Tuesday', nor would she until the performance itself. Her main concern was Grandad and Max, their fighting, and killing. She'd have to have another word with them and they had better behave.

Laetitia sat quietly and played with her doll, which was wet and bedraggled, much like she was. That morning Grandad wouldn't let her paint her pirate face, which wasn't right, was it. After lunch, she went to the toilet, like always. There she managed to paint on a quick pirate face. She didn't have a mirror when she was sitting on the toilet, which was inconvenient, and she'll talk to Grandad about that later. Laetitia ended up with a spotty face, blue and red being the predominant colours. From a distance, and if you didn't know her, she appeared to have some nasty contagious disease, and best given a wide berth. Fortunately, most people on the beach did know her, so she didn't affect sales too much.

While playing with her doll, Laetitia kept a sharp lookout for the nasty muffee man. If he turned up again, she was going to see him first and deal with him in her own incontestable way. She was going to add to her attack one of her pirate songs that she had impressed Grandad with earlier. That way, she could kill three things with one attack. Deal with the nasty muffee man for Jessica, because she's her big sister. Impress Hans with her pirate lookout duties, because she wanted to. Amaze Lucy with her song so she could sing in the show, because she wanted to be the star.

She could multi-task, could Laetitia.

That's when Laetitia saw them, the six teenage boys. They kept their distance, watching, because they had heard about the two pretty English girls giving away beignets. The beignets weren't necessarily the attraction, but the English girls were. They knew they stood no chance of getting their attention; they knew their limitations. They wanted to earn bragging rights; oui, we checked them out; non, they wouldn't talk to us; oui, they must be lesbians, and other such nonsense bragged by young teenage boys.

They spotted Laetitia who had taken up a commanding position five yards in front of them. They had to pass Laetitia to get to the beignets, and then check out the English girl and her fat friend. The little devil girl with the black frilly thing around her neck had humiliated them once before, and they didn't want that to happen again.

'We've come for the beignets,' said the bravest of the six.

'Where's your money,' demanded the pirate lookout.

'We were told they were free.'

'You put money in the box, get it.'

'How much?'

'How much have you got?'

The six teenage boys, who were wary of Laetitia, emptied their pockets and bags until she was satisfied.

'That's all we got.'

'Follow me and don't try anything funny.'

They followed Laetitia and didn't try anything funny.

Would you?

Exactly!

'Hi boys,' welcomed Jessica, 'you look hungry, help yourselves.'

They did look hungry, and it wasn't for the beignets. Jessica and her fat friend were living up to their expectations. English girls were the best. Every French boy knew that. Laetitia gently kicked the honesty box to remind them of their obligations.

'*Merci*,' said the bravest of the six while putting all his money into the box. The other five did the same.

'That's generous, boys,' commented Ellie, 'you can all come again.'

'*Merci beaucoup, mademoiselle*,' answered the bravest.

The six teenage boys were mesmerised by Ellie. Yes, she was fat, and for them, titillatingly so. She had a warm, generous smile, and filled every inch of her size sixteen swimsuit. While clandestinely studying Jessica at close hand, they all acknowledged that English girls were indeed the best. Who could argue?

With menacing glares from Laetitia, they moved away, sat next to Ewan and his two trusty pirate captains, and ate their beignets.

'Hi, Julien,' said the bravest of the six, who was their self-elected leader, 'how's things?'

'Can't be better,' Julien replied, while strumming his guitar so the buccaneer beauties could practice their dance routine. In fact, most of the occupants at that end of the beach were clapping, you know, that synchronised clapping the French were prone to do, and Lucy and the others were hamming it up a bit, enjoying the attention.

Laetitia forgot her animosity towards the six teenage boys, who clearly knew Julien. Hadn't Ellie smiled pleasantly and said nice things to them? Laetitia had done her bit, done them over good and proper, and now they were doing what she said. What more could you ask from a pirate lookout sporting an evil looking outfit and contagious diseased spotty face? She was sure Hans had noticed her excellent work, and that's what mattered most.

On that last point, Laetitia was correct. Hans had noticed her courageous deed, and he was mightily relieved to see the six teenage boys being polite, and friendly. To Hans, Laetitia was just a little kid dressed like some weirdo, with strange face decorations, and inclined to smell, though useful to have around because of her aggressive habits.

Ewan and Noé were oblivious to ever having seen the six teenage boys before and happily made friends, got themselves beignets so that they could have a fastest beignet eating competition, won by Noé.

Ever alert, Laetitia stood up and marched down the beach armed with her bedraggled doll, stopped, hands on hips, and waited. She had spotted the nasty muffee man and two plagistes.

They saw Laetitia, and stopped.

Did they think her contagious? Was her threatening manner intimidating? Perhaps it was the smell. On the other hand, had they noticed that several of the men on the beach, the big ones with tattoos, had stood up in a menacing manner, ready to defend Jessica and gang?

'Don't think you can get away with it,' shouted one of the plagistes, 'you need a licence?'

'Furcuff,' shouted she who might have been contagious and definitely sported an unpleasant smell.

'If you're back tomorrow, we will report you to the municipal police.'

'Furcuff.'

With that last insult, the two plagistes stomped away, back to their restaurants, which, since Jessica had started business, hadn't been doing that well. The third man, the nasty muffee man, stood his ground and cocked his hand in the shape of a gun, and directed it towards Jessica.

'I have connections,' he said, 'in the m—'

'Charrrrge, let's get'em, this is our beach, furcuff.'

...and other such pirate lookout expletives.

'Charr—'

Once again, our little six-year-old girl with a contagious diseased spotty face, while running wildly down the beach, tripped over her black tutu skirt with drooping frills. Did she cry, of course not? She was brave with the heart of a pirate lookout. Despite hurting herself with that fall, she forced back her tears and watched her bedraggled doll fly through the air and hit the nasty muffee man full on his leg.

'—rrge.'

The man in question gave Jessica one last menacing stare, again cocking his pretend gun, then turned around and strode down the beach to pacify poor beignet boy, whose trade was almost non-existent. What he didn't manage to say was he had connections in the municipal police. If you were selling beignets on the beach, how would you ever get a licence?

Her doll, her best favourite doll, had done the trick and scared away the nasty muffee man, despite Hans not coming to her rescue. She didn't need him anyway; he was useless, like her cousin Ewan. She sat on the beach, happy as happy could be, and sang her song, the one Grandad liked earlier, and picked a few scabs from her knees, the big ones anyway.

'Lucy, can't you do something about that noise,' Jessica sighed, 'she's bad for business.'

'Best not to,' Lucy advised.

'You're probably right. I blame that bath she had, the one with soap. She hasn't been the same since.'

To anyone watching Jessica and her gang on the beach, life continued as normal. Little did they know?

For example, Ewan and his two trusty pirate captains had had a nasty fright when the man with the dark slicked-back hair and long sideburns that reached his chin, the one with a Barbary pirate family, threatened them with his pretend gun trick. He was definitely after their treasure. Why were six French kids suddenly sniffing around being all friendly and things, that wasn't natural, was it. They must be working with sideburns man to steal their pirate treasure maps. It was obvious.

Jessica and Ellie exchanged a fleeting, knowing look. The local mafia was warning them. On the beach, they knew they were safe. They had noticed how the men on the beach, the big ones with tattoos, had stood up, ready to defend their honour and ~~profits~~ donations. They were safe on *Black Pearl* because they had Grandad, and they knew no one got past his hammock and lived to tell the tale. They knew that literally, because when searching around the chartroom they found a sawn-off shotgun, which Grandad kept cunningly hidden. While it wasn't loaded, they didn't doubt for one minute that Grandad had a ready supply of cartridges nearby, though they couldn't find those.

Lucy, in her role as casting director, recognised an opportunity when she saw one. She knew her show lacked good able threatening pirates because Ewan and his two pals were anything but threatening. Grandad and Max didn't count because they were a liability. Then as luck would have it, six teenage boys turned up. Just like that.

'Do you want to be pirates in my show, the one at Chez Claude?'

All six regarded her in confusion.

'Max is one of my pirates, so you'll be helping him.'

If you were a young teenage boy, then Max, who they saw as a worldly kind of chap, burdened with being tall, handsome, and bronzed with a physique of a Greek warrior, was everything they aspired to be, eventually. While they knew they had to wait a bit, but to be associated with Max, and being a pirate, was a start, wasn't it.

'Good, that's agreed then,' said Lucy before the six in question had time to answer. 'We better start with the pirate dance, the one Max did. Copy Laetitia, she's probably the best at doing it.'

When Grandad took his usual late afternoon walk along the beach, he again met Lucy, who kind of barred his way, and instructed him, not asked or gently coerced, to go to Chez Claude and get his act together with Max, or else. Grandad wasn't going to argue.

'Grandad is still pulling old biddies on the beach and slathering all over them, it's disgusting,' Lucy informed Jessica. 'You said you were going to deal with it?'

'I'm working on it,' replied Jessica.

While getting their act together, Grandad and Max enjoyed a few beers on the terrace of Chez Claude.

'What's the rope for?' asked Max, nodding at the rope hanging from the old tree on the terrace. The tree was a godsend for the restaurant because it provided much needed shade for the midday diners.

'Lucy hasn't mentioned it yet,' Grandad pondered. 'You've got me thinking. I know how you die, because I have to do the killing. I am not sure how I die though. Lucy said not to fuss because it will become clear on the night. You don't think…'

'She wouldn't intentionally hang you,' Max replied without much conviction.

'It's not her nature, not normally. This has become an obsession. I heard her muttering things like surrealistic realism in the subconscious mind and juxtaposing contradictory fantastic imagery onto a hostile audience, and that'll get the punters in.'

'She has been doing a lot of background research on my laptop,' posed Max, 'and everything goes into her notebook.'

'You don't think hanging your Grandad is covered by Lucy's surrealistic juxtaposing ideas, do you?'

Max gave an authentic example of a Gallic shrug while pouring two more beers. 'I'm sure it won't hurt.'

'We had better do what Lucy says,' said Grandad.

'Which is?'

'Get our act together.'

'What do you propose?'

'We'll do our bit like we practiced the other night, and when I kill you, you fall down nearly dead, and in your last gasp, you stab me, then I fall, and we both die together. I'm sure we can both do good dies for Lucy.' Grandad wasn't going to risk any hanging trickeries by Lucy, no matter how juxtaposing her intensions were.

'Are you sure that's what Lucy wants?'

'I'm dead sure,' Grandad answered with conviction while gazing at the rope hanging from the old tree on the terrace. 'If that's not surrealism, then nothing is.'

'What's surrealism?' Max asked.

'I'll be hanged if I know.'

When they all returned to *Black Pearl*, they were physically and mentally exhausted, and extremely happy. It had been an eventful day.

'What have you all been doing?' Grandad was curious, because he could hear and see things going on at the boathouse end of the beach, the end where the children seemed to gravitate in the afternoons.

'Nuffin.'

Grandad had prepared a huge pot of Yorkshire stew with dumplings made with herbes de Provence. It was a favourite of his, because he added Moroccan spices and cream to thicken. It wasn't really a Yorkshire stew. Grandad called it that to give it a name. He left it in the oven, low, and that was that. It was a particularly useful meal for when you didn't know when the others might turn up and what friends they might bring.

You might think it to be an unsuitable meal for a hot Mediterranean evening. It wasn't.

Apart from its logistical usefulness, children loved it. To start with, it was tasty. Conveniently, most things inside the stew were indistinguishable from each other. Those with dislikes are therefore never disappointed because whatever they disliked couldn't be recognised. With lots of juices for dunking your baguette, you couldn't go wrong.

Julien and Thierry had come along so that the Black Pearl Band could do its final rehearsals.

After the meal, the younger ones around the table seemed a bit worried, exchanging glances and mouthing things like, well has she or hasn't she?

'Come on you lot, give me a break,' said an exasperated Jessica, 'I said I'd do the dishes, didn't I.'

'Julien, you tune your guitar,' directed Lucy in a business-like manner, 'and I'll check that Ewan knows his lines. Ellie can check the costumes with Grandad.'

'Metoo, metoo.'

'You're the lookout, Laetitia, so you already know what to do.' While Lucy was a little insensitive, she was under a lot of pressure. 'You can play with your dolls if you like.'

'*Hi*, Mum, it's me.' Laetitia was on the mobile.

'xxxx'

'What noise?'

'xxxx'

'It's the band.'

'xxxx'

'Lucy's band, don't you know anything'

'xxxx'

'What tone of voice?'

'xxxx xxxx'

'Oh, that one...'

'xxxx'

'Jessica's busy doing the dishes in the galley with Thierry. He's cool and plays the bongo drums.'

'xxxx'

'The kitchen, don't you know anything.'

'xxxx xxxx'

'Sorry, I forgot.'

'xxxx'

'It ain't my bedtime and Grandad's busy, gotta go, furcuff.'

'xxxx xx—'

Chapter 13
The morning of *The Opening*

Everyone woke early, except Laetitia who was dog-tired and needed her beauty sleep. Was it nerves? It was for Lucy. The rest had other things on their mind.

Ewan could sense he was getting closer to his hidden pirate treasure. The previous evening he had spread his maps on the chartroom table and had carefully examined the bay through Grandad's binoculars. On the hills were two big rocks visible from *Black Pearl* but not from the beach. The rocks had to be in line with a tree, which had to cross another line drawn from the end of the pipes and the jumping cliff. The tree was the problem. There were lots of them. Which one was the oldest? If you were that close to discovering hidden pirate treasure, wouldn't you get up early?

Jessica was unsettled about the mafia business. The threat of the municipal police didn't concern her that much, because they were no more than glorified traffic wardens. One thing for sure, she wasn't going to stop her beignets business on the beach, it was too lucrative. She had to devise a getaway plan if the municipal police turned up.

Ellie was simply happy, happy, happy, and happy. At a break in Lucy's rehearsal the previous evening, she and Julien had slipped away to the front of the klipper where it was darker and more private. Julien had demonstrated a few simple cords on his guitar. He had wrapped his arms around her and delicately moved her fingers over the frets. This movement wasn't as simple as it seemed taking into account the size of both protagonists in question. All the same, they managed quite agreeably. Ellie's heart was pounding and she could feel Julien's warm body on her back. She had closed her eyes, waiting...

'Come on you two,' Lucy shouted. 'We've gotta get Ewan's song right.'

The moment had passed.

All this getting up early had caught Grandad by surprise and he fell out of his hammock.

'Damn,' uttered Grandad.

'Careful, Grandad, or I'll make you do the dishes,' Jessica teased, which made him stand up suddenly and bang his head on the boom of the mainmast.

'Damn, damn, damn...'

'I'll pretend I didn't hear that.'

Breakfast was quickly organised with pancakes as the main attraction. Grandad had prepared the pancake mixture the night before while the others were rehearsing. Toppings included Nutella, fig jam, honey, lemon juice, and his favourite, fromage blanc sprinkled with sugar. Delicious.

'Help, help...'

'Better leave some for Laetitia,' warned Lucy, 'or she'll go mad. I'm sure there're ghosts Grandad, cos Laetitia talks to them in bed. They all have names.'

'Grandad, can I borrow the Zodiac,' Jessica asked.

'Of course you can.'

'We need to get things to Chez Claude,' Lucy added.

'It's not a problem.'

'We won't be leaving the bay.' It was Ellie this time.

'It's fine.'

This was a further example of children getting an affirmative answer when they weren't expecting it, and having rehearsed their argument, they were going to give it anyway.

'You know you said that I'm the pilot of *Black Pearl* and Ellie's the sailing master?'

'Yes...' Grandad could spot a leading question a mile off, a nautical mile at that.

'We've read those books you lent us and they were very interesting, weren't they, Ellie.'

'Oh yes, very interesting, especially the anchoring bits.' Ellie knew her lines despite not knowing where this conversation was leading.

'We want to put all our knowledge to practice, don't we Ellie?'

'Yes,' said Ellie on cue, 'most definitely.'

'Yes...' Grandad knew he had to be careful. He realised Jessica was leading him somewhere, but he didn't know where, not yet anyway.

'Oh good,' Jessica declared, 'that's agreed then.'

'What's agreed?' Grandad enquired. He hadn't agreed anything.

'We're having a journey, perhaps tomorrow,' was Jessica's final remark. 'Don't worry, Grandad, we know you like little adventures.'

'Metoo, metoo.'

Grandad wasn't normally the worrying type, unless told not to. Nevertheless, Jessica was right because he did like little adventures.

'Laetitia, why is your face green?' queried Grandad.

You couldn't call it a typical morning for the youngsters, because each was preoccupied with their own things. Except Laetitia who stayed aboard *Black Pearl* looking after Grandad and playing with her dolls.

She kept a good lookout having unintentionally discovered her peripheral vision. She could happily play with her dolls, have an intellectual discussion with her ghosts, practice her singing and she now judged her version of 'I am a Pirate King' far superior to Ewan's, and do her looking out. Most things she reported to Grandad were questionable, because you didn't normally get whales in Pramousquier bay or fleets of pirate ships, or giant crabs bigger than *Black Pearl*. Grandad happily acknowledged each reporting and said he would deal with the oncoming danger forthwith.

Lucy had to sort out Max, because he didn't grasp what she needed.

'I need more space, Max.'

'Lucy,' pleaded Max, 'I need room for the tables.'

'Where are my beer barrels?'

'Chef is sorting it out.'

'What about the sound system?'

'It's all ready.' Max didn't want Lucy meddling with his sound system.

'Remember, don't fool about when Blackbeard kills you tonight, do it like I said.'

'We'll do it like you said, I promise. Charlie has explained.'

'Good, that ticks all my boxes,' said Lucy. Regrettably, she had lost a page from her notebook. She didn't think it had anything crucial on it, she hoped not anyway. Despite that, something nagged at the back of her mind she had to sort out, though couldn't remember what.

Max had a bounce in his step, more a jaunty walk, a swagger, like a pirate. The summer had been good, better than ever before, despite Lucy and the others disturbing his normal routine. What a boost to trade they've been. He knew about Jessica and her little enterprise at the other end of the beach, and he had heard about the complaints from the other plagistes, but that was their problem.

When he arrived each morning at Chez Claude, he didn't know what to expect, except that his laptop would be immediately confiscated, and then things followed, all unexpected, all bringing a smile.

Ewan's morning with his trusty pirate captains had been frustrating. It had involved the onerous task of checking trees between the Maures Hills and the sea. It was hot work and most trees they couldn't get to easily, not without climbing over fences or sneaking into people's gardens. Did a thick trunk make it old, or was it its height. Some trees appeared to be old, except they weren't, like cork oak with its rugged bark. Olive trees, someone told them, were sometimes hundreds of years old, and the one on the roundabout near Le Lavandou was supposed to be over a thousand. That one was too far away.

Hans and Noé were reluctant tree hunters, and their zeal for pirate treasure hunting was definitely on the decline.

More to the point, all three were getting nervous about the show that evening. They knew they had to do Max's pirate dance, which wasn't a problem. They knew that Ewan had to sing his song, again that wasn't a problem. The dancing and jigging on beer barrels was a different matter. They had only done it on the sand, and Lucy kept confusing them with the number of barrels. Then she got six more pirates who weren't real pirates at all. What was that all about?

And another thing, what about the wailing Laetitia's been doing for days, because no one had told them about that.

Because the evening would be busy with the preparations for Lucy's opening night, they had ~~lunch~~ dinner at Chez Claude. Grandad had ordered steak haché et frites, with a side salad, followed by a pudding of their choice. Max's steak haché weren't your normal burger. They were made using quality fresh beef, infused in Chef's special marinade, with added herbs. Max's frites weren't frozen from the fridge but were hand cut by Chef, chunky and crisp.

'How many barrels, Max?' Lucy demanded to know.

'Leave Max alone for now,' said Grandad, 'you can see he is busy.'

'But—' argued Lucy.

'No buts.'

'But—' pleaded Ewan in support of Lucy, because this was crucial information he needed to know.

'Which bit of leave Max alone don't you understand?' Laetitia decided to add her bit here, since Lucy still hadn't given her the singing part she wanted.

'Scrote,' was Lucy's response.

'Max,' Laetitia shouted, believing she had the better of that exchange, 'can I have some more *frites, sivooplay*.'

Chapter 14
Afternoon of *The Opening*

Jessica and her beignet gang had an efficient operation on the beach, very professional.

Too professional for the two plagistes and beignet boy's controller, who, as promised, had informed the municipal police. They had paid to have a licence to trade on the beach and it was their livelihood at stake.

Eventually, a hot and weary member of the municipal police arrived.

He hadn't wanted to go.

His superior informed him that French justice had to be upheld, and if municipal licencing laws were infringed unchecked, then the very fabric of French society would be at risk. Meaning his backhanders for issuing trading licences might be in jeopardy.

It was hot that afternoon and the only place the policeman could park his van, which didn't have air conditioning, was behind Chez Claude, the other end of the beach. The policeman was not very tall, and he considered himself stocky, rather than fat. When he parked his van, Max saw him.

'You can't park your van there, it is private property and for customers only,' warned Max.

'I'm on duty and—'

'I said customers only.'

'*Menu, s'il vous plait.*'

The poor policeman duly bought himself an ice lolly because it was the cheapest thing on offer at Chez Claude. Pacified, Max left him alone then sent a text message to Jessica warning her of the danger.

The policeman, with his right hand twitching on his gun, and left hand holding a fast melting ice lolly, made heavy work of his three hundred yard march to the other end of the beach. His boots sank into the soft sand, making walking difficult and causing him to sweat profusely. Such was the lot of the poor policeman that hot afternoon.

'Hey guys,' Jessica said to the others after receiving her text message from Max, 'I think we're almost done for today, not many beignets left now, do you think you can handle it by yourselves, we got things to do.'

'Yep, no problem,' Lucy replied, taking control of the situation.

'I'll take the donation box,' said Jessica.

By the time the sweating policeman arrived, Jessica and Ellie had long gone in the Zodiac. The first obstacle he came across was Laetitia, armed with her favourite doll. Despite her small size, she was an imposing figure, with her green face and drooping frilly outfit, even for him, who must have seen a thing or two in his long and distinguished career. To those on the beach, he was part of the animation, an easy mistake to make when observing a small, sweaty, fat man sporting a melting ice lolly, and dressed as a policeman.

'What do you want?' Laetitia didn't like the gait of the new arrival and decided she had better check him out.

The poor policeman, who was there under duress, didn't know what to think. The creature before him, with a smell worse that his own, talking in a foreign language, wasn't what he expected. He had been informed that a gang of dangerous immigrants from North Africa had invaded the beach and were selling illegal contraband and drugs.

'Do you want a *beignet*?' Laetitia asked in a demanding manner.

He was confused.

'*Beignet*, you know, *beignets, beignets*...**baynay**.'

Laetitia had fallen in to the stereotypical role of an English woman abroad. If the hapless creature in front of you appeared not to understand, say it louder, and if that didn't work, louder still. We could forgive Laetitia her cultural faux pas because she still wanted to impress Hans with her pirate lookout duties despite him being useless, and at the same time impress Lucy who still might give her that singing role she so wanted.

'*Beignets*?' was all the policeman could think to say, and not knowing what to do, he gave Laetitia the remains of his melting ice lolly.

'*Merci*,' said Laetitia, finishing the ice lolly with delight.

'*De rien*.'

'Help yourself,' Laetitia said to her new friend, the portly policeman, pointing to the few remaining beignets.

173

'*Merci, mademoiselle.*' He was partial to beignets.

Laetitia had taken control of the giving away of beignets. Lucy and the boys were preoccupied with learning their beer barrel dance with the other girls doing their thing nearby. For those who care for technical details, Ewan and his two friends had four pretend beer barrels that day.

Only two of the six teenage boys had turned up. It was Saturday and the others had left for home having finished their holiday.

With Laetitia's tuition, they perfected Max's pirate dance, although Lucy wasn't completely happy because it wasn't the artistic performance she sought. She wanted big rough pirates to compensate for Ewan and his two trusty pirate captains, who were a bit weedy. Now all she had were two more weedy pirates, admittedly, less weedy that Ewan. As a seasoned director, she knew she had to make do with what you were given and to simply get on with it.

Our friendly neighbourhood municipal policeman, remembering his official duties, surveyed the scene around him. He saw two little girls, one playing with her doll, and the other messing around with a gang of boys. Two other small girls were doing twirls, arms held high, like pirouettes if you were being kind. The boys appeared to be doing some game in the sand, prancing in and out of circles. He could do that.

The policeman took off his belt and holster, which was heavy and cumbersome, and gave it to Ewan to hold. He hesitated because of the gun, only slightly, because, unbeknown to his superiors, his gun had never been loaded in the past ten years. It was a foolish thing to be carrying when on traffic duty or handing out the odd parking fine. While he had never suffered from police rage, like one or two of his colleagues, he didn't want to tempt fate.

'You do it like this,' explained the policeman, while he nimbly leapt from one pretend beer barrel to another. He knew his beach games, and quickly invented a new game for the boys to play. He enjoyed himself, despite it being hot and sweaty.

Ewan was in awe of holding a gun. He touched the handle, as did the others. It was steel and heavy. It was real.

It was Laetitia who saw them first, the two plagistes and beignet boy's controller. All Ewan saw was the man with dark slicked-back hair and long sideburns that reached his chin, the one after his treasure.

Laetitia, the green-faced six-year-old sporting a black frilly tutu skirt around her neck, and we know it had seen better days, and the whiff of a pungent smell, stomped up the beach to accost the three intruders who had come to witness the issuing of the on-the-spot fine for illegal trading without a licence. She stood in their path, holding her best favourite doll, the bedraggled one, at arm's length, directly in front of her, like a voodoo doll. Then she launched into her own rendition of 'I am a Pirate King' as a last ditch attempt to impress Lucy.

The voodoo trick and dreadful wailing noise stopped all three in their tracks. They felt they had right on their side, so the controller, the one with the dark slicked-back hair and long sideburns that reached his chin, made to push Laetitia aside, and that was a big mistake.

Ewan, with the holster and gun slung around his neck and under his right armpit, just like you saw in those old spaghetti western films, came to Laetitia's rescue. Now he had a gun, he was going to warn off any treasure hunters whose family were probably Barbary pirates who did the plundering and things. Ewan stood between Laetitia and the man with sideburns and gave him the look, y'know, that pirate king look that could make the whole populace of a Caribbean island tremble with fear.

'Go ahead punk, make my day.' Ewan had often heard Jessica say that, and it sounded menacing when she said it.

The policeman came to investigate. He gently took his holster and gun from Ewan, and buckled it where it should have been, around his ample stomach.

Holding her gently by the hand, Ewan took Laetitia back to their place on the beach, proud of his little cousin.

'Well done little cousin,' said Ewan, 'you're my little star now.'

'Will you let me sing the pirate song with you tonight?'

'Yeah, why not, but don't let Lucy know,' Ewan whispered, 'y'know how sensitive she is about these things.'

Ewan was sure he had at last seen off any treasure hunters whose family were probably Barbary pirates. The gun did the trick and Ewan was high on adrenalin. He wouldn't have been so blasé about allowing Laetitia to sing otherwise, not without Lucy knowing. He was now Laetitia's best boy ever. He's not useless, not now, not like useless Hans.

'Are you the ones who made the complaint about illegal traders on the beach?' The policeman had recovered his poise, with his right hand twitching over his gun once more, be it not loaded. He directed his query at the two plagistes and controller.

'Yes,' answered the man with sideburns.

'Where might these illegal traders be?'

'Over ther—'

'Do not, I repeat, do not think of informing me that those little girls over there are illegal traders of contraband and drugs.'

'*Mais ce n'est pas juste,*' protested one of the plagistes.

The policeman, who wasn't so friendly now, grabbed both plagistes by the arm and made them observe Laetitia, who was sitting at the feet of her favourite boy, her no longer useless cousin, Ewan. Lucy was busy knocking the other four boys into shape, who easily got the hang of the policeman's beer barrel game. Virginia was trying to explain to Nina that when holding your hands in the fifth position, which was some sort of ballet pose, pretend you were holding a small beach ball above your head, like what she was doing.

'Can you not see?' the policeman demanded. 'They are children playing on the beach.' He took the details of the two plagistes and the controller, carefully examined their Identity Cards, and informed them in a loud voice that they were being reported for wasting valuable police time, and that a large fine would be the least they could expect.

Everyone on the beach cheered, or clapped, or both, appreciating the new animation on the beach that day. Some realised what was actually going on, and resented the plagistes taking up so much space on the beach with their vastly over-priced matelas and parasols. The policeman pointed down the beach with his left arm, and allowed his right hand to twitch over his gun.

That effectively ended the Pramousquier beach beignet war, although none of the others were aware of it. Lucy, being preoccupied with last minute changes, missed the goings on and didn't want any buccaneer beauties holding pretend beach balls, thank you very much.

'Hungry work,' declared the policeman while eating the last beignet.

'*Que faites-vous ce soir?*' Lucy asked the policeman.

Chapter 15
The Opening

The unedited Notebook of Lucy Tarantino
Black Pearl, **Pramousquier**

I am now calling myself Lucy Tarantino because Jessica said he was a cool director, so I checked him out on Max's laptop. He does satirical nonlinear storylines and that kinda fits in with my new subconscious juxtaposing surrealistic realism approach.

What a disaster! Everything that could go wrong certainly did, and everything that should have gone right certainly didn't.

When we arrived at Chez Claude, everything was set up like I planned. The beach was a pirate camp with a barbecue and things. There were tables everywhere. The terrace was the same, with flames, candles, and pirate flags all over the place. It looked cool.

Max had set up a kinda stage next to the salon at the back of the terrace, like how I told him, near the plugs for the sound system. That's when I saw the rope hanging from the tree and then I remembered I had forgotten about that, so I tied it to the side, like what pirates would do. The Black Pearl Band was to be in the salon, behind the stage. There was something missing.

It was the beer barrels, so I asked Max where they were. He told me that Chef was sorting it, so I said he'd better or he was dead meat.

I told Max that Chez Claude looked cool, real cool.

Grandad left *Black Pearl* earlier than the rest of us, in the red kayak, cos he didn't want to interfere with our getting ready. That could have been a mistake, cos when we all got to Chez Claude, I'm sure he'd had too much to drink.

Chez Claude was full, so was the beach, and Max had set up an extra bar on the beach. I didn't get nervous, not like Ewan who kept moaning about not knowing how many beer barrels there were. My two extra pirates turned up and luckily, Grandad had made plenty of pirate hats, like how I told him.

When doing satirical nonlinear juxtaposing directing, that required a lot of organising. Ellie helped me, of course, and Max's laptop was useful. Julien was ace cos he was the musical director and the only one allowed to meddle with Max's sound system. He had added some of his own bits and it was complicated so I didn't touch it. Julien had done everything, like how I told him.

Jessica and Thierry got together in the corner. They thought no one saw them but I did. They just talked in secret, thinking nobody could hear.

'Did you get them, Thierry?' asked Jessica in a whisper, and he had, which was definitely suspicious. I didn't hear the rest cos I was busy.

Max wouldn't let us start until after nine, cos he wanted everyone to arrive and get a few drinks inside them, cos they might need it, he said. I'll talk to him about that later.

Julien and the Black Pearl Band started with a mixture of pirate songs, like an overture. It was real good and everyone liked it.

Then Nina, Virginia, and me did our buccaneer beauties dance and sang the 'Poor Wandering One' song, not all of it cos some of it was boring. We did the 'Take Heart' and all the 'Ah, ha-ha-ha,' bits. It was mostly 'Ah, ha-ha-ha,' cos Nina and Virginia could only manage that. Max spoilt it a bit cos he joined in 'Au, hu-hu-hu,' all French like. We had to do that twice and the second time Laetitia joined in. She only did her wailing, which, I'll tell you, wasn't appreciated. I don't know why everyone cheered. I could see some of the old biddies didn't appreciate it cos they had tears in their eyes.

After one or two other bits, it was time for Blackbeard to kill Redbeard and that was so embarrassing, cos Grandad and Max came on singing, 'What Shall We Do with the Drunken Sailor', and that wasn't in my playlist, definitely not. The band must have been in on it cos they played the tune. Everyone joined in with the chorus.

When it came to the killing bit, they definitely got that wrong. Pirates don't fight with a mop and broom, and I definitely told Max not to do that getting Grandad in a headlock, cos all Grandad did was drink more beer and a pirate wouldn't do that with your head in a headlock, not in a fight to the death. Why was Max wearing a tea towel around his head with bits of lettuce sticking out, wait until I see him. When ~~Grandad~~ Blackbeard escaped from the headlock, he managed to kill Redbeard properly, then Redbeard decided not to die immediately and he killed Blackbeard, and that wasn't in my script, was it. Grandad and Max then rolled around the floor doing their dying for nearly a minute before they were dead, all to the 'Drunken Sailor' tune. All right, everyone clapped and cheered. You would expect that cos they were French and that's what they did.

Poor Ewan and all his pirates rushed on to the stage to kill Blackbeard and found him already dead. They got that wrong because Hans was supposed to play the pirate king for that bit, because he was bigger. Maybe I forgot to tell Hans. Anyway, it didn't matter because Blackbeard was already dead.

That's when I saw the beer barrels, all two of them with a wooded plank on top, and not looking too safe. That's when I promised that Chef would be dead meat when I saw him next. I knew Ewan and his two pirate captains wouldn't be pleased with the beer barrels.

The band played the introduction to 'I am a Pirate King' while Ewan climbed onto the beer barrels, but the other pirates wouldn't join him like in my script. Instead, they started Max's pirate dance, even the slightly less weedy two new pirates joined in. I couldn't see Laetitia cos she was supposed to do that.

'I shall live and die a pirate king,' Ewan shouted, cos that was in my script, but not falling off the beer barrels. That wasn't in my script at all. Then he started crying cos his leg was bleeding. What a weed. Who needs a twin brother?

Then Laetitia appeared swinging on the rope, doing her wailing.

That wasn't in my script either.

It was just as well cos it took the attention away from Ewan doing his bleeding and crying. Not everyone appreciated Laetitia's wailing cos I could see tears in the eyes of those old biddies again. Even Grandad had tears in his eyes except that might have been because Max whacked him hard a couple of times with his mop while they were doing their fighting bit.

Mind, Ewan did manage to stand up and Laetitia rushed over and gave him a big hug, definitely not in my script, and when the band again started playing 'I am a Pirate King', he hopped up onto the beer barrels and sang it beautifully, in his pirate hollering way.

The others did Max's pirate dance again, including Laetitia. That went well, like in my script, except Max and some others joined in, like a crocodile chain. Like I said before, the French always seem to do things like that. Then everyone stood up, cheered, and clapped at my useless twin brother.

It was time for the pirate pranks, which the buccaneer beauties did on the pirates. They didn't know what hit them cos we had practiced them on the beach and they didn't know. The easy one was when Nina got on her hands and knees behind Noé, and then Virginia pushed him so he tripped up backwards. I was supposed to catch him and kinda didn't. He didn't cry though, not like my useless twin brother. Then Virginia did a cartwheel over Noé, which frightened him a bit.

Then Laetitia joined in!

She wasn't supposed to and she hadn't practiced like the rest of us. She charged at the two extra pirates, the less weedy ones, who tripped over Noé and fell down. Then she threatened Hans because he didn't help her and he looked frightened. I don't think Laetitia realised it was pretend. Everyone cheered, so it was probably all right.

Then I had my surprise.

I had closed the curtains, which were like thin net ones, and then all the lights went out. That's when the fat policemen came on, the friendly one we met on the beach, to do his beer barrel dance. I had texted Julien from the beach to get a projector, and he had. Using Max's laptop, I projected 'A Policeman's Lot is Not a Happy One', the Tony Azito version from *YouTube*, onto the net curtains from behind so everyone could see. With the music on Max's sound system, my policeman, a real one in his uniform and gun, did his beer barrel dance without the beer barrels, cos they weren't safe. He even tried to copy Tony Azito and did it real good. Everyone booed, of course, and someone said his wife fainted. I didn't see that because I was behind helping Julien. At the end, everyone stood up and cheered. My policeman even remembered to arrest Ewan, the pirate king, cos that's what he was supposed to do.

Then the band started to play Grandad's favourite Rolling Stones song, 'Ruby Tuesday'. Julien shouted, 'it's your turn, Lucy,' and Max picked me up and took me to the front, so I had to sing it all by myself in front of all those people. The old biddies definitely weren't happy about it because some had tears running down their faces, like Grandad. Then Jessica made me sing 'Walking in the Air', which definitely wasn't suitable for a buccaneer beauty despite all the clapping. But it's the truth.

Everyone stood up, cheered and clapped. Max and Chef held me up high over their heads and that's when I managed to tell Chef he was dead meat. Julien and the band played more songs until late.

Grandad said I was his little angel, so I put him right, 'buccaneer beauty, Grandad, buccaneer beauty.'

Jessica and Ellie gave me big hugs, and I liked Ellie's best cos it was all cuddly and soft, and Jessica said, 'Good one, Lucy, good one.'

Ewan was limping a bit and he gave me the thumbs up. He'd never done that before.

Laetitia was asleep on the VIP table, with a fierce pirate face Jessica had done earlier that evening. She was wearing Jessica's frilly tutu skirt, the one that whiffed a bit and had seen better days. She was a scrote.

Like I said, it was a complete disaster. I had better get some sleep now. I've never written so much in my life before, not all in one go.

Signed

Lucy Tarantino

*E*wan was ecstatic.

Immediately after his bleeding and crying episode, he glanced up at Laetitia swinging on that rope doing her pirate lookout wailing noise and saw the oldest gnarled tree ever. There it was all the time, on the terrace of Chez Claude. It wasn't very tall, which was as well, because Laetitia might have killed herself. That hidden pirate treasure was as good as his. He wasn't going to share this new piece of information with his two trusty pirate captains either. They'd lost interest anyway.

No wonder Ewan hopped up onto the beer barrels and sang his heart out.

*G*randad was bursting with pride, with his grandchildren and their friends doing all their amazing things, and singing, and dancing, and the band was incredible, and they did all this in the few days they had been in Pramousquier, a lot of it on *Black Pearl*.

Jessica had spotted Gigi, the lady who had given her and Ellie tea the previous day, watching from the corner.

'Hi,' welcomed Jessica, 'glad you could make it.'

'I never expected it to be so good,' replied Gigi.

'That's my Grandad over there,' said Jessica.

'You mean the one with the charming ponytail?'

'That's him. I think he'd appreciate some comforting. I have to go because I'm needed in the band. Whatever you do, please don't tell him his ponytail is charming. It's gross.'

Gigi meandered across the terrace unassumingly, and stood beside Grandad.

Result, Jessica said to herself, over to you Grandad, you're on your own now.

'You must be the grandfather, the owner of that fine ship in the bay?' said Gigi.

'They did this all on their own,' replied Grandad wiping his nose on his sleeve.

'Here, use my handkerchief.'

'Thanks.'

Good move Grandad, women always fall for all that emotional approach, go in for the kill while hubby is not around, willed Jessica from behind her flute. The show was reaching its finale. Jessica then got the band to play 'Ruby Tuesday' with Lucy singing.

'Isn't that such a beguiling cover version,' Gigi remarked.

'The Rolling Stones did the original.'

'Did they?'

'That's my little granddaughter singing.'

Grandad, don't blow it, a little bit of emotion is okay, but women don't go for men who blubber all over them…

Grandad did some serious blowing of his nose into the handkerchief he had borrowed and when he turned round to return it, Gigi was gone. Pity, he said to himself, she was quite attractive.

Grandad, you blew it, was Jessica's thinking on the matter.

Gigi was next to a tall aging hippy character with uncontrollable, bedraggled, grey hair partially hiding a craggy face that had seen life to its full. 'What do you think?'

'You will never see this happen again,' replied the aging hippy. 'It is the greatest concert ever.'

After the performance, everyone involved in the show enjoyed a midnight barbecue and drinks on the beach. Lucy was over the moon with her triumph and played the role of feigning modest director.

'Oh, what a disaster,' she kept saying, with the back of her right hand lightly resting on her forehead, 'what a disaster.'

'Can you do it again next Saturday?' pleaded Max, having had the most successful night ever. 'You can use my laptop any time, Lucy, any time.'

'Oh, how could I?' feigned Lucy once again, 'what a disaster.'

'Is that a yes then?'

'Oh, how could I?'

Max thought about this a bit more and decided he couldn't realistically put Lucy and her enthusiastic cast through that again. He didn't think he could repeat the success and the spontaneity of the fabulous production that had just taken place.

He managed to get plenty of photographs and he would make up some large posters to hang around Chez Claude. He would also have some postcards printed and then start selling them in a day or so.

There must be something in that realistic juggernaut method Charlie talked about the other day, thought Max. It must be an English thing!

'You're probably right, Lucy,' Max said gently, 'we'll leave it at that, I think, because it can't get any better.'

Max immediately saw the disappointment in Lucy's eyes and his own emotions nearly got the better of him. He knew he had made the right decision. He picked up Lucy and gave her the best hug ever, not as enjoyable as Grandad's, or Ellie's, obviously, but the third best ever.

If you were a ten-year-old girl, hugged by a tall, handsome, and bronzed man with a physique of a Greek warrior it would make you feel better, wouldn't it? Many eyes in Chez Claude witnessed that display of affection, several with envy.

'Thanks, Max,' replied Lucy. 'We had a good time, didn't we?'

Grandad got legless, with Max. It was all that rum.

At around two in the morning, Jessica rounded up the others, except Laetitia who was fast asleep on the VIP table, and returned to *Black Pearl*. She and Ellie had some serious planning to do. About an hour later, Grandad staggered towards his red kayak, but saw three, and tried to figure which one was his.

'Charlie,' shouted Max from the terrace, nodding towards the VIP table, 'I think you've forgotten something.'

Chapter 16
Escape

It was Sunday, the morning after, and everyone was up and on the go, everyone except Grandad.

*E*wan was up at dawn. He again put all his bits of paper and maps on the chartroom table and then carefully examining the landmarks through Grandad's binoculars. He tried to be as quiet as possible so as not to wake Grandad in his hammock, a difficult task for a busy treasure hunting pirate king.

Ewan need not have worried because Grandad was out for the count, having had a few pirate punches too many the previous evening. How he managed to return to *Black Pearl* in the kayak, with Laetitia, was a minor miracle. Max had kept a careful eye on him.

'Solved it,' Ewan whispered to himself.

He drew a line on his map from the high rocks on the Maures Hills to that tree he had found last night, the old one at Chez Claude, and extended the line into the bay. He could see the jumping cliff on the left hand side of the bay, and all he had to do was find the end of the pipe in the sea, then draw a second line and see where they crossed. If he could find the end of the pipe, he didn't need the map because he could see the other marks.

Ewan was nervous. He had to find the end of that pipe. Having got his snorkel and mask, he quietly climbed down the steps on the side of *Black Pearl* and entered the sea, which was warm and calm.

'*Eins, zwei, eins, zwei…*'

It was Gisela having an early morning swim, the one wearing a blue bathing cap and making a big splash doing the backstroke.

'Good morning, young man,' said Gisela. 'It is good to see you swimming this early.'

'Hi, Gisela,' said Ewan, 'are you going to be around long?' He didn't want Gisela poking her nose into things not her business.

'I can stay around a little longer if you like,' replied Gisela. 'I'll keep an eye on you while you have a swim.'

Such a sensible boy, Gisela thought…

That wasn't what Ewan meant, was it. He didn't want busybody Gisela keeping an eye on him, not while he was hunting for hidden pirate treasure.

'Thanks,' said Ewan, though he wasn't thankful at all, but Gisela wasn't to know that, was she. 'I'll have a swim to see if there are any fish.'

Finding the end of the pipe wasn't easy because most of the pipe was under the seabed. He found it between two white buoys, like an old urn with the open-end upwards at an angle, covered in barnacles and seaweed, like camouflage. He then swam in the direction of the jumping cliff, until, when peering towards the land, the high rocks and old tree were in line.

Ewan inspected the seabed through his mask, but the water was deep, deeper than he would normally go. He looked around for caves and holes but couldn't see any obvious ones. This wasn't where he usually explored and it was all new to him. He saw that the sandy seabed gave way to rocks and seaweed nearer to the jumping cliff.

Then he saw it.

It was like a cage, with one side and the top open. Ewan didn't know what it was. It looked big and heavy, like a bit of a submerged building. Similar to the end of the pipe, it was camouflaged and difficult to see. It was the perfect place to hide treasure, Ewan thought.

The water was deep. Even Noé couldn't swim that deep, and he was the best. Only Grandad could swim down that deep. Ewan had a go but it was no good. He barely got half way. What about the conger eels like it warned on his treasure map? The cage might be full of them, and, like Jessica, you didn't mess with conger eels. What's got into Jessica? She didn't swear much now and she was pleasant at times. That made him at risk of doing the dishes, and he'd prefer to have a dunking to remember than do the dishes, but not the Chinese burn.

Ewan could see something but he wasn't sure.

He knew that was where the hidden pirate treasure was, he just knew, and that, according to Ewan, was that. He, Ewan, the pirate king of Pramousquier, had found it. Not the hidden pirate treasure, not yet anyway because the water was too deep. He had found where it was hidden, and nobody else had, only him, all alone.

'Are you okay?' Gisela asked, as Ewan gasped for air when he surfaced.

'Yeah, I think so, although my ears have gone weird and it hurts behind my eyes.'

'Pop your ears like this.' Gisela held her nose and blew hard, and she went cross-eyed doing so, and red in the cheeks. 'You might need to do it several time.'

Ewan then remembered he had to do that on the way down, when swimming deep, like Grandad said. He had forgotten. Maybe she wasn't batty after all, he thought. With a bit of luck, all the splashing she did might frighten away the conger eels. 'Thanks, Gisela.'

Ewan did as he was told, and his ears weren't so weird, although his eyes still hurt. Then he took a deep breath, and swam down once more. This time, on the way down he twice held his nose tightly and blew hard. It still was no good. The cage thing was too deep and it hurt behind his eyes. He surfaced once more and Gisela saw the pain on his face. It was genuine pain from behind his eyes, not disappointment for not reaching the cage. That could wait now he had discovered where the pirate treasure was. He needed some training and that's where Grandad could be helpful because he was good at swimming underwater, the best he knew.

If there's hidden pirate treasure down there, then it's been there hundreds of years already, so no real danger of others finding it. He needed a plan, how to dig underwater, how to handle conger eels, things like that. If he didn't find the hidden pirate treasure that year, then he would next year, that's for sure.

'I can see someone shouting from your boat,' Gisela said kindly. 'I think they want you.'

'Thanks again, Gisela.' This time he meant it.

Ewan swam back slowly, enjoying his moment.

'What have you been doing?' queried Lucy pleasantly when Ewan got back on board while making corrections in her notebook.

'Nuffin, honest,' was Ewan's dishonest reply. 'When's breakfast?'

'I'm writing my memoirs, so don't disturb me.'

*G*randad vaguely remembered waking up and hearing voices.

'Why does Grandad keep saying he's dying,' queried a worried Laetitia, 'he's not going to die, is he?'

'No, he won't actually die,' explained Ellie kindly. 'He only feels like he's dying, like pretend.'

'That's okay then.'

Grandad was aware of the motion of *Black Pearl*, and it was different to other mornings. It wasn't the motion of a ship at anchor. It was the motion of a ship under sail.

'Damn,' said Grandad falling out of his hammock in a panic.

'When's breakfast, Grandad?' asked Lucy pleasantly. 'You said you were the cook.'

'Damn, damn, damn,' said Grandad while trying to stand up and banging the boom of the mainmast with his head once more, because it wasn't where it was supposed to be, except this time he didn't feel a thing because his head was already hurting from all that rum he had had the previous night. And what's that sail doing up, he asked himself.

Grandad decided to take things more slowly, so he sat down and gathered his senses. That didn't work, because all he could gather was that *Black Pearl* was under sail, far away from land, with Jessica at the helm and Ellie tending the sheets on the mainsail.

'Damn!' Grandad exclaimed once more. 'It's that rum Max gave me, I'm hallucinating.' With that, Grandad managed to climb back into his hammock and went back to sleep.

'Does that mean Grandad's doing the dishes?' Ewan asked hopefully, because he certainly didn't want to do them.

'Breakfast is served in the saloon,' Julien shouted, 'It is French toast.'

'Ace.'

'Awesome.'

Metoo, metoo.'

Despite what you might think, things were thoroughly organised on *Black Pearl*. The weather was kind, with a light south-westerly wind, making excellent sailing conditions, particularly if you're on course for

Saint-Tropez. That's where Jessica and Ellie were heading with their young crew, including Julien and Thierry.

Ellie had weighed anchor without a hitch, and then organised the two elder boys in hauling up the mainsail, followed by the mizzen. Once the sails were up, *Black Pearl* looked a magnificent display of nautical finesse. Jessica had left early to arrive at Saint-Tropez in daylight hours.

After about two hours sailing, Grandad made a more cautious approach to waking up. He opened his eyes and once again recognised the motion of his precious klipper sailing smoothly through the water. He was experiencing something unreal, a dream, like an illusion.

He pinched himself.

Hard.

'Ouch.'

It wasn't a dream after all. It was real and not an illusion.

At first, the harshness of the sun blurred his vision, so he laid there while his eyes became accustomed to the light. He glanced to the port side of *Black Pearl* and saw land in the distance, maybe two or three miles away. To starboard, he saw open sea, with a crisp, clear horizon. He looked up and saw the two sails taut with the wind, though nothing to cause alarm. He spotted Laetitia half way up the mainmast, with her best favourite doll, talking to herself, except we know otherwise. She was actually facing aft, though Grandad forgave her for that minor remiss of lookout duties.

At the bow was Ewan, astride the bowsprit wearing his pirate hat, talking to his parrot. He sat there, daydreaming about his treasure, as contented as could be. Behind him on the sunbed was Ellie, with Julien gently strumming his guitar, music Grandad didn't recognise. Ellie stood up and walked down the leeward side, checking the sheets and stays, and once satisfied, returned to her sunbed.

At the helm was Jessica giving instructions to Thierry, like a seasoned old hand. She then handed the helm over to Thierry, watched him for a few minutes until satisfied, then disappeared into the chartroom. All was in order. They were sailing in a westerly direction and Grandad felt happy, extremely happy, despite the throbbing head.

'Coffee, Grandad,' offered Lucy, 'you look like you need it.'

'Thanks.'

Lucy had placed a mug of hot coffee on the dining table and some baguette, which seemed to have been fried in….

'Julien taught me how to make French toast,' Lucy explained, 'it's kinda good for hangovers.'

'I'm not sure about that,' which was true, because Grandad's stomach churned over a few times at the sight of Lucy's version of French toast.

'You better eat it, or you're…'

Lucy stopped herself saying he was dead meat, because it was Grandad.

'…or you'll be sick.'

Grandad made a gentle descent from his hammock and sat next to Lucy. The coffee was strong and sweet and much appreciated, and Lucy's French toast wasn't bad either.

'Grandad, you're lucky you still have your ponytail, cos Jessica was going to cut it off when you were asleep. We stopped her.'

'Was she now?'

'Hi, Charlie,' Ellie shouted, 'you okay?'

'I'm fine,' Grandad replied, 'you've done a good job setting the sails.'

'Thanks.'

After finishing his coffee and making a reasonable go at eating the French toast, Grandad wandered aft to see how things were. Thierry was quite competent at steering, he noticed. He should be, because his family were into boats, although they didn't have one at that time.

'Hi, Grandad,' said Jessica coming out of the chartroom, 'you okay?'

'I'm fine. You seem to have everything under control.'

'We're lucky with the weather.'

Grandad went into the chartroom and was surprised to see charts, proper ones, on the chartroom table.

'I hope you didn't mind me getting some charts, Grandad, because you needed them,' explained Jessica.

'You're probably right.'

'I am right, Grandad, and take that from a girl who has just passed eleven GCSEs, with five *A* grades, one with an *A* star, and five *B* grades. The results came through a couple of days ago, although I only found out last night.'

189

'Congratulations and how did Ellie do?'

'About the same.'

'I bet your parents were pleased.'

'I think they expected more A grades.'

'I think you both did well and we'll celebrate tonight.' Grandad was pleased.

'Celebrations in Saint-Tropez, cool,' said Jessica. 'Did I say we're going to Saint-Tropez? We should make it before dark.'

Grandad found out he was the proud owner of nautical charts covering the coastal sea area from Marseille to Monaco.

'These would have cost a small fortune. Where did you get the money for all these?' Grandad knew Jessica didn't have much cash and nautical charts weren't cheap.

'Don't ask, Grandad.'

Jessica's beignet business had been successful, as we know, and the profit easily covered the cost of the charts. Then she had an added bonus. During the *Pirates of Provence* show the previous evening, she noticed mafia man in the corner, watching her. After a while, mafia man approached her.

'*Mademoiselle, s'il vous plaît,*' mafia man said politely.

'What!'

'I hope we can be reasonable about our little dispute.'

'What dispute?'

'I have to make a living and so do my boys, and the summer season is very short.'

Jessica did have pangs of guilt about poor beignet boy because he had been selling beignets on Pramousquier beach for as long as she could remember. She had collected a considerable amount of money and had been able to buy the charts Grandad needed.

What did you think Jessica was going to do with the money?

'So what do you propose?' Jessica asked mafia man.

'We have all enjoyed your animation on the beach and I would like to make my own donation to that box of yours.'

Mafia man put his hand into his back pocket, pulled out a wad of money, and peeled several notes of large denomination into his other hand; he paused, looked Jessica in the eye, and then added two more.

'Two conditions,' continued mafia man. 'No more beignets on the beach, agreed.'

Mafia man handed the cash to Jessica. 'You said this was a donation, right, nothing more?'

'Of course.'

'Agreed,' said Jessica, taking the money, because she needed a little more for what she was after, 'and no hard feelings.'

Mafia man smiled and shook hands with Jessica. 'I am pleased we have come to an amicable agreement, and no hard feelings.'

As mafia man went to walk away, Jessica suddenly remembered something. 'You said two conditions, what's your second condition?'

'Please can you keep that little devil creature away from me, the smelly one dressed in black.'

*G*randad didn't ask where the money for the charts came from. He fought back his tears, because he got a bit emotional, and gave Jessica a good Grandad hug.

'So where are we?' asked Grandad, getting down to business.

'Approaching Cap Lardier, you can see it ahead. We'll pass quite closely, but there's plenty of deep water,' Jessica explained. 'I can get good positions from my useful gadget.'

'You mean your iPhone, Jessica, iPhone 6s.'

Jessica stared critically at Grandad, who kept a straight face.

Grandad picked up the dividers and checked Jessica's route on the charts. 'We are doing about four knots, so we should get there okay, I'll suggest to Ellie we hoist a couple of the foresails to speed us up a little.'

'How do you measure the speed in knots, Grandad?'

'I'll show you,' and he did.

'That's easy, once you know,' Jessica commented.

'Lucy put on a good performance last night?' said Grandad.

'The best,' Jessica replied, 'she did ever so well. We'll have a double celebration in Saint-Tropez.'

'You have everything under control so I'll have a shower now.'

Jessica gave Grandad another critical stare. 'Best use soap, Grandad.'

On his way to the stateroom, Grandad was accosted.

'Grandad?'

'Yes, Ewan.'

'Can you teach me to swim deep without my head hurting?'

'Of course, but I'll have to buy you a new snorkel and mask. The ones you're using now are getting too small for you.'

'Awesome.'

'*It* simply isn't acceptable,' stated Mother from Hell, again on the phone to her sister-in-law, Marina. 'I'm their mother, and I have a right to know what's going on.'

'You said you spoke to Laetitia, didn't you, on Skype?' Marina was trying to sound reasonable, although she was apprehensive because Lucy had also spoken to her.

Contacting your mother on Max's laptop, late at night, with all that pirating and frolicking at Chez Claude, was probably not the best of decisions. At the time, Lucy was over the moon after her overwhelming and rapturous applause, and wanted to share her success with her mother.

'*M*um,' Lucy gushed on Skype the previous evening, 'it was a disaster and they all clapped like mad, how embarrassing.'

'How is Grandad, is he okay?' Marina queried, because there had been no answer on his mobile whenever she had tried phoning.

Grandad's mobile probably needed charging, something he often forgot to do. He mostly switched his mobile off to save the battery and, being prudent, only switched it on to make a call. Taking into account his mobile only has a small memory and Grandad never erased things, his memory had been full for ages. Grandad was not the most sophisticated of mobile user. Consequently, trying to contact him was always a bit hit-and-miss.

'Yep, he's fine except he keeps kissing old biddies on the beach, and it disgusting. Did I tell you it was such a disaster?'

'What, Grandad kissing old biddies?'

'Yep,' Lucy replied. 'Then I saw him chatting up a pretty lady in the bar. I think Jessica arranged it cos she thinks Grandad needs sorting except I'm not supposed to know. They still clapped like mad and it was such a disaster.'

'It doesn't sound like a disaster to me,' Mum responded kindly, 'it sounds like a big success. Did you say Jessica is arranging dates for Grandad?'

'Yep.'

'Can I speak to Grandad, please?'

Lucy glanced over to the bar area and saw Grandad with a glass of beer balanced on his head and if it wasn't for his ponytail, it would have fallen for sure. There was a crowd around him, led by Max, cheering and counting to twenty for some reason. Even ten-year-old girls, excited after an overwhelming success, knew all about discretion, something parents didn't appreciate.

'He's a bit busy at the moment. He's definitely okay, I promise.'

'What's that noise, it sounds like broken glass?'

'I didn't hear any noise, Mum.'

'Can't you switch on the video so I can see you?' What Mum really meant was so that she could see what was going on.

'It's not working.' See what I mean about ten-year-old girls reaching the age of discretion. That was something ten-year-old boys, like Ewan, failed ever to do. 'Gotta go Mum, Laetitia wants to talk to Aunty Jo. Say hello to Aunty Marina, Laetitia.'

'Hello, Aunty Marina.'

'*M*um,' babbled Laetitia, 'Ewan let me sing and I was the star and I swung on the rope from the tree but I didn't fall well only a little fall and the policeman came to arrest Jessica but she escaped and Ewan played with a real gun and frightened the nasty muffee man who was going to beat me up and I've eaten lots of beignets and I don't smell and Grandad says I don't need to flush the toilet because I'm too small and I'm a scrote and I've seen lots of ghosts but they're my friends and I can climb the mast higher that Ewan because he's can't but he's not useless and I'm the star gotta go furcuff.'

Laetitia didn't once pause for breath. She then returned to her VIP table, because she was tired.

'Hello, hello, are you there, Laetitia, can you hear me, Laetitia, Laetitia?' Mum shouted. 'Skype is so fucking rubbish.'

What Laetitia's Mum said about Skype was a little unfair because Laetitia had walked away having said all she wanted to say, and she was pleased with having got all that off her chest. Laetitia didn't know how to disconnect Skype. She was only six. With the video off, Mum could hear all kinds of strange noises. What would you expect to hear when pirates were partying late at night with rum flowing freely? When not knowing what was causing the noise you start to imagine all sorts, which was as well, because on that occasion, what was actually taking place was far worse than Laetitia's Mum's imagination.

'Hello, is there anybody there? Can you hear me? Hello…'

'I don't know what's got into Laetitia since she arrived in France,' continued Jo to her sister-in-law, Marina.

'What do you mean?'

'It's the bad influence of your father, if you ask me, with all that fucking swearing she does. He never answers his mobile and that's inconsiderate and irritating.'

'I would never call my father perfect, far from it. One thing is for sure, he never swears. The worse thing he ever called me was a rotten piece of rhubarb, and that shocked me at the time,' Marina informed her sister-in-law, Jo, the one she considered a silly bitch. 'If your children swear, then it's because they're copying you.'

'There you go again, always defending your fucking father like he's some fucking god or something.'

'You should listen to yourself.'

'That irresponsible father of yours is allowing my poor Laetitia to swing on ropes from trees,' moaned Mother from Hell. 'Hasn't he heard about Health and Safety?'

'It sounds like they are having a good time?'

'What is all that about climbing the mast, then?'

'Fun, perhaps?'

'What do you know about the police coming to arrest Jessica?'

'What are you talking about?'

'What do you know about Ewan playing with a real gun?'

'What, Ewan with a gun?'

'I've got your fucking attention now, haven't I?'

They successfully rounded Cap Lardier and with the wind almost astern, and two foresails successfully hoisted, *Black Pearl* was doing six knots.

Grandad gazed at the coastline between Cap Lardier and Cap Taillat through his binoculars. It was a wild and rugged coastline and difficult to get to from land, although not too difficult because years earlier, he had been there.

'What are you thinking, Grandad?' Jessica had seen Grandad surveying the land with interest, in a king of reflective mood.

'See that beach over there, near Cap Taillat, that's the Bastide Blanche. It's very secluded. I went there when your father and Aunty Marina were very little. It was Easter and very windy and we had a picnic. There was no one there, only us.'

'Did you swim?'

'The water was cold. Aunty Marina swam anyway.'

'What about Dad, did he swim?'

'No, but he paddled in the water a bit.'

'Shall we stop and explore?'

'We'll stop on the way back.'

What Grandad didn't tell Jessica was he had also been to the Bastide Blanche years before with his late wife, before they were married. Again, it was Easter and they had risked the rough ride in their 2CV. The weather was pleasantly warm and the beach was empty, as it usually was then. They had a picnic, a simple meal of baguette filled with camembert cheese, a bottle of local rosé wine, and…

'Grandad, you're dreaming again.'

Jessica kept a cautious distance as they passed Cap Camarat because of the rocks extending out to sea. After Cap Camarat, they headed north and lost the favourable south-westerly they had had earlier. There was a more blustery wind from the east blowing inland, a typical sea breeze. While Jessica managed to trim the sails for the new wind, their speed reduced to a bare three knots and *Black Pearl* drifted towards the land, not dangerously so, but enough to be a nuisance.

'Time for the engine,' Grandad declared. Both Jessica and Ellie didn't want to use the engine but Grandad explained that, if they didn't, it would mean arriving at Saint-Tropez much later than planned. 'We'll keep the mainsail hoisted to reduce the rolling.'

Julien prepared a good lunch, but not as enjoyable as Grandad's. There was no baguette on board though when Julien found Grandad's own baked bread, he was impressed. In recent years, the French had been trying to bake brown or wholemeal bread, not always with success. He wanted Grandad's recipe, and would urge his father to bake it and see how it sold.

'Those are the famous Saint-Tropez beaches,' declared Grandad, indicating the land on the port side. 'Over there is Pampelonne Beach, and a bit further north, Tahiti Beach.' The others peered at the wide expanse of coastline with many plagistes and low hills behind.

'I bet it was a good place for pirates to hide,' said Ewan, who was considering his new passion for treasure hunting.

'Seems good to me, there're no rocks to jump from.' Ellie was thinking more of the safety side of things.

'With those smart yachts at anchor, I bet there are some gorgeous men there.' Jessica was thinking more of the social side of things.

'And gorgeous women,' added Thierry.

'Parking is very difficult,' added Julien, being practical.

'The beaches are miles from Saint-Tropez,' Jessica said, having studied the charts carefully.

'Metoo, metoo.' Laetitia wasn't even listening. She wanted to let everyone to know her opinion just in case she was missing something.

What those on *Black Pearl* didn't know was that all eyes from the beach, including those on the smart yachts, the gorgeous men, beautiful women and celebs, were watching them as they sailed north towards Golfe de Saint-Tropez. They saw a real ship, with the mainsail hoisted, with huge flipper things hanging over the side amidships. They saw something different, something chic, probably owned by some rich financier, with loads of young nubile women to entertain the men.

They couldn't see Grandad with his scraggy beard and gross ponytail, sitting on a plastic chair, nursing a hangover, steering with his feet, while he cleaned his toenails with a screwdriver. Nor could they see seven hungry youngsters sitting around the deck table eating like the hungry animals they were. Ewan had invented a new game. Who could hold the most food on their tongue without dropping it – Laetitia won!

Black Pearl rounded Pointe de la Rabiou at the entrance to Golfe de

Saint-Tropez, and while sailing in a north-westerly direction, made its final approach to Saint-Tropez.

'We might need to anchor outside the port,' Grandad informed his now experienced crew of seven. 'Berths this time of year can be difficult to get, especially at short notice.'

'Grandad, I'm the pilot,' replied Jessica. 'Our berth is available and ready. I have already made the arrangements.'

'Mmm…' Grandad was still worried because the outer port, the new port, generally held the smaller boats and there wasn't much room to manoeuvre. The inner port, the old port, was where all the large yachts owned by the rich, chic, celebs, and anyone with enough money berthed. These needed to be booked months, if not years, in advance; and were very, very expensive.

'Thierry's uncle works in the Capitainerie du Port,' Jessica explained. 'One of the big yachts in the old port has gone sailing and won't be returning for a couple of days, so we can stay two nights. Thierry's uncle got permission from the owner so we could us it. There were some favours swopped, I think. Our berth is on Quai Suffren, opposite the Bar du Port. It's a good position, I'm told.'

'Excellent.' Grandad was pleased because anchoring near Saint-Tropez could be dangerous with all the movements in and around the port. 'Thank you, Thierry.'

'Thank Uncle Pierre,' replied Thierry. 'I told him all about *Black Pearl* and he's looking forward to our arrival. He's partial to a glass of pastis.'

'*Pas de problème.*'

Grandad explained to everyone the manoeuvres he would require for berthing and it would mean all hands on deck with fenders so as not to damage any of the yachts, which cost a fortune.

Late afternoon, *Black Pearl* cruised into the Port de Saint-Tropez with the lighthouse and long arm of the outer breakwater to the left. Grandad followed the outer breakwater, passing the new port on the right and entered the old port, much painted by artists for over a century, and *Black Pearl* turned sharply to the right.

'There's the berth,' Thierry shouted. 'I can see Uncle Pierre waving.'

Those in the restaurants, bars, shops, tourists and locals around the old port, gazed at the new arrival. A real ship had arrived. Grandad had kept the mainsail hoisted, mainly for effect, because it looked good.

People waved at Laetitia, who was half way up the mainmast, doing her pirate lookout duties. She was wearing her usual pirate costume, the bedraggled black drooping frilly tutu skirt, and she was playing with her best favourite doll, the one that had seen her through many campaigns on the beach. For those interested, her face was black because the other colours were depleted having been used for Lucy's show. She wondered what all the fuss was about and why people were waving at her. She kept a sharp lookout, just in case that nasty muffee man was about.

Grandad judged it best to keep Laetitia up the mast, out of harm's way, because, wanting to be helpful, she had a nasty habit of undoing ropes causing havoc at inconvenient times. She also had a knack for undoing knots, which was an unfortunate knack for a six-year-old. Of course, Laetitia knew better because only she knew how to help Grandad sail his pirate ship and she had discussed this at length with her friendly ghosts, which was definitely something the others hadn't.

'Furcuff,' shouted Laetitia in the nice way to those waving at her because there was no sign of the nasty muffee man.

It was fortunate that the wind, noise of the engine, and the bustle of the old port drowned out her welcome. She was having doubts about her use of furcuff because, despite the odd reactions she sometimes got, she had noticed that Jessica no longer said it. She had also noticed that Lucy was fond of saying cool, like Jessica, and that sounded like a teenager, didn't it.

'Cool,' she shouted.

Ewan had returned to the bows and once again straddled the bowsprit, feeling sorry for himself. In the last hour or so of the journey, *Black Pearl* had rolled in the slight sea swell and he was feeling a bit sea sick, although he wouldn't admit it to anyone, particularly his twin sister, Lucy. Grandad had recognised poor Ewan's plight and had left him alone. Once in port, Ewan began to feel better and spoke to his pretend pet parrot. He was going ashore soon and when he ran out of money, like pirates did, then he might have to sell his parrot. Ewan wasn't sure he could do that, not unless he wanted to buy an ice cream.

'Remember what I said,' Grandad reminded his crew.

Opposite the berth, the one from where Uncle Pierre was waving,

Grandad again turned sharp right, so that the stern of *Black Pearl* faced the quay. He put his engine in reverse, and the klipper slowly moved backwards.

'Drop the anchor.'

Ellie had already paid out some of the anchor and chain, so that it was above the seabed, just as it said in the book. She paid out more chain and knew the anchor was at the bottom, because the chain became taut, leading ahead as the klipper went astern.

'Keep the chain tight, Ellie, and someone move the Zodiac to the bows.' While sailing, they towed the Zodiac and it needed moving because the stern of *Black Pearl* would be end on to the quay and the Zodiac would otherwise be in the way.

'Fenders ready,' Grandad shouted. That was not necessary, because the crews, in their pristine white uniforms, from the two immaculate yachts that would be *Black Pearl's* immediate neighbours were already ready with huge fenders to defend themselves from ninety tons of old Dutch klipper flying a pirate flag.

'Stern ropes ashore.' Uncle Pierre slipped the eyes of the two stern ropes over bollards on the quayside, and Julien and Thierry heaved the klipper between its two neighbouring yachts.

'Hold the anchor and make fast the stern ropes.' *Black Pearl* moored snugly between its two neighbours and despite Grandad never having done such a manoeuvre before, it was a slick operation for anyone observing with a nautical eye.

'*Mes amis,*' said Uncle Pierre to anyone nearby and, once the gangway was in place, he then boarded *Black Pearl* giving the watching crowd a slight wave. The youngsters nearly knocked him off the gangway when they made a mad dash for the shops. Lucy had spotted NAF NAF. Uncle Pierre knew his etiquette and kicked off his espadrilles.

'Hi, Uncle Pierre, meet, Charlie.' Thierry then also disappeared, with Julien, after the others.

'Julien,' shouted Grandad, 'book a decent restaurant for tonight.'

'*Pas de problème.*'

'*Magnifique, Monsieur Charlie,*' admired Uncle Pierre. 'It is a privilege to have such an unusual ship in the Port. As you can see, we are used to these large modern yachts built without taste or style.'

'I must thank you for arranging such a convenient berth.'

Already artists around the quayside were sketching and painting *Black Pearl*, hoping to catch the eye of tourists or, perhaps, the owner of such a fine ship.

'It is nothing,' said Uncle Pierre.

'Would you like a drink,' asked Grandad. 'I have an agreeable pastis I bought in Marseille you might like to try.'

'A small one, perhaps…'

Some may find Saint-Tropez too touristic, a little tacky perhaps, over-priced maybe.

If you looked more closely, you could still see a traditional village of fishermen and shopkeepers, which it was before the arrival of artists and the famous. If you saw beyond the glamour and glitz, it was still there, just. After a while, the magic took over and it was a place to enjoy and explore. It was not that big a town and you never knew who you might bump into.

Jessica and gang ambled up this alley and down that, just window shopping, because they knew they had all the next day to shop at leisure. After buying the charts for *Black Pearl*, Jessica had to make one priority purchase, and she could now afford it after extorting money from the Marseille mafia. Near the quay, not far from *Black Pearl*, she found a shop that had some adorable things within her budget.

When Julien asked what everyone wanted to eat that evening, Lucy quickly answered.

'Indian?'

'Awesome.'

'Metoo, metoo.'

"Sounds good,' agreed Ellie, 'tandoori in Tropez.'

'I'll go along with that,' added Jessica.

Thierry shrugged, which could have meant anything.

'Good choice,' said Julien. 'I know a place not far from here.'

It was early evening by the time they all returned to *Black Pearl*, and it was probably too long a period of time to leave Grandad and Uncle Pierre with a bottle of the very best Marseille pastis.

'Hi, Grandad, you okay?' asked Jessica.

'I couldn't be better,' slurred Grandad amiably. 'Meet my friends.'

'Cool,' greeted the pirate lookout, 'I'm Laetitia.'

'This is Anatoly,' Grandad continued, 'who is the owner of the yacht next to us, the big one to our right. He kindly brought a bottle of Russian vodka to welcome us to Saint-Tropez.'

The bottle was now half empty, as was the bottle of Marseille pastis, which didn't go unnoticed by Jessica. Russian mafia, Jessica imagined. I had better keep an eye on him for Grandad, you can never be too careful in the south of France.

Grandad introduced Jessica, Ellie, Lucy, Ewan, Julien, and Thierry. Laetitia had already introduced herself, as we already know.

'My full name is Lucy Tarantino,' Lucy informed Anatoly, who didn't think Grandad did justice when introducing her. 'I'm kinda not famous yet, except probably in Pramousquier.'

'I am glad to make your acquaintance, Miss Tarantino,' replied Anatoly. 'You must be interested in films, I think. I once invested in one of Quentin's films but it wasn't the financial success I hoped.'

'This is Ksenia who is Anatoly's niece,' said Grandad, quickly moving the introductions on before Lucy started asking for money for one of her productions. 'She is about your age, Jessica, and is learning English. I've agreed to give her conversation lessons.'

'Call me Susha,' said Ksenia, 'all my friends do.'

Ksenia was on board to keep an eye on her uncle.

Anatoly's wife much preferred the Black Sea. She found the south of France too pretentious for her liking and she didn't speak the language. Therefore, she invited Ksenia, her sister's daughter, to accompany her husband for six weeks over the summer.

With a business empire difficult to comprehend, and with politicians, mafia, and many others after their slice of his wealth, Anatoly was tired. He wanted some peace, quiet, and rest. He had a big, expensive yacht with all its luxuries to ease the stress and tension from body and mind; but it didn't. It was too big and despite owning it for the past two years, he still found it impersonal. The crew was too large and he never had any privacy. His business associates, competitors, politicians, mafia, and the many others all wanted invitations. All he wanted was a quiet and relaxing time, and perhaps the odd distraction.

Then guess what turned up?

A quaint old Dutch klipper of the pirate ship variety. It was crewed by a bunch of kids, and a chubby, grizzly old man sporting a scraggy beard and gross ponytail. Anatoly would have wanted a ship like that, if he weren't a rich Russian patriarch. He had an image to maintain.

'Isn't that the American actor, Jack Nicholson,' Anatoly remarked to his captain. 'Didn't I once finance one of his films? They must be making a children's film or something. Maybe it isn't too late to invest.'

Anatoly's captain then told his crew about the famous American actor on *Black Pearl* and that they were making a children's film, then the crew, in turn, told...

It didn't take long for the rumour to get around Saint-Tropez, which loved to receive real, proper, famous celebs, rather than has-been singers, models, soap actors, and footballers. Hadn't the Capitainerie du Port moved out that big yacht to make room for the new arrival?

Ksenia and her Uncle Anatoly got along fine.

Despite her long legs and being extremely attractive, Ksenia wanted to study at Moscow State University, then move to Harvard Business School for her postgraduate studies in corporate and commercial law. She had some hard work to cover over the summer holidays before returning to her studies in September. Don't get the wrong idea. Ksenia was no geek, just another healthy teenager of the Russian variety giving her parents a hard time. Nevertheless, she had ambitions.

'What is the problem?' asked Uncle Anatoly.

'I've got to pass the entrance examinations first,' Ksenia replied.

'I can fix it for you,' offered Uncle Anatoly.

Although tempting, that wasn't what Ksenia wanted because once at Harvard things would get harder, and she wasn't sure Uncle Anatoly could fix things there. While Ksenia could have anything she wished, she had other plans. She was ambitious and wanted to achieve on her own merits. She worked hard and wanted to study at Harvard. Since Anatoly didn't have children of his own, Ksenia would without doubt be running Anatoly's business empire one day. There would be no bodies floating down the Volga on her watch.

'*Hi* Susha,' said Jessica, 'much going on in town?'

'They're mainly tourist traps,' replied Ksenia.

'We're eating out tonight at an Indian place not far from here. Why don't you and your uncle join us?'

'We would love to, wouldn't we, Uncle Anatoly.'

'Indian!' exclaimed Anatoly. 'What an excellent idea.'

Their chosen restaurant, while not too expensive, was one of the most popular in Saint-Tropez. They were surprised they didn't need a reservation! That had nothing to do with the rumour that Jack Nicholson was in town filming with some kids – those very same kids in front of the owner wanting to make a reservation at short notice.

We think Anatoly might have overcome his confusion over Grandad and Jack Nicholson, except you never knew with Russians, particularly Anatoly, who was always suspicious. It was obvious, to Anatoly at least, that a famous American actor would want to hide his identity. Be that as it may, Grandad and his young crew interested him, and they were good company, a distraction.

'I am pleased you can join us, Anatoly, because we are having a double celebration tonight, a party to remember,' said Grandad, feeling remarkably better after a few drinks. 'You'll join us, won't you Pierre?'

'*May wee...*' Despite Uncle Pierre being used to pastis, the vodka had done its damage. He sounded almost English and would have been devastated had he known.

'Okay everyone, showers, baths, and smarten up,' Grandad ordered. 'Let's get moving.'

'What about you, Grandad?' urged Jessica, seeing the state he was in.

'I think it's time for an apéritif,' offered Grandad to his two new friends, Pierre and Anatoly. 'I have a rather good whiskey somewhere, single malt, and twenty years old. I am sure you'll like it.'

'Grandad!'

Chapter 17
Calm before the storm

A poor translation from the *Var-matin*, the regional daily newspaper:

Jack Nicholson – *'J'adore Saint-Tropez'*

Once again, the *Var-matin* brings to its readers headline news before the national newspapers.

Saint-Tropez again welcomes the rich and famous to its shores. Jack Nicholson, the American Oscar Award winning actor, was seen dining at one of Saint-Tropez's top restaurants near the old port. Among Nicholson's best known films are, *One Flew Over the Cuckoo's Nest*, and as the Joker in *Batman*. He arrived on an old Dutch klipper, a modern day pirate ship, with a crew of child actors, and berthed next to a large luxury yacht owned by a Russian business mogul with mafia connections.

Nicholson, in 2001, was the first actor to receive the Stanislavsky Award at the 23rd Moscow International Film Festival and was photographed dining with President Vladimir Putin.

In true Nicholson style, he arrived at the Saint-Tropez restaurant drunk, with his two drunken companions, the Russian business mogul, and a senior official from the Capitainerie du Port.

When asked what he was doing in Saint-Tropez, Nicholson answered, 'we are celebrating the success of our latest production, *Pirates of Provence.*' The child actors all cheered and started singing pirate songs to everyone's amusement. From the singing, it was evident that the children were talented and entertaining. Nicholson had grown a beard and stylish ponytail for his latest role.

Nicholson was last seen in France with a beard in 2002, when he attended the Cannes Film Festival. He has also visited Saint-Tropez before, staying at *La Ponche* not so long ago.

The Russian business mogul stated, 'I am interested in films, I like art, it can be very profitable, and I often invest in American films. This is my humble contribution to world culture.'

One of the child actors, when asked what was her name and who was the director, answered her name was Lucie and the director was Tarantino, famed for films such as, *Kill Bill*, and *Inglorious Basterds*. The child actor, Lucie, who was wearing a pair of oversized adult spectacles, with cracked lens, stated that the director's approach was, 'doing satirical nonlinear juxtaposing stuff, which is cool.' This might explain why Nicholson is making another film in view of recent claims that he has retired because he had difficulty in remembering his lines. Lucie explained that, 'with the juxtaposing stuff, who needs to remember lines, we're talking Tarantino, aren't we.'

We all look forward to the film being released in France.

Surprisingly, Grandad woke early.

No headache!

He had slept below decks in preference to his usual hammock, because tourists and locals had crowded the quayside near the stern of *Black Pearl* and persisted in taking photographs. Admittedly, *Black Pearl* was pretty with the Saint-Tropez lights reflecting on the calm waters of the old port, mingling with the reflection of the moonlight, but photographing Grandad struggling to climb into his hammock at two in the morning was a bit much. Grandad gave up and decided to sleep in his comfortable stateroom.

Grandad crept through the chartroom where, surprisingly, Julien and Thierry were fast asleep, alone. Grandad smiled, because they were good kids, all of them.

After a couple of false starts, he had drunk quite a lot remember,

Grandad found the stateroom only to find Laetitia in his bed, fast asleep with her collection of favourite dolls, her best favourite doll firmly clasped in her arms. With Laetitia talking to her friendly ghosts and Lucy up all hours writing her memoirs, they had become uneasy roommates. Laetitia had decided that Grandad's room was the place for her, and he never slept there anyway. It was comfortable, and it had its own loo. She could talk to her friendly ghosts undisturbed and without Lucy's frequent, 'What a disaster,' 'How embarrassing,' and 'Cool,' three of her current favourite expressions.

What more could a pirate lookout want?

There was plenty of room in the saloon, and Grandad found the floor the most comfortable place, rather than the bespoke daybed that became a bed at night for anyone to sleep on.

After waking up without a hangover, Grandad took a long, hot shower, and went up on deck. It was a beautiful morning. The sun had risen, the sky was blue, and the old port deserted. He saw that Bar du Port across the road had opened for early risers, like him. He lowered the gangway and walked to the café for a large café crème, followed by an espresso. He sat there, thinking about life in general. Despite missing his wife, life was still good, very, very, good in fact.

Grandad paid the waiter, who explained where the best boulangerie was. He strolled along the old port and paused at la statue du Bailli de Suffren. Here was an eighteenth-century seafarer who had spent most of his seafaring career battling against the British, almost like a hobby. Grandad continued, then turned left up Rue Georges Clémenceau and found the boulangerie. There was a short queue of older people, who like Grandad, wanted their bread fresh. He bought a selection of bread still warm from the oven and different to the usual baguette. On an impulse, he also bought two large tartes tropéziennes, fresh, inviting, and expensive. These were round flat brioche filled with a yellow cream, made from a secret recipe. The tarte became famous in the mid-'50s with origins from the more humble Poland.

Grandad leisurely prepared breakfast.

Nothing much went on in Saint-Tropez until late morning, when the shops opened and the street artists slowly assembled around the old port awaiting the arrival of the tourists, who probably had spent the previous two hours in a traffic jam approaching Saint-Tropez.

The first sign of life from the others was Ewan singing from the front of the klipper.

'Morning, Grandad, what's for breakfast?' Ewan enquired.

'It's early, Ewan.'

'We all have things to do.'

'You can help bring things on deck, but don't wake the girls.'

'Okay.'

Ewan can be a happy soul, and as we already know, had a very short-term memory. In the galley, he grabbed a tarte to bring on deck, and again made the fatal mistake of singing outside Jessica's cabin.

'Summertime, and the livin' is easy…'

'That's one of my favourites, Ewan,' said Jessica pleasantly, 'good one.'

'Hi, Jessica, Grandad's got custard cakes for breakfast.'

'Custard cakes!' exclaimed Ellie. 'Wait for me.'

'Help, help…' cried Laetitia and after a short pause added. 'It's okay, I can do Grandad's loo. Save some cake for me.'

'Grandad, are you sure there are no ghosts, cos Laetitia been speaking to them all night. If there are no ghosts then you gotta sign my book as proof,' demanded Lucy.

'Are they my glasses?' queried Grandad, scrutinising the owl-like spectacles precariously balanced on the end of her nose.

'Are yours cracked?'

'They weren't,' was Grandad's careful reply.

'Then these cannot possibly be yours, can they?'

'Well…'

'You know I'm right, Grandad, admit it.'

Julien and Thierry slept right through the awakening on *Black Pearl*, which goes to demonstrate how resilient teenage boys' sleep can be, something parents simply don't tolerate.

'Is it like this every morning?' asked a half-awake Ksenia.

'Yes it is,' answered Grandad. 'Where did you sleep?'

'In the spare bed in Lucy's room.'

'Does your Uncle know? I would hate him to be worried.'

'Yes, he knows. We need a salad with breakfast, and fresh fruit.'

With that, Ksenia went on deck and shouted in Russian, then a head appeared out of one of the ports on her Uncle's yacht and a brief conversation took place. 'It's coming.'

'Who wants French toast?' offered Julien with bleary, sleepy eyes.

'What's going on?' It was Thierry, who didn't seem to understand that on *Black Pearl* the day began with a proper breakfast.

Whatever happened to Uncle Pierre the previous evening was anybody's guess. When he did arrive home, his wife gave him such a telling off for being out so late, getting drunk, and without letting her know. He certainly wouldn't do that again in a hurry. 'Saint-Tropez is no longer safe,' she said, 'with all those Russians around.'

As for Anatoly himself, he also was an early riser, and went directly to his communications room where a steady flow of coffee was at hand. From there he conducted his business empire until noon, and nobody was to disturb him. He was supposed to be on holiday, having a break, and taking things easy!

The cafés around the old port were now mostly open, and shopkeepers, artists, artisans, and other workers were having a typical French breakfast of an espresso, croissant, and a nicotine fix. Some were reading the morning papers, and those who had reached the Saint-Tropez page of the *Var-matin*, casually glanced at *Black Pearl*, from where the laughter and shrieks were coming. They were used to film stars, celebs, the rich, and famous disturbing their peace and tranquillity and longed for the winter, when Saint-Tropez returned to the sleepy fishing village it once was. In the meantime, they welcomed the spending spree, but not from the film stars, celebs, the rich, and famous. Your everyday tourist did the spending.

'What are your plans for today?' Grandad asked.

'We have a few things to do.' Jessica was the spokesperson.

'Yep, we have a few things to do,' agreed Lucy.

'Yeah, y'know, things to do.' It was Ewan this time, being helpful. 'Metoo, metoo.'

'Retail therapy, mainly.' Ellie was hoping to clarify matters.

'They need my assistance,' added Ksenia

'They're helping,' said Jessica, nodding towards Julien and Thierry.

'What time do you want lunch?' Grandad hoped for an answer.

'Usual time,' replied Lucy.

'Yeah, y'know, when we're hungry,' added Ewan.

'You do remember about the party tonight, don't you Grandad?' Jessica asked. 'It was your idea, remember.'

'Party—'

'The one you agreed to last night.'

'It wasn't a dream then,' mused Grandad.

'We have it all organised.'

'We heard you swear, Grandad, so you're doing the dishes.' It was more an order from Lucy than a request.

'Did I?'

'Yep, rule two, remember.'

'You shouldn't swear in front of little kids like us.' The harmony between Lucy and Ewan was out of character.

With the unanimous agreement from the others that it was Grandad's turn to do the dishes, much to Ewan's relief, they all disappeared to wash, dress, and get ready to hit Saint-Tropez with what little spending money they had. Except Jessica, of course, she had loads of money as we already know.

Grandad had finished the dishes before his grandchildren and friends emerged from below decks. We use the word grandchildren deliberately, because gone were the pirate costumes and bikinis. Even Laetitia looked pretty, although that wasn't a word normally used within her hearing, because she didn't do pretty, not knowingly, anyway.

Grandad slipped some extra cash to Jessica, for the younger ones. They might see something they want.

'Thanks, Grandad.'

'Follow me,' said Ksenia. 'I know this little shop…'

And off they went.

Grandad went about his nautical chores, checking his tanks, washing the decks, those sorts of things. He also had time to examine his collection of new nautical charts. Jessica, or whoever had helped her choose, had done a good job.

Tourists started to arrive and the artists slowly took their positions immediately adjacent to the yachts on Quai Gabriel Péri and Quai de L'Epi. After his chores, Grandad ventured ashore for a coffee, and then to do his shopping. As he left *Black Pearl*, quite a few tourists took photographs. Grandad suspected it was something you had to put up with if you berthed in the old port. Grandad crossed the road to the nearest café and ordered an espresso.

Anatoly watched Grandad do his chores. He had a crew to do such things, but still envied Grandad who had to do his own nautical tasks, even the dishes. He joined Grandad for a coffee.

'Good morning, Charlie,' said Anatoly.

Grandad signalled to the waiter for an espresso for Anatoly. 'We're having a party tonight. I hope you can come.'

'You have already invited me.'

'Did I?'

'Yes, when you were doing your yoga impressions on the table, you were very good.'

'Was I?'

'Yes, and I promised to bring some Russian vodka and champagne.'

'Thank you, that's very generous.'

'It's nothing. Your capable young niece, Jessica, is handling all the arrangements, along with her friend. My niece is also helping.'

Saint-Tropez had all the shops a small town needed, small supermarkets, butchers, bakers, newsagents, and so on. It also had the added bonus of having all the leading designer shops crammed into the narrow streets and passages. The wealthy, like Anatoly who volunteered to help Grandad shop, could be seen ambling around with an ice cream wearing a tatty pair of shorts and t-shirt indistinguishable from the likes of Grandad, similarly rigged-out, also with an ice cream, conveniently bought at Barbarac on Quai Gabriel Péri, the best ice cream shop in town.

Shopping in Saint-Tropez wasn't all bad news for Jessica and gang. Ksenia knew the town and could advise the others where to go. While her uncle might be wealthy with more than a few roubles to spare, Ksenia was financially independent and survived on the small allowance her parents gave her during her studies.

While Jessica had cash, which was burning a hole in her pocket, she knew what she wanted. She had sent Thierry and Julien to do some preliminary investigations and anyway, she didn't want inept boys around when she had some serious retail therapy in mind.

Jessica carefully bought trendy outfits for Laetitia and Lucy from NAF NAF, which for them, was as good as it gets. For Ewan, Jessica bought a new snorkel and mask as suggested by Grandad.

Ellie had a good look around the shops. They appeared to cater for size ten and under and not size sixteen and over more suited for her shape. She knew that was how things were.

They played a game.

Each had ten thousand euros to spend and only an hour to do it. They loved rummaging around the designer shops and even tried a few things on. Surprisingly, the shopkeepers were quite tolerant with their antics. I'm sure that had nothing to do with the *Var-matin* article, which had a couple of photographs, one with Grandad doing his pretend yoga position on the table, and the other of his support actors doing pirate impressions. They found that ten thousand euros didn't go very far!

They stumbled upon the Place des Lices, where old men were playing boules underneath the plane trees while at the same time enjoying the occasional pastis at the Café des Arts in the corner. Laetitia wanted to play and one old man allowed her to double with him in a match against two others. As you would expect, with Laetitia's version of the rules, which were unknown to anyone in France, they won.

They walked towards La Citadelle, away from the built-up area. This was a park favoured by dog walkers, for obvious reasons.

'Laetitia, you like dogs, don't you?' said Jessica pleasantly. 'Can you see Madame with all those lovable pooches?'

'They're so cute, aren't they,' and off Laetitia went to play with Madame's dogs.

'Yep, they're definitely adorable,' and off went Lucy.

Jessica had spied Madame with all the dogs and deduced that such a woman must be missing something, like a man, a man kind of like Grandad, who had been doing his best to pull old biddies on the beach but without much luck. The woman in question was wearing a black blouse and black jeans, had her hair in a large bun, and used a cane to help her walk.

She loved her Grandad, so setting him up with a woman was the least she could do. Her first venture with the super-sophisticated lady at Chez Claude, the one Grandad blubbered all over, was a disaster. Grandad needed help, and who better to help him than herself, his loving Jessica.

'Hi,' said Jessica, '*bonjour Madame.*'

'*Bonjour Mademoiselle,*' Madame replied. 'You are English?'

'Yes, aren't they adorable,' said Jessica while giving the nearest mutt a tickle behind its ears.

'Can I hold the lead, Madame,' pleaded Laetitia, 'pleeease...'

'Of course,' said Madame, who was obviously kind, because only a kind Madame would have four dogs. 'You can call me, Brigitte.'

'Brigitte,' said Jessica, 'my Grandad loves dogs, doesn't he Ellie?'

'Does he...ouch, oh yes, he loves dogs.' The sly kick worked.

'And parrots,' added Ewan.

'And fish.' Laetitia didn't want to be left out, did she?

'Fish, you mean like dolphins?' asked Brigitte, who had a thing about saving dolphins.

'Dolphins?' Laetitia wasn't sure about the dolphins. She'd never seen Grandad eat them, had she, or parrots.

'Grandad's got a klipper in the old port. It's a sophisticated soirée and leisure centre for the more discerning traveller, you can't miss it.' You can forgive Jessica's change of description from a cool party boat. They were in Saint-Tropez, after all.

'We're having a party tonight,' added Ksenia, 'you must come, Brigitte.'

'You're not English?'

'No, Russian, and I have interesting conversations with Charlie.'

'Charlie is my Grandad.' Jessica could have hugged Ksenia for having invited Brigitte. She was trying to work that one into the conversation. 'He's like, cool, with a pigtail and dead young for a Grandad.'

'I adore beautiful young men,' said Brigitte dreamily, her eyes drifting away into memories. If this Charlie was enjoying interesting conversations with this beautiful Russian girl with long legs, then he must be something, was Brigitte's general thinking.

'That's Charlie, isn't it guys?'

'Grandad!' Lucy was taken aback.

'Charlie?' queried Ellie. Then she cottoned on to Jessica's plan. 'Charlie, absolutely, dead young, that's right, and beautiful.'

'Grandad!' Lucy again.

'It's the pirate ship in the old port,' added Ksenia, 'if you can make it about eight. Best not bring the dogs, the noise might frighten them.'

'About eight, you said, maybe, maybe...'

Jessica wasn't sure if Brigitte had taken the bait. They might have laid it on a bit heavy with describing Grandad as young and beautiful.

Brigitte wasn't as silly as she made out.

She had read the *Var-matin* that morning and she knew that a famous American actor was in town. It was a real famous actor, a proper actor, although she couldn't remember his name. He was on a pirate ship with a load of child actors doing some filming. She recognised some of the faces from the photograph, particularly the two pretty ones in front of her. The fat one was also pretty and Brigitte decided she liked her. These child actors patently didn't know who she was. They clearly liked animals, and the little girl was undoubtedly cute, despite the smell.

Brigitte lived about two miles away and rarely visited the town itself but her husband wanted to do some shopping. She accompanied him and he dropped her off near La Citadelle, where it was normally quiet, so she could walk her dogs.

Brigitte no longer cared much for her faded beauty or conceited younger days. She had done that. She didn't feel old or used up. Now she wanted to pursue her interests, and age disgracefully. She remembered the name of the famous American actor, Jack Nicholson. He liked dogs. She saw that in a film once. He has clearly been around and might be interesting and he did look alluring with his ponytail while dancing on the table. She had seen the picture in the *Var-matin*.

As Jessica and the girls walked away, Ellie had to say something.

'Jessica, she's ancient,' she whispered, 'how can you think Charlie would be interested in her?'

'She's a vast improvement on some of the ones Grandad had been trying to pull on the beach, isn't that right, Lucy?'

'Yep,' agreed Lucy. 'Some were terminal, like in a coffin, and all that kissing, it's disgusting.' Her mind was on other things, such as what did juxtaposing mean, because she had forgotten. Furthermore, did it really matter about smashing Grandad's glasses, probably not because apart from all the squinting, he didn't seem too concerned.

'She might not come anyway,' said Ellie. 'She'll probably be in bed by eight.'

On their way back, Jessica and gang went into the church, which was not far from where *Black Pearl* was berthed. The church was small and offered relief from the heat and sun. Jessica took the others to the altar, and to the left was a bust.

'That's Saint Tropez himself,' Jessica declared.

'Grandad told us about him last year, didn't he,' added Lucy.

'Who was he,' asked Ellie, 'what did he do?'

'Dunno,' replied Laetitia, who liked being helpful.

'Just some bloke,' concluded Ewan, wanting to clarify to the others that he knew a thing or two.

We'll skip describing lunch on *Black Pearl*, because we know it would have been a feast, particularly with Anatoly adding one or two Russian recipes prepared by the head chef from his own yacht.

Anatoly didn't know which champagne to bring to the party, so after lunch he, Grandad, and Uncle Pierre had to test several bottles, which wasn't a good idea, was it? They settled for Russian champagne, and although a little sweet, was probably better suited to the menu Jessica and gang were planning for that evening.

Chapter 18
The storm

'**Fucking** *AirJet!*' It was Jo, Mother from Hell to Jessica, Mum to Laetitia, Aunty to Lucy and Ewan, and daughter-in-law to Grandad.

'What are you moaning about now? The flight arrived early, neither did we have to stand, nor pay to go to the toilet, so quit complaining.' It was Marina, who reluctantly accompanied Jo on the flight to Hyères airport.

Jo had got herself into such a state, she decided to immediately fly to France to sort out, what in her mind, needed sorting. Her husband, Dominic, Grandad's son, would have nothing to do with it. There were no reported broken bones, no complaints from either Jessica or Laetitia, so what was there to get in such a state about?'

Apparently, according to Jo, there were lots…

'Be reasonable,' pleaded Dominic, 'they've only been away a week.'

'I'm flying out, and that's all there is to it.'

Marina decided it was best to tag along, mainly to keep an eye on Jo and make sure she didn't become too much of a nuisance. In any case, she decided she needed a short break from being a busy and successful barrister specialising in women's rights, so exerted her own right in taking a few days holiday. It was August, and not a busy month for women's rights. They were too busy minding their children during the summer!

What made Jo suddenly want to fly out to the south of France?

Was it concern for the wellbeing of her two daughters? Was it pent-up hostility for Grandad sneakily naming Laetitia behind her back all those years ago? Was it resentment that her two daughters were seemingly having a good time with Grandad?

Life at home was anything but happy, with Mother from Hell and her elder daughter, who was the most devious, deceitful conniving shitbag ever to walk the planet, continually at each other's throat. Life at home was so bad that Dominic had planned the best and simplest method for committing suicide, should ever the need arise. Caught in the middle, Dominic had to walk a delicate path between mother and daughter. They both damned him, of course. It was equal damnation, so at least he was being impartial to both sides.

Jo and Marina arrived at Hyères. The sun was hot, the sky blue, and the sea inviting. The airport was almost on the beach, and Marina had allowed Jo to sit at the window seat on the left-hand-side of the aircraft to see the magnificent view of the coastline as the pilot approached the runway. Whenever arriving, Marina had that feeling of excitement, a joy of what was to come. It hadn't always been like that. She was never the perfect teenager, far from it. She had had her dark moments.

'It's fucking hot,' Jo commented.

They picked up the hire car, avoiding the *AirJet* chosen partner, because that's where the long queue was. They were soon on their way in a little Fiat Panda with Marina driving because she knew the way. The journey to Pramousquier was only forty or so minutes.

Jo tried ringing Grandad, then Jessica.

'Still no fucking reply,' Jo complained.

It was late afternoon when Marina parked the Panda outside Grandad's villa. She didn't find Grandad or the children there, that's for certain. The old woman who lived there was confused because Jo walked straight in, uninvited.

'Where is he then,' she demanded. 'I bet he decided to hide when he saw us arriving. I tell you, he's evil, and he's bad. He's even found himself a fancy woman, and that didn't take long, did it.'

'*Bonjour Madame, puis-je vous aider?*' It was the poor confused old woman's husband in his underpants, having had his afternoon siesta disturbed.

'So who are you, the fucking gardener?'

'*Pardon?*'

Being a busy and successful barrister, Marina suspected something was not quite right, so with a few pertinent questions, ascertained that the old couple had bought the villa from a charming English man several months ago.

The old couple were appalled that they, as the children of the charming Englishman, didn't know that he had moved. What kind of children were they?

As the old couple knew Grandad was recently widowed, it occurred to them what was going on. They glanced at each other and knew what and what not to say. With the draconian French inheritance laws, where, by law, the children inherit a sizeable chunk of the estate, it was obvious that the charming Englishman was acting craftily, who wouldn't, and being elderly themselves, they understood. Why should the children get their hands on any inheritance? They would only spend it.

'We know nothing, nothing,' was all Marina could get out of them.

The only way the elderly couple could get Jo out of the villa was by threatening to call the gendarmes, the military force acting as armed police over the civilian population.

'See, I told you he was bad,' Jo informed her sister-in-law.

'I am sure there is some simple explanation—'

'—which he forgot to inform us about,' added Jo, 'and in the meantime, we have no idea of the whereabouts of our children. I think we should go to the gendarmes and report a kidnapping.'

Despite what Marina thought, things weren't good. 'Let's go to Chez Claude, have a cup of tea, and speak to Max.'

So they did.

The tea wasn't particularly enjoyable, but it never was in France. While drinking her tea, Marina picked up the *Var-matin* to see what the local gossip was. She could read French.

Dad, Dad, Dad, Marina contemplated, what are you doing? What are you up to? What caper is this, and pretending to be Jack Nicholson, the American Oscar Award winning actor, on a pirate ship, filming. She had to force herself not to giggle. She was now quite pleased with her decision to accompany her silly bitch of a sister-in-law. Dad was up to something, he always was.

'What are you looking so smug about?' asked Jo.

'Nothing.'

'What's going on?' The question was directed at Max.

He didn't know what to say.

'*Rien.*'

Firstly, he didn't know Grandad hadn't informed his family of having sold the villa. He certainly wasn't going to inform the two agitated ladies, well, one at least, in front of him that Charlie had actually bought an old Dutch klipper, much admired in the bay. He had his loyalty to Grandad, didn't he? Secondly, he could appreciate the concern of the two mothers not knowing where their children were.

It was always women, Max mused, who put him in impossible situations and there was no getting away from it. That Grandad was possibly the culprit and cause of his impossible situation never occurred to Max.

'The children are happy,' reasoned Max.

Marina coughed, holding the *Var-matin* in a prominent position. Max had known Marina for a long time and knew she was no fool.

'I think they might be in Saint-Tropez, *oui*, I remember now, they are having a happy time in Saint-Tropez.'

Max knew that was true. Hadn't he been invited to the party on *Black Pearl* that very evening, in the old port? Dress code, pirate, his text message had said. Wasn't he at that very moment finishing for the day, going to get himself tidied up, and then make his way to Saint-Tropez?

Marina coughed again.

'It just so happens I am going to Saint-Tropez this evening and I can give you two ladies a lift if you like.'

'That would be very helpful,' replied Marina.

'I'm not happy with going on some wild goose-chase around the south of France. We should inform the gendarmes,' said an unhappy Jo.

'Trust me,' stated Marina.

'What,' answered Jo righteously, 'trust you and your father? I'd rather stick needles in my eyes.'

'Isn't that a quote from *Terms of Endearment*, a Jack Nicholson film, isn't that right, Max?'

'I'm not familiar with that particular film,' he answered cautiously. 'Leave your car here because parking in Saint-Tropez is difficult. We will go in my car. First you must freshen yourselves because Saint-Tropez in the evening can be exciting.'

'Where are we going to sleep?' whined Jo, also known as Mother from Hell, and we can appreciate why.

'Trust me,' Marina said more sternly this time.

Jo wasn't stupid, a silly bitch perhaps, but not stupid!

Something had changed Marina's demeanour and Max now appeared quite relaxed. They were going to Saint-Tropez, which wasn't so bad, and as Max had said, it could be quite exciting.

In the late afternoon, when the shops opened and the restaurants prepared for the evening rush, the mood in Saint-Tropez changed. Cars disappeared and people took over. The municipal police closed off Quai Suffren and Quai Jean Jaurès to cars around five in the afternoon and the rest of the port at nine. It was like a carnival, and it took place every evening during the summer. It was puzzling where all the people came from, particularly with the difficult parking.

Day-trippers, tourists, and locals vied for tables in the restaurants, particularly those with views of the glamorous yachts, and those without a prior booking were promptly turned away. You never knew who you might see unless you had read in the *Var-matin* that Jack Nicholson, the American Oscar Award winning actor, was in town, on a pirate ship in the old port filming – a Tarantino film, it said.

The artists, who had invested their time painting *Black Pearl*, with its black pirate flag flying from the mizzenmast and the iconic Saint-Tropez buildings in the background, were not disappointed. Street entertainers took their place around the port, hoping for good takings.

It was not surprising that *Black Pearl* attracted a lot of attention from the day-trippers, tourists, and locals, all interested and hoping to snap a photograph of the klipper, or some of the actors, particularly the pretty girls in the *Var-matin*, or even Jack Nicholson himself.

Grandad was pleased he had raised the gangway, because the crush ashore, particularly the local paparazzi armed with large cameras, threatened to board *Black Pearl*. Grandad didn't know the paparazzi were after him. He hadn't read the *Var-matin*, had he?

Jessica and gang had done a good job preparing for their pirate party, particularly when Ksenia had the head chef from Anatoly's yacht at her disposal. Anatoly had ordered a proper pirate outfit that morning from his communications room, and it arrived promptly. Such things were available in Saint-Tropez. Grandad and his young crew already had their costumes, and they easily kitted out Ksenia.

Lucy, being responsible for the entertainment, quickly adapted *The Pirate of Provence* production into what she called, *La Soirée de Saint-Tropez*. This was a much more glamorous affair in keeping with their surroundings and her juxtaposing contradictory method she was now keen on doing. What this translated into was the Black Pearl Band, which she renamed the Provençal Pirates specifically for the Saint-Tropez market, was to have a bit of a jamming session with the best of her pirate songs, a bit of Rolling Stones, some *Yé-yé* Vintage French, and then, she nearly forgot, a bit of surrealistic stuff.

'Got that boys? 'Lucy said, the boys in question being Julien and Thierry and not forgetting Jessica, who we assume was an honorary boy for the evening. They all nodded obediently, so that was all in order.

'Metoo, metoo.'

Lucy noticed Laetitia lurking nearby, who wasn't going to be left out, because she was the star and everyone said she was cute, which wasn't a nice thing to be called, was it. Madame's dogs were cute.

'You'll be helping Grandad, won't you, Laetitia, you're his Little Miss Helpful.'

Laetitia reckoned she wasn't any Little Miss, that's for sure. While she didn't mind being Helpful for Grandad, she had other plans for the show that evening. She hadn't been rehearsing her songs for no good reason. Anyway, Grandad didn't need any help because he was sitting in his hammock with Sasha, talking about boring things.

Far from being boring, Grandad and Sasha were discussing tenses.

'There are three tenses in the English language, I was taught that at school,' argued Sasha.

'You just said you were taught that at school. What tense is that?'

'Past tense.'

'I teach now; what tense?'

'Present tense.'

'I will teach you tomorrow?'

'Future tense.'

'The verb form hasn't changed, I only added, will, before, teach, to indicate the future. The future tense always requires an extra word and you can do this in many ways. So technically, there are only two tenses in the English language.'

As Laetitia surmised, they were talking about boring things.

'Don't tell Uncle Anatoly will you, he might arrange for my teacher's legs to be broken,' pleaded Ksenia.

Julien had contacted a couple of his musical friends to help with the band and if asked why by Lucy, and without her permission, he would answer, he was only being surrealistic, like she said. Fortunately, he never had to test his plea, because all she said was, 'Glad you could make it, boys.'

Chapter 19
The calm after the storm

By eight, it was getting dark and the lights from the cafés and restaurants illuminated the road around the old port.

Sophisticated women sat in the old port cafés, hoping to get into conversation with some of the yacht owners or guests. They were eager either to get an invitation, or alternatively, slip aboard a large yacht behind other guests, and then party the night away shoulder to shoulder with the rich and famous.

Black Pearl was an obvious target with Jack Nicholson and Tarantino aboard. Also, there was a gaggle of talented young starlets, future megastars without a doubt. And Russians. With this in mind, Anatoly placed an evil-looking minder on the quayside near the gangway, a Ukrainian Oddjob lookalike to, with the occasional help from Laetitia, keep away any potential gatecrashers.

Laetitia had other things on her mind. Because she considered herself the star of Lucy's show, she didn't want to miss her cue. She felt that both her twin cousins were jealous of her success and had plans to leave her out of the action. We know that wouldn't happen, not if Laetitia had anything to do with it.

Jessica had invited all their friends from Pramousquier, including, Noé, Hans, Virginia, and Nina. Their grandparents came as well, because they provided the taxi service. With the enticement of a party on *Black Pearl* in the old port de Saint-Tropez they didn't need much persuading.

Uncle Pierre came with his wife, Chantal, who, having read the *Var-matin*, seemed to have miraculously forgiven him his previous misdemeanours.

'You call him Charlie, you little rascal,' she said. 'I imagine you have to be tactful in your job. Your secret is safe with me, *mon cher.*'

Uncle Pierre wasn't much of a reader, least of all the *Var-matin.*

What was his wife was insinuating? What secret! He didn't want to say anything in case it jeopardised his reprieve.

The deck table was set with the buffet. One of Anatoly's catering staff in a pristine white uniform helped to serve drinks. Everything was in order. Ellie was in charge of the catering, and you wouldn't be surprised to know that she felt the need to test the food on offer. Quality control, she claimed. With most of the guests dressed as pirates, it was definitely a swanky affair to those watching from the quay.

The evening started with the gentle sounds of Thierry adjusting his bongo drums and Julien and his friends tuning their instruments. Jessica did a bit of spitting to get her flute to work properly because it was a humid evening. The Provençal Pirates sat on top of the chartroom, which was divided by the boom of the mizzenmast thus providing seating for the band. They opened the soirée with a selection of slower Rolling Stone's tunes.

'Great gig, boys,' encouraged Lucy.

We forgot to mention that Max's car was a Quatrelle, an early classic Renault 4, an icon of French automobiles. When owned by the likes of Max, who never did mundane things like car maintenance or servicing, such a car was extremely unreliable. It broke down near Gassin, when Max was taking his short cut. With an hour or so of poking and banging under the bonnet, he got it going again as he always did.

Marina and her silly bitch sister-in-law, Jo, who complained throughout the whole journey, arrived at Saint-Tropez later than planned. While parking was a nightmare, if you owned a beat-up Quatrelle, then you parked anywhere. It wasn't a problem. The municipal police much preferred utilising their time towing away the likes of a Porsche or Ferrari.

Max and the two mothers arrived at a crowded Quai Jean Jaurès. *Black Pearl* looked pretty, with coloured lights hanging between the two masts, with laughter and merriment. Marina and Jo couldn't see much because of the crowd.

Max pushed his way through the crowd, but it was hard work.

'Isn't that a Gilbert and Sullivan song?' inquired Marina.

Max shrugged in his traditional Gallic manner. It was from Lucy's

Pirates of Provence production, wasn't it?

The deck floodlighting from Anatoly's yacht lit up the stern of *Black Pearl* and the crowd was hushed. The gangway, which protruded from the stern, was hanging parallel to the ground, about two feet above the quayside. It was the best Lucy could improvise for Ewan's walking the plank prop, while singing his pirate king song.

Since the Provençal Pirates were perched on top of the chartroom and the mizzenmast boom, they were clearly visible.

'Isn't that Jessica playing the flute?' said Marina.

'She never plays the fucking thing at home.'

'Why do you always use such coarse language?'

'Life, that's why,' replied Jo. 'What is Jessica doing on that boat?'

'She's playing the flute very well.'

'I shall live and die a pirate king.' It was unmistakably Ewan shouting his opening line, on the gangway, pretending to walk the plank, in his pirate outfit. Where he managed to get the stuffed parrot from is anybody's guess.

'Hurrah…' from the chorus, which was the band, pirate captains, and buccaneer beauties.

After a few opening chords by the band, Ewan sang 'I am a Pirate King' with a touch of pirate dash, Tom Jones, and Mick Jagger. The crowd, which had gathered on the quay, loved it, particularly when the pirate lookout did her swinging trick from the mizzenmast, joining in with the singing. It not only looked dangerous what Laetitia was doing, it was dangerous.

'That's my Ewan,' said Marina proudly. 'Can you see that little one swinging on a rope from the mast, brave don't you think?'

'That's Laetitia! Max, what do you know about all this? What's going on?' Jo was in a panic.

The best Max could do was offer another Gallic shrug, which didn't help matters.

It should have been Noé swinging on the rope, except he had never done it before. Anyway, Laetitia was working from her own script.

'I told you your father was bad.'

'Don't be such a silly bitch.' Despite that, Marina was a bit worried. Wouldn't you be if you suddenly saw your little six-year-old niece swinging from the mizzenmast, bouncing off this and that, and wailing like a banshee, followed by that appalling fall?

'Isn't that Jessica's best party skirt, the tutu one that cost me a fortune, hanging around Laetitia's neck?'

Both Jo and Marina, with Max's help, unceremoniously pushed their way to the front of the crowd to get to *Black Pearl* to see what was going on. Unfortunately, or fortunately depending upon your point-of-view, they were prevented getting any further by the Oddjob character. All they could do was watch.

The Provençal Pirates then played the 'Policeman's Lot' tune, and everyone did Max's infamous pirate dance around the deck, with Grandad leading, followed by Brigitte holding onto his bum for dear life, then Uncle Pierre and his wife, Ellie with Anatoly holding on firmly, then the buccaneer beauties, the two pirate captains, Ksenia and everyone else. Don't forget Laetitia, who tagged along at the end. She didn't limp much considering her fall. It wasn't her fault. It was the ropes fault. Remember, she had a knack for undoing knots and ropes. She couldn't tie a knot to save her life, not yet anyway.

Anatoly had had a lot of Russian champagne, with vodka chasers, so hanging on to Ellie was more out of a necessity. Remember, he had Ksenia keeping a close eye on him.

'There's your father flirting with that old woman,' said Jo frostily, 'and your mother still warm in her grave.'

'That's, that's Bri—' spluttered Max in awe.

'I don't care who it is.'

Admittedly, Brigitte was hanging onto Grandad intently, and with an air of familiarity. On the other hand, she was old and walked with a cane, and Grandad probably provided much needed support for someone not familiar with Max's pirate dance.

Max wondered how Charlie did it. Not only did he see him flirting with the first lady of France at Chez Claude, but here he was again, with the first lady of Saint-Tropez hanging on to his bum as if her life depended on it.

After the pirate dance, if you could call it a dance, the Provençal Pirates broke into the opening cords of 'Ruby Tuesday' with Lucy on the gangway, gazing into the sky. You could have heard a pin drop.

Lucy's voice was clear and note perfect and some would claim they witnessed tears in the eyes of Oddjob. Jessica's background flute melody was note perfect and complimented Lucy's singing perfectly.

'That's my Lucy,' stated Marina proudly.

'That's my Jessica,' said Jo with more pride than she would admit.

'Yes,' added Marina, 'Jessica is quite talented.'

'They're good kids,' Max said with fondness. There was no denying it. He definitely had tears in his eyes.

Max then watched Charlie climb into his hammock with a woman who was young, blond, long in the legs, and very attractive. Life wasn't fair, he pondered. Then again, nobody ever promised that it would be.

'See your father now,' said Jo, the silly bitch sister-in-law. 'He's almost in bed with that blond tart. He's bad, I'm telling you.'

'No wonder you have a daughter going through her awkward period. If I had a whinging and swearing mother like you, I would be awkward, and I mean bloody awkward. No wonder poor Jessica calls you Mother from Hell, you are.'

'What are you talking about?'

'We've witnessed a remarkable performance by our children, something to be proud of. All you can do is moan. Get a life and don't be such a silly bitch.'

'If you're going to take that atti—'

'Aren't you proud of Jessica? She played beautifully. I could cry with the performance of my twins. Everything they all did was incredibly good. You would think they've done it before, wouldn't you Max.'

'You certainly would,' agreed Max truthfully.

'Laetitia seems to be okay now?'

'She's a tough one,' added Max.

'All the children were excellent,' admitted Jo. 'I am proud of Jessica. I didn't expect it, that's all. Do I swear a lot?'

'Yes,' confirmed Marina.

'I don't realise I do it.'

'It's not surprising your children swear.'

'What do you expect with my crappy job?' answered an irritable Jo. 'I am a junior governor, the token female governor, in an all-male prison. Everyone swears and none more so than the staff. It's all I ever hear. Then I have to go home to face the family, including a teenage daughter going through her f— through her awkward period.'

Marina didn't know what to say and gave her sister-in-law's hand a kindly squeeze. It was the best she could do.

'It's your father. He winds me up,' added Jo more calmly. 'Did I tell you how he tricked us in naming Laetitia?'

'Many times,' Marina replied with patience, because she had often heard the story. 'Dad isn't bad. The grandchildren love him. He gets into all sorts of mischief, but he's not bad.'

'Laetitia!' exclaimed Max. 'It is a beautiful name for a cute and lively little girl. Everyone loves Laetitia and the name suits her. She is Laetitia. How can you not love the name? It is a romantic name, a bewitching name, a name fit for a little princess, or a tearaway ferocious pirate. You must love the name, surely?'

'I didn't say I didn't like the name—'

'Then stop moaning.'

'I could do with a drink.'

They crossed the road and sat at the Bar du Port, a hip, hi-tech spot fronting the old port and *Black Pearl*. The waiters were clearing away the tables before smoothly moving into DJ-driven night-time revelry.

'A bottle of white wine, please,' Marina requested, 'the cheapest.'

'*Deux bouteilles, s'il vous plait,*' added Max.

When the Provençal Pirates had a break, Jessica took a glass of sparkling water and sat by herself on one of the padded sunbeds immediately behind the bowsprit. She wanted some time alone.

Having a soirée on Grandad's cool party boat in Saint-Tropez port, with the patronage of the Russian mafia, was as good as it would ever get for a teenage Jessica, and she knew it. Playing in the band, sailing *Black Pearl*, selling beignets, sorting out the mafia, being with Julien and Thierry, who were kind and never groped you like the boys back home, and making friends with Ksenia, were brilliant. The whole summer holiday had been the best ever.

She was sixteen and confused.

Julien and Thierry, although a couple of years older, were soon going to university to do some serious studying, and I mean, serious studying. They were happy, enjoying life, laid back about things, knew what they wanted and got on with it.

A friend of Jessica's had once said to her that you only had to work as hard as needed. Why overdo things when it wasn't necessary?

Jessica knew she could have done better with her GCSEs. Her results were still among the best, so what was the problem? In spite of that, something was nagging at the back of her mind. Was it guilt, disappointment, or resentment? She didn't know.

'A penny for your thoughts?' Ellie had seen Jessica by herself.

'I've got to sort out what *A*-levels I'm doing next term.'

'I've still to settle what I'm doing so we can do it together'

'Jessica, quick,' said Laetitia, all excited and eating something strange on a piece of baguette, 'I've got something to tell you.'

'What's up, my little star?' Jessica asked. 'You okay now, it was a bit of a fall you had. You have to be careful with those ropes.'

'I'm okay now,' replied Laetitia. 'Grandad put his special cream on my knee and a plaster. It's stopped bleeding.'

'That special cream of Grandad's,' Jessica whispered to Ellie, 'is spit. He used to do it to me.'

'Did it work?' queried Ellie.

'It did, until I was eight.'

'Bye, gotta go, I'm hungry,' said Laetitia, 'cool.'

'Wait a minute, Laetitia. What did you want to tell me?'

'I nearly forgot. What's Mum doing in the bar across the road?'

Chapter 20
Finally…

It was quite a shock for Grandad when Marina and Jo turned up. He had been found out. He knew he would, sooner or later. He had hoped it would be later, rather than sooner. There was no escaping.

The first he knew about his daughter, Marina, and his daughter-in-law, Jo, being aboard *Black Pearl* was when somebody tapped him on his shoulder.

'Good champagne, Dad,' said Marina. 'You can explain everything in the morning. That should give you time to prepare your defence.'

'Oh, damn?'

'You're doing the dishes, Grandad.' It was Ewan, mightily relieved because Jessica wasn't swearing much now. 'Hi, Mum, hi, Aunty Jo.'

'Terrific party.' It was Jo being pleasant, and he wasn't used to that. 'Your Russian friend is very hospitable.'

'He's kindly offered us cabins on his yacht,' added Marina.

Then Marina and Jo wandered off, just like that. There was no shouting, no threats, no trying to throttle him.

It must be the vodka, Grandad thought. It can have strange effects!

He had been trying to avoid Uncle Pierre's wife, Chantal, who kept asking him about films he had never heard off. Then there was that other old battle-axe a bit on the plump side. What was all that about dolphins? Mind, if she were a few years younger…

'Jacques,' Brigitte had asked sensuously, 'tell me about the lovely little dog in that film.'

'It's Charlie,' Grandad explained, 'that's my name. *Je suis Charlie.*'

'I know all that, Jacques, you don't have to explain, *je comprend.*'

Jessica had noticed how hopeless Grandad was with Brigitte despite building him up as young and beautiful, perhaps that was a mistake. She decided to give up her quest to fix Grandad with a woman. Let him to roam the beach trying his arm at pulling old biddies and sneaky kisses.

What could you do with him? He was a lost cause.

Brigitte was now with Max, and oddly, he was simply standing there with his tongue hanging out. Anatoly's vodka again, no doubt.

'*Voulez-vous danser avec moi?*' she asked Max.

He stood there, speechless, his feet not moving.

'*J'adore les beaux jeunes hommes.*'

'*Merde!*'

It was some party.

Early next morning, not long after the party had finished, Grandad woke and briefly inspected the deck of *Black Pearl*, and could not believe what he saw. No disorder, no empty glasses or bottles, everything was tidy and ship-shape. Unknown to Grandad, Anatoly's crew had done a good job cleaning up, as they always did.

He lowered the gangway, and wondered across the quay to Bar du Port for a large espresso, then a second, just to make sure. He wanted time to think. He was hoping, praying, that seeing Marina and Jo the previous evening was only a bad dream. He knew it wasn't. Luckily, the two mothers were busy enjoying the party and at one stage, were having a long discussion with Max, which didn't look good, because they all kept glancing in his direction. Later, his daughter-in-law, Mother from Hell, Jo, slapped him on the back and called him, 'Jack,' and went away giggling.

It was morning, nearly the time to explain everything, and he hadn't prepared his defence, not yet anyway.

He glanced over to Anatoly's yacht, not for inspiration but for signs of Marina and Jo. He couldn't see them.

On top of everything else, he had to leave the berth before midday. He had a few nautical tasks to do before leaving Saint-Tropez, sorting out his grey and black water tanks, and taking on more fresh water. Take one thing at a time, and take deep breaths, he reasoned, was the best way forward.

He caught the waiter's eye, and signalled for the bill.

First things first, he needed to do a bit of shopping. He had almost run out of his homemade bread, so he had better get plenty of those fine baguettes he saw the previous day, and put them in the freezer. The tarte tropézienne went down well, so he decided to get some more.

When he returned to *Black Pearl*, he passed Thierry on the gangway, 'I'll be back soon.'

Grandad went to the galley, and as quietly as he could so as not to wake the others, prepared breakfast. He prepared something similar to the previous day, which seemed to go down well. He added porridge, cooked with cream and fresh figs, which were coming into season. It would be like a brunch. When leaving Saint-Tropez, everyone would be busy and there wouldn't be time for a proper lunch.

Grandad began to feel better with all that planning.

'Hi, Grandad, what's for breakfast?' It was Ewan. 'You've got those giant custard cakes again, awesome.'

'Can you help lay the table?'

'No problem.'

'You're supposed to sing to us in bed, Ewan,' Jessica shouted, 'what's up?'

'There is a klipper in Saint-Tropez, they call the Black Pearl, and it's been the ruin of many poor girls, and God, I know you're one...'

'Good one, Ewan.' Jessica was now out of bed, and joined Grandad in the galley. 'Get that, Grandad, the Animals, Vintage English.'

'Good party, Jessica,' said Grandad, 'and yes, I got it.'

'What a surprise with Mum suddenly turning up. Did you see her, she got plastered.'

'Yes, quite a surprise.' Jessica seemed quite casual about her mother arriving.

'I had to help carry her aboard Anatoly's yacht. I took some photos of her with my gadget. They'll be useful one day.'

'iPhone 6s, Jessica, not any old gadget.'

'You're learning...'

'Who wants French toast?' It was Julien, with bleary, sleepy eyes.

'Metoo, metoo, cool.'

'Grandad, last night you said your number was up,' queried Lucy with a certain amount of indignation. 'Well, you're not dead. How surrealistic is that?'

'It's early yet, Lucy.'

'Okay.'

*O*n the deck table was a feast. Sasha had brought a fresh fruit salad, yogurt, a Russian version of porridge, and freshly squeezed orange juice.

'Eat up everyone,' Grandad said. 'We've got a busy morning and we have to leave by midday.'

'Where're we going?' Lucy asked.

'Don't know, I'm only the cook,' replied Grandad.

'We going to that isolated beach, the Bastide Blanche. We can anchor there for a couple of days, and then move on. We've checked the weather, haven't we Ellie, and there's a mistral coming from the west. It should be sheltered there, if it reaches that far.

'Ace.'

'Awesome.'

'Metoo, metoo, cool.'

'What's Thierry doing in the chartroom with that chap?' Grandad queried, more from curiosity than anything else.

'Nothing,' replied Jessica quickly.

Up to no good was Grandad's general thinking.

'Is there room for two more for breakfast?' It was Marina, accompanied by her sister-in-law, Jo.

'Mum, you're hung-over,' commented Jessica, 'you okay?'

'You're quite right, I'm hung-over, and no, I'm not okay,' groaned Jo, who had already self-diagnosed her own ailment with accuracy. 'In fact, I feel like I'm going to die.'

'Not you as well,' commented Lucy, 'you can take surrealism too far, Aunty Jo.'

'Dad, aren't they your glasses that Lucy's wearing?' queried Marina.

'Apparently not, mine have got lenses in.' Lucy had done some alterations to Grandad's glasses, because she couldn't see much through the cracked lens.

'Mum, we gotta lot of talking to do,' declared Lucy, opening her note book, 'and you've gotta lot of explaining, hasn't she Grandad.'

'Well…'

'What's this?' queried Jo.

'What's what?' It was Ewan this time.

'What's all this food doing on the table?' Jo was puzzled because there wasn't a pizza or a packet of cornflakes in sight.

'Breakfast, Mum,' said Laetitia. 'This one's Russian porridge and that one's Grandad's with squashy things in. That's Julien's special eggy-bread.'

'Yep,' added Lucy, 'eggy-bread is good for handovers, isn't it Grandad.'

'Well...'

'The fresh fruit salad is delicious,' said Ellie. 'It's my favourite.'

'The custard cake is awesome,' was Ewan's contribution.

'Do you have this every morning?' Jo queried.

'It's only breakfast, Mum,' Laetitia explained. 'Grandad says it's the most important meal of the day, don't you Grandad.'

'I can vouch for that, it's what he always told me,' added Marina, while helping herself to fresh fruit salad, yogurt, and coffee. 'Russian porridge, you said...'

'I better try the eggy-bread,' said Jo, 'and coffee, black, no sugar.'

'Max explained everything last night,' said Marina quietly. 'We'll fill in the gaps later.'

'Where's this Bastard place, Jessica, is it far?' queried Jo.

'Bastide Blanche, Mum,' corrected Jessica.

'I was close,' said Jo, who wasn't being a Mother from Hell, not at that moment, anyway.

'It's working,' shouted Thierry from the chartroom, directing his comment to Jessica. 'Leave some *tarte tropézienne* for me.'

'If we're anchoring at Bastide Blanche, then we'll need more supplies,' said Grandad.

'We'll accompany you shopping, won't we Jo,' offered Marina.

'Good idea, I need some new shoes.' Jo had found buying new shoes was always a good remedy for a hangover.

'We would help, but we need to sort out our *A*-levels, don't we Ellie,' said Jessica.

'*A*-levels? You said you wanted to be a beautician or something?' commented Jo quietly.

'Mum, I was winding you up.'

Jo, who didn't want an argument, left it at that. Jessica doing her *A*-levels was what she had always wanted.

Marina had gently held Jo's hand to keep her calm. It's surprising what a couple of bottles of wine can do for family bonding, particularly when followed by Russian champagne and vodka, and a fabulous party in the old port of Saint-Tropez. Mother from Heaven – okay, that's stretching it a bit – was finding it difficult not to swear, and finding it unnerving to find a happy and relaxed Jessica. A-levels! That was a turn-up for the books. She hadn't expected that.

*G*randad was in the chartroom.

'It's a Marine GPS, Grandad,' Jessica explained. 'It displays your position, latitude and longitude, your speed, things like that.

'It's second-hand, like a display model. Thierry managed to get an adaptor so it can work on your electricity supply. You can unplug it and it works hand-held on rechargeable batteries for about eighteen hours. It is waterproof and floats and you can hang it round your neck or strap it to your wrist while sailing.

'It displays your position on the little screen, like on a chart, see, we're in Saint-Tropez port. When you sail it plots your track, and you can plan your route and things. I've already planned our route to Bastide Blanche. You have charts, so you can go where you like, in safety.'

'Jessica, how can you afford this?' He should have bought charts and a Marine GPS, himself. He simply never bothered. 'I can pay for this.'

'Don't come all emotional on me, Grandad,' Jessica said. 'We all worked hard to get this. We're planning where to go after our stay at Bastide Blanche. We might go west, Antibes, Monaco, or maybe Capri.'

Initially, Jessica had in mind to get Grandad an iPhone 6s. They were expensive and not waterproof, and not a practical proposition. Thierry, with the help of Uncle Pierre, managed to get the handy little Marine GPS through a friend of a friend, because, surprisingly, there was none available in Saint-Tropez. It was exactly what was needed, something robust, and not complicated to use. It was expensive. Fortunately, Max put his hand in his pocket and contributed to Jessica's fund. With the profit he had made on Saturday night, it was the least he could do.

'My own gadget,' Grandad said, 'and I don't need a sextant.'

'When we get to Bastide Blanche, we'll give you some serious staff development on how to use it properly.'

Marina and Jo decided that a cruise on *Black Pearl* was what they needed. If breakfast were anything to go by, the food would be good.

While Julien and Thierry had to return to Le Lavandou for their summer jobs, they arranged for *Black Pearl* to return to Pramousquier before the end of the holidays. Jessica and Ellie made plans to visit Ksenia in Russia when they had saved enough money. Anatoly contributed a couple of cases of local wine to Grandad's supplies, and a few bottles of Russian champagne to be on the safe side.

When everything was ship-shape, *Black Pearl* slipped out of Saint-Tropez, with Laetitia up the mast doing her pirate lookout duties with her best favourite doll helping. As they passed the Capitainerie du Port, Uncle Pierre gave a wave, sad to see his favourite boat leaving.

At first, Jo was horrified when she saw her little daughter climb up the ratline to take up her usual pirate lookout position, with Jessica's black frilly tutu skirt hanging from her neck. Why worry, Jo thought, Laetitia appeared happy enough. There was Jessica steering *Black Pearl*, with Ellie doing things with the anchor, and everyone hauling ropes and sails like seasoned sailors.

Marina had taken her position on the sunbeds behind the bowsprit, keeping out of the way. Jo was still nursing her hangover, in Grandad's hammock, watching the children getting on with things, while Grandad passed around baguette butties to his crew for sustenance.

'Grandad,' shouted Laetitia from her lookout post, 'what's for tea?'

'Don't you mean supper, darling?' corrected Aunty Marina, which we know was the wrong thing to say.

'Mum, I think we better have that talk now,' Lucy informed her mother while opening her notebook. 'This might take some time.'

'Killer sharks, dead ahead, cool.' Laetitia had to get in the last word, didn't she?

About the author

For many years, TG Snowball was a travel-hardened minor academic managing British higher education with collaborative partners worldwide. He has also been involved in various projects as a consultant for the United Nations. Before becoming an academic, he spent several years as a ships navigator, plying his trade worldwide.

Being a professor, he has about fifty or so academic publications (journals, readers, conference papers, and so on), which includes short spells as a technical editor for a shipping journal.

Travel has been the nature of his career and he has visited over eighty countries, including spending about eight months in China, and working in Oman and Israel among other places. He currently spends the summer months in the south of France, swimming, drinking the local wine, and writing.

www.TGSnowball.co.uk